BLOOD
BROTHERS
Family Secrets
Book One

Donna Jean Picerno

For My Mom
With Love

chapter 1

arah slumped forward and rested her head on her husband's hospital bed, then closed her eyes and worried for the thousandth time if he was going to make it. *Please, Lord, don't take him away from me. We just got married; there is so much more we have yet to do together. I don't think I can go on without him.* She jumped when she felt a hand placed on her shoulder.

"Mrs. Evans, may I have a word with you?" Dr. Knolls asked.

"Sure," she said and wiped the tears from her face, then turned to face the doctor.

"The leukemia is getting worse; Michael's organs are shutting down. If we don't find a donor soon, I'm afraid he isn't going to make it. Is there anyone else you can think of who hasn't been tested yet?"

"We've tested everyone I know." Her voice quivered. "There must be something else we can do?"

"We've already tried an autologous transplant; his body rejected it. I'm sorry, but his only chance of survival is to have an allogenic transplant. We need to find a donor right away." Sarah bit her bottom lip to hold back her tears.

"It's late, and he is resting now. Why don't you go home and get some rest too? We can talk more tomorrow."

"I will. Thank you, doctor."

After Dr. Knolls left, Sarah stood by her husband's bedside and ran her fingers through his short brown hair and murmured to him, "Hold on, baby, we're going to find a donor real soon; I just know it. You get some rest, and I'll be back tomorrow." She bent down and gave him a tender kiss on his lips.

She grabbed her purse off the chair and walked across the room. At the doorway, she turned back to glance at him one more time as her eyes swelled up with tears. "I love you," she whispered before stepping into the hallway.

A blast of cold air hit her face as the sliding glass doors rolled open and Sarah stepped out into the frigid night. It had started snowing over two hours ago, and the ground was covered in white. Sarah pulled her hood up over her head and looked down at the ground, attempting to keep the snow from hitting her face. She let her car run for several minutes with the heat blasting and the defrosters on. She began to cry. *Lord, we need a miracle. Please help me find a donor now!*

When Sarah got home, she changed into her pajamas, went to the bookshelf, retrieved their wedding album and several other photo albums, then climbed into bed. She reached up and removed the messy bun from her head, then ran her fingers through her curly blond hair, letting it cascade down her shoulders to the middle of her back. She flipped open the wedding album and smiled at the picture in front of her. *We were so happy. It's hard to believe that was only one year ago.* She stared at a picture of Michael standing at the altar in his black tuxedo beaming down at her with so much love in his eyes. She flipped the page, then giggled when she saw a picture of her and Michael kissing. A whole foot taller than his five-foot-two wife, he picked her up a foot off the ground and planted a kiss on her lips.

It was just two months later, shortly after they returned from their honeymoon, when Michael received the diagnosis. Sarah gazed at the picture and wished she could turn back time. When she finished looking at the wedding album, she placed it aside and picked up one of Michael's family photo albums. She smiled as she turned the pages of the album and watched the progression of Michael's childhood, from chubby baby to toddler to teenager; Sarah thought he was adorable at every stage.

She looked at the pictures for over an hour before exhaustion kicked in, and she fell asleep with the lights on, and the albums spread across the bed. When she awoke, she looked at the clock on the bedside table and was surprised to see that it was morning. She hadn't slept for more than two hours in a row since Michael was hospitalized. In a hurry to get to the hospital, she jumped out of bed, sending the photo albums flying everywhere.

She bent down and picked up one of the family photo albums, and a photo fell out. She retrieved it up and stared at it; it was a picture she had never seen before. Two boys stood smiling with one arm around each other; they were holding fishing poles, each with a fish hanging from it, their chests puffed out as if they were proud of themselves. She recognized the one boy as Michael but did not know who the other boy was. She wondered who this boy who had a strong resemblance to Michael could be. She flipped the picture over and read the writing on the back: Michael and Dylan 1998.

Sarah called her sister-in-law with a newfound spark of hope. "Hi Megan, it's Sarah. Can I come over? There is something important I need to talk to you about."

"Is Michael okay?"

"Not really. I'll explain when I get there."

"I'm on my way to work right now. Why don't you meet me at the store?"

"Great. I'll be there in twenty."

Sarah quickly showered and dressed, grabbed the photo off her nightstand, put it into her purse, and left the house. Her mind raced as she drove to her sister-in-law's antique store. Could this boy be the answer to her prayers?

She walked into the store and double-timed it to the office in the back. "Megan," she yelled, "where are you?"

"In here," Megan replied.

Sarah entered the sunny office and found Megan standing at the windowsill watering her plants. She walked straight up to Megan and pushed the photo of the two boys into her chest. "Who is this boy with Michael?"

Megan put her water canister down, glanced at the photo, then took it from Sarah. "Where did you find this?" she asked, pivoting away from her.

"In an old photo album. Who is he?"

Megan let out a sigh and took a seat at her desk. "It's our brother, Dylan."

Sarah leaned across the desk and got into her face. "What? You have a brother! Why didn't anyone ever mention this?" Sarah waved her arms in excitement and started to pace. "I can't believe you and Michael would keep this from me. I've been driving myself crazy, looking for a donor, and you're telling me that you knew he had a brother all this time. Don't you realize this could be the answer to our prayers?"

"Calm down, Sarah. Have a seat, and I will tell you everything. Do you want a cup of coffee or something?" She placed the picture on her desk and walked over to the coffee maker.

Sarah took a seat and huffed. "No, I don't want a cup of coffee. Just tell me where I can find Dylan. We don't have much time. Michael is getting worse."

"I'm sorry. You don't know how much I wanted to tell you. When Michael got sick, I begged him to ask Dylan to be tested, but he refused. He forbade me from telling you because he knew that you would pressure him about it."

"You're damn right, I would. This is a matter of life and death,

Megan. I don't understand. How come you don't have any contact with Dylan?"

"It was a difficult time in our lives, and Michael and I don't like to talk about it. My father had an affair on our mother. Dylan is a result of that affair."

Sarah took a moment to take in what Megan had just said. "I'm sorry if you didn't want to talk about it, but that is no excuse. You should have told me. Michael should have told me!"

"Michael hates Dylan. He doesn't want anything to do with him."

"That's crazy. It's not Dylan's fault your father had the affair. Look at this picture." Sarah jabbed a finger at the picture. "They were so close once. What happened?"

"Yes, they were friends, but Michael didn't know they were brothers back then. Our parents were friends. They were always at our house. We went on vacations together and everything. I think that picture was taken at my parents' cabin by the lake. It wasn't long after that trip that my mother found out about the affair. It destroyed their marriage. My mother committed suicide when she found out Dylan was my dad's son. Michael blamed Dylan and cut him out of his life."

Megan sighed, "I tried to keep in touch with Dylan for a while, but Michael found out, and he was furious. He told me I needed to decide; it was either him or Dylan. I loved my brother; I didn't want to lose him."

Sarah took a minute to absorb everything she just learned. "That's terrible. I can understand why Michael doesn't like to talk about it, but he should have told me. I'm his wife, for God's sake. Is there anything else he is keeping from me?"

"I don't know, Sarah. That is a question you're going to have to ask Michael."

"Oh, don't worry, I will. But first, I need to get him better. What I don't understand is how Michael could find it in his heart to forgive your father but not Dylan. Dylan's not the one who had the affair."

"It took years for Michael to forgive our father. It was only on my dad's deathbed that Michael was able to forgive him. I suppose he might have forgiven Dylan too if things had been different, if Dylan had been a good person."

"What do you mean if Dylan had been a good person? So, he has some issues; who doesn't? I'm sure that finding out about the affair was hard on him too."

"No, you don't understand. Dylan is a really bad person. He is in jail."

"For what?"

"Murder."

"I'll show you," Megan did a Google search on her computer and brought up an article on the murder of a young woman, then turned the screen around to face Sarah. "Here, read this."

Sarah said nothing as she read the article. It stated that Dylan Hogan had been sentenced to thirty years of incarceration at the Ohio State Correctional Facility for Men for the murder of Stacy Richards, a twenty-three-year-old college student who was brutally murdered in her apartment.

"I know Michael needs a miracle right now, but Dylan is not it. Let this one go, Sarah. I don't think that Dylan would even agree to be tested, and besides, there is only a thirty percent chance that he would be a match anyway."

"I have to try. We are running out of time. Do you want your brother to die?" He needs to be tested." Sarah stood and snatched the picture from the desk.

Megan got on her feet too and grabbed Sarah's arm. "Wait, Sarah. You're making a mistake."

Sarah yanked her arm out of Megan's grasp and stormed out.

chapter 2

S arah was scared to death as she entered the Ohio State Correctional
Facility for Men. She had never been in a prison before. She
folded her hands in front of her to keep them from shaking.

"Who are you here to visit?" the guard asked.

"Dylan Hogan."

She handed Sarah a clipboard. "Fill this out."

Sarah placed her name and Dylan's name in the appropriate col-
umns on the list and was immediately escorted to a holding room where
a group of other visitors were waiting. She took a seat and patiently
waited as names were called and people left the room. After fifteen
minutes, a woman called her name. She stood and followed the woman
into another room, where she placed her personal items into a plastic
bin and walked through a metal detector. After retrieving her items, the
guard pointed her in the direction of another guard holding the leash
of a drug-sniffing dog. Once she was cleared by the guard and dog, she
was told to put her belongings into a locker.

"Can I take this with me?" Sarah held up the photograph.

"Yes. Have you ever visited here before?"

"No."

"This is a closed visit. That means you will be separated by glass, and you will need to talk on a telephone. You will have twenty minutes to visit provided the prisoner behaves himself. The visit will be cut short if the prisoner acts up or decides he doesn't want to speak to you any longer. Is that understood?"

"Yes."

The guard unlocked the sliding door and then locked it again behind them. When they reached the visitation room, Sarah took a seat at booth number three and waited. Sarah recognized Dylan as he entered the room on the other side of the glass. He had kept his similarities to Michael as he grew up but wore his hair a little longer than Michael did. He had many of the same facial features as her husband, and she wondered if he also had Michael's dimples. She watched as he scanned the row of visitors, skipping right over her as he did all the others. He looked at the guard who pointed to Sarah's booth. He frowned but took a seat and picked up the phone.

Sarah put the phone to her ear and spoke first, "Hello, Dylan. My name is Sarah Evans, and I am married to your brother Michael."

Dylan's face changed from confusion to anger. "What do you want?"

"It's Michael. He's sick."

"What does that have to do with me?"

"He needs your help." Dylan made a face but didn't speak. Sarah continued, "He has leukemia. His organs are shutting down. He needs a stem cell transplant right away. I am here to ask you to be tested to see if you are a match."

Dylan frowned, "Why would I do that? I haven't talked to Michael in years. He hates me. Does he even know you are here?"

"No, not exactly, but that's only because he is out of it. I know you and Michael were friends once. Can't you do this for an old friend?" Sarah held the picture up and placed it against the glass.

Dylan moved closer to the glass and stared at the picture. He smiled and then quickly looked away from the image, his fond expression fading. Sarah removed the picture from the glass and placed it in her lap.

"Look, lady. That was a long time ago. We aren't the same boys anymore. I can't help you." He placed the receiver back into the holder and started to get up.

Sarah's heart began to race. She raised her hand to him. "Wait! Please, I'll do anything. What do you want?"

Dylan turned back and looked at Sarah. He picked the phone back up and placed it to his ear.

"The only thing I want is to get out of here. You going to hire me a good lawyer? Get me an appeal?"

"Yes." Sarah's grip on the phone tightened.

"What do I have to do?"

"All I need right now is a blood sample to see if you are a match."

"They won't let you just take my blood."

Sarah popped up from her seat. "I'll get the paperwork. I'll be back." She hung the phone up and called for the guard.

She left the prison and went straight to the Goldstein & Finch Law firm.

"I need to see Ryan. It's an emergency," she said, running up to the reception desk.

"Do you have an appointment?" the receptionist asked.

"No, I just told you it's an emergency. I need to see my cousin right away."

"I'm sorry, but Mr. Finch is with a client right now."

Sarah ignored the receptionist and headed toward Ryan's office.

"You can't go in there; he's with a client."

Sarah swung the door open and charged into the office as the receptionist followed behind her, apologizing, "I'm sorry, sir. I told her you were in a meeting."

Ryan looked up at his cousin and said, "It's okay, Julie. I will handle this. You can go back to your desk." Just then, the phone began to ring.

"Yes, sir." She left to answer the phone.

Ryan turned to his client. "I'm sorry for the interruption. Did you have any other questions for me?"

The man turned to look at Sarah with sympathy in his eyes and said, "No, nothing that can't wait. I can send you the rest of my concerns in an email."

"Thank you, Mr. Townes. We will be in touch." He shook hands with his client and walked him to the door.

After the client left, Ryan closed the door and said, "This better be important."

"It is. I wouldn't have bothered you if it weren't."

"What is it?"

"Michael is getting worse. He needs a stem cell transplant right away. We haven't found a donor yet. I just found out he has a half-brother. He is willing to get tested to see if he is a donor, but I need your help. He's in prison. Can you draw up the paperwork necessary for me to get a blood sample from him?"

"You said he is willing to give a sample?"

"Yes, but I don't know what the prison will require."

"Do you have the donor consent form from the hospital?"

"Yes, I have one of them right here." She pulled it out of her purse.

"I will draw up the papers that the prison will have to abide by." He pulled a pad of paper out of his desk and started asking questions.

"What is Dylan's full name?"

"Dylan Hogan."

He wrote it on the paper. "Where is he incarcerated?"

"Ohio State Correctional Facility for Men." Again, he wrote that down.

"What hospital is Michael in?"

"Columbus Springs Hospital."

"Okay, I think that is all I need. I will draw up the papers, and you can pick them up tomorrow."

"I'm sorry," Sarah said, shaking her head, "but Michael doesn't have much time left. Can you please do them now? I can wait."

Ryan picked his phone up and said, "Can you please send a paralegal into my office right away? Thank you." He scribbled some notes onto the paper, and a minute later, there was a knock on his door, "Come in."

"You wanted to see me?"

"Yes. Thank you for coming so quickly. I need you to draw up these papers right away." He tore the sheet of paper from the pad and handed it to the paralegal.

"Yes, sir," she said, taking the paper and then leaving the office.

After she was gone, Sarah said, "Thank you so much, Ryan. You are a lifesaver. There is just one more thing I need to ask of you."

"What is that?"

She hesitated a moment, then took a deep breath and cast her eyes downward. "I know you aren't a defense lawyer any longer, but you are the only lawyer I feel comfortable asking such a favor of. Would you be willing to represent Dylan? He needs a lawyer to appeal his case."

"What is he serving time for?"

"Murder."

He leaned back in his chair and placed his hands together in front of his face. "Oh Sarah, what have you got yourself into?"

"I don't know yet. All I know is that my husband is dying, and I have to do something to help. Please, Ryan, I'm desperate."

"I don't know. Let me look into his case before I give you an answer."

"Fair enough. Also, if he's not a match, you don't have to represent him."

Sarah and Ryan discussed Ryan's children and other family matters for several minutes until Julie rang his phone and announced that his next appointment had arrived.

"My next appointment is here. I can call you when the papers are done?"

Sarah got to her feet. "That's okay. I'll wait."

Ryan walked her to the door. "Are you sure?"

"Yes."

Sarah took a seat in the waiting area and watched as Julie worked on her computer and occasionally gave her a disapproving look. She watched for the next two hours as two clients came and went through Ryan's office. She smiled at the paralegal when she saw her exit her office carrying a piece of paper and tapped on Ryan's door. Hoping it was the papers she was waiting for, Sarah jumped up and followed the woman into Ryan's office. Ryan looked them over and then said, "Good job. Thank you very much."

"You're welcome, sir." The woman smiled and left the office.

Ryan signed his name on the papers and then handed them to Sarah, "Here you go. Have a seat." Sarah took a seat and watched as he picked up the phone and pressed a button. "Julie, can you please get me the phone number for the Ohio State Correctional Facility for Men? Thank you."

A minute later, he had the phone number and called the correctional facility. When he got off the phone, he said to Sarah, "You have an appointment at ten a.m. tomorrow. Bring the paperwork, and you will get your sample. Good luck, Sarah. I hope everything works out and Michael gets better soon."

Sarah came around the desk and hugged her cousin with tears in her eyes. "I don't know how I can ever thank you enough. I'll let you know if he is a match."

She left the law firm and went to the hospital to check on Michael, optimistic about their future.

"Hey, baby. How are you doing today?" she asked her unconscious husband.

The doctor came into the room to do his rounds. "Good afternoon, Sarah."

"Good afternoon, Dr. Knolls. I have some good news. Michael has a half-brother. He has agreed to be screened."

"Really? And you didn't know about him?" Dr. Knolls raised his eyebrows and gave Sarah a curious look.

Not wanting to get into it, she said, "No, it's a long story."

Dr. Knolls hesitated a moment, giving her time to explain. When she didn't say anything further, he said, "Have him come in right away, today if possible, and I will run his bloodwork."

Sarah squirmed in her seat. "He can't come here. He's incarcerated. I had my cousin, who is a lawyer, draw up the paperwork for me to retrieve his bloodwork. I have an appointment tomorrow."

"Okay, just remember there is only a thirty percent chance he will be a match. I don't want you to get your hopes up."

"I have a really good feeling about this, doctor. He's going to be a match; I just know it."

Dr. Knolls ignored her comment and started taking Michael's vital signs.

chapter 3

Sarah arrived at the prison at 9:30 a.m. the next day to allow extra time to get through security. Instead of being sent to the visitor waiting room, the guard escorted her to the warden's office.

"Please have a seat, Mrs. Evans." The warden pointed to a pair of chairs on the other side of his desk. "I understand you are here to obtain a blood sample from one of our inmates, Dylan Hogan."

"Yes, he is my husband's half-brother. My husband has leukemia and needs a stem cell transplant right away. I need a sample of Dylan's blood to see if he is a match." She handed the warden the paperwork and then sat on her hands to keep them from shaking. The warden took a minute to read the papers and inspect the signatures, then said, "Mr. Hogan did not sign the consent form."

"I know, he agreed to be tested yesterday when I visited him. I'm sure he will sign them today."

The warden picked up his phone. "Please have Dylan Hogan delivered to the infirmary." When he hung the phone up, he stood and said, "Let's go." Sarah followed the warden out of his office and down the hall, through several locked doors and eventually to the infirmary. When they got to the prison hospital, Dylan was not there yet.

Sarah took a seat and only waited a minute before Dylan was escorted into the infirmary in his orange jumpsuit, his hands and feet shackled. He looked Sarah over and smirked before taking a seat. The warden spoke first, "I understand that you have agreed to be tested for a stem cell transplant."

"Yes." He looked at Sarah. "Do we have a deal?"

"Yes," Sarah replied.

"Okay, I will be tested," Dylan said.

The warden turned to the guard and said, "Unlock his hands." The guard unlocked his handcuffs, and the warden put the consent form in front of Dylan. "Sign here," he said, pointing to the signature line.

He signed the form, and then the prison nurse placed a rubber band around Dylan's arm and tied it tightly, cleaned the area with an alcohol-absorbed cotton ball, and then inserted a needle into his arm and removed one vial of blood while Dylan looked away. The nurse printed out a label with Dylan's name and placed it around the vial, then put it into a clear baggie and handed it to Sarah.

"Thank you," Sarah said to the nurse and then turned to Dylan. "This means so much to me. I can't thank you enough."

Dylan said, "You're welcome. When will you come back to visit me?"

The warden raised an eyebrow and turned to look at Sarah, making her uncomfortable.

"Tomorrow," Sarah said with a red face and looked away from the warden.

The guard put the handcuffs back onto Dylan's wrists and pulled him up from his chair. "See you tomorrow," Dylan said as the guard dragged him in the direction of the door.

The warden escorted Sarah through the prison and back to the entrance. He waited as Sarah retrieved her purse and coat and then said, "Good luck, Mrs. Evans. I hope Dylan is a match and your husband gets better soon."

"Thank you," Sarah said. She practically ran out of the prison and across the parking lot to her car. She drove straight to the hospital at top speed; she had to check the speedometer and slow the car down more than once. *Please, God, let him be a match. I can't lose Michael.*

When she got to the hospital, Sarah went to the nurses' station and asked to have Dr. Knolls paged and then went to Michael's room. She wasn't prepared for what she saw. Michael was so pale. She went to his bedside and touched his face. "Hi, baby. I'm here." Michael was burning up. She pressed the button for the nurse.

"Did you need something?" The nurse's voice came over the speaker.

"Yes, my husband is burning up. He needs something for his fever."

"We just paged his doctor. He should be here shortly."

"Thank you."

"Hold on, baby. Dr. Knolls is on his way," Sarah said and then kissed his feverish forehead. "He'll give you something to bring your fever down. I love you. Do you hear me, Michael? We're going to get through this." She took his hand and stroked it.

Dr. Knolls came into the room, "Hi, Sarah."

"He's burning up, doctor. You need to get his fever down."

"I know. He's been fighting a fever all night. I will increase his medication, but Sarah, his body is trying so hard to fight the cancer. I don't know how much longer he can go on."

Sarah marched over to the chair by the window and retrieved the vial from her purse. She handed the doctor the vial, "Here, this is a blood sample from his brother."

"Okay, I will have it tested right away."

"Thank you, doctor."

Dr. Knolls left, and Sarah took a seat by her husband's side. She knew from the past that it would take twenty-four hours to get the test results. Sarah passed the hours sitting next to her unresponsive husband by researching Dylan's trial on her cell phone. She began to feel uneasy as she read his case. *What kind of person did I get involved with? It doesn't matter; if he can save Michael's life, that is all that matters. After Michael gets better, you can sever ties with him.*

Sarah stayed by Michael's side all day into the evening, ignoring her stomach as it growled; eventually, his sister Megan came to visit.

"How is he doing?" Megan asked as she came into his room.

Sarah closed the article she was reading on her phone and looked up at Megan, "No change."

Megan touched her brother's hand. "He's burning up."

"I know. Dr. Knolls increased his medicine, but nothing seems to be working."

She placed a hand on Sarah's shoulder, "How are you holding up?"

"I'm okay. I'm waiting on Dylan's test results."

"Have you eaten today?"

"I had a protein bar earlier."

Megan grabbed Sarah by the elbow and pulled her out of the chair. "Come on, let's go to the cafeteria and get something to eat before they close."

"Okay," Sarah said and leaned over Michael's bed. "We'll be right back."

They took the elevator down to the first floor and went to the cafeteria, and ordered food. Once seated at their table, Sarah said, "What can you tell me about Dylan?"

"Not too much. We haven't been in touch with him for years. What do you want to know?"

"What was he like as a child?"

"He was okay, I guess. He and Michael were best friends. They were inseparable."

"And they just stopped being friends because of what your father did?"

Megan pushed her food around on her plate and avoided eye contact. Sarah could see she was uncomfortable talking about the past.

"Please, Megan. I need to know what type of person Dylan is and understand why Michael feels the way he does about him."

Megan took a deep breath before she responded. "They were both mad at my father for destroying their families, but they remained friends. My mother was devastated; she couldn't bear seeing Dylan. I think it was a reminder of what my father had done. Dylan wasn't allowed over at our house any longer. I guess it was the same for Dylan's mom, too, because Michael wouldn't go to their house either. They would sneak around hiding out together."

"What changed?"

"My mother became obsessed with the affair. She couldn't put it behind them. My parents were in the middle of getting a divorce when my mom committed suicide."

"That's terrible, but why blame Dylan? It was your father's fault, not his." Sarah placed her hand under her chin and leaned her elbow on the table, curious to hear what she had to say.

"I think Michael thought my mother could have gotten over the affair if it hadn't produced a child. Michael was the one who found our mother. She overdosed on pills. He ran straight to Dylan's house and attacked him. They haven't spoken since. They hate each other. Michael didn't speak to our father for years, but he did forgive my dad just before he died."

"That's so sad."

"Yes, it is. Sarah, I don't know how Michael is going to feel if Dylan is a match. You may have to prepare yourself that he will be furious with you."

Sarah removed her elbow from the table and leaned back in her chair and contemplated what Megan had just said. "I know, but I'm willing to take that risk. I won't let his stubbornness kill him."

They sat in silence for a minute before Sarah asked, "What do you know about Dylan's case?"

"Just what I read in the papers. I didn't go to the trial. They found him guilty of manslaughter."

"He says he didn't do it." Sarah raised her eyebrows, "Do you believe him?"

"I don't know. I haven't seen him in years. I don't know what kind of person he is anymore."

"Have you ever talked to Michael about his case?"

"Yes, Michael is sure that he is guilty."

"But is that just because he hates him?"

"I don't know. It's possible. Why are you so interested in his case? I know you're a journalist, always looking for the next story, but leave this one alone. It's in the past. Michael won't be happy to have this story come out. It was a very painful time for him. He hasn't even told you about it. He definitely doesn't want the whole world to know."

"Maybe you're right. Dylan asked me to help him file an appeal. It got me thinking, what if he is innocent?"

Megan thought for a moment, then said, "And what if he isn't? Do you really want to get yourself involved with a killer?"

"No. Right now, I just want to get my husband better. If I have to help Dylan with his appeal in order to do that, then that is what I will do." Sarah stood up and grabbed her half-eaten tray of food to take to the trash can.

Megan followed her lead and followed her to the exit. "Look, I can see that there is no chance of talking you out of this, but can I just give you some advice?"

"Sure." Sarah dumped the contents of her tray into the garbage and then placed the tray on the conveyer belt.

Megan placed her tray on the conveyer belt too and then put her hand on Sarah's shoulder. "Try not to let your emotions get in the way of your ability to accept the facts. Promise me that if the evidence shows that Dylan is guilty, you will let this thing go. I don't want to see you get hurt."

"I promise."

chapter 4

The clock displayed 2:17 a.m., and Sarah still had not fallen asleep. She had been tossing and turning in bed for the past three hours, unable to shut her mind off. *This is ridiculous,* she thought, then reached for her cell phone on the nightstand. She Googled Dylan Hogan's name again and got the same results she had already read multiple times. Feeling frustrated, she decided to take another approach and Googled Stacy Richards, the twenty-three-year-old victim Dylan allegedly murdered.

Sarah learned that Stacy and Dylan had been dating for seven months when Stacy was murdered. Dylan's semen was found inside her, and the prosecutor used that fact to build a case against him. Dylan claimed that he and Stacy had sex the night she died, but he went home afterward, and Stacy was still alive when he left. An autopsy revealed that Stacy was two months pregnant at the time of her death. Dylan denied that he knew anything about the pregnancy, and the prosecutor claimed that Dylan wanted Stacy to have an abortion and when she refused, he killed her.

Sarah fell asleep thinking about Stacy and Dylan's relationship and wondering if Dylan had murdered Stacy. She only got four hours of sleep when the sound of her phone ringing woke her.

Still lying in bed, she reached over and grabbed the phone and put it to her ear, "Hello," she answered, half asleep.

"Mrs. Evans, it's Dr. Knolls. I'm sorry, did I wake you?"

She sat up and looked over at the clock. "It's fine. I needed to get up anyway. Did you get the results?"

"Yes, I wanted to call you right away. He's a match, Sarah. Dylan is an acceptable donor."

"Oh, thank God! That's great news! How soon can we do it?"

"There is some prep that must be done before Michael's body will accept the stem cells, but I think he will be ready in two days."

She flipped the comforter off and put her feet on the floor. "I need to go see Dylan and make arrangements with the prison." She jumped out of bed and rushed to her dresser, pulled clothes out of it, and threw them on her bed as her mind raced with thoughts of everything she needed to do. "Thank you so much, Dr. Knolls."

"You're welcome, Sarah. I'll see you soon."

Anxious to get to the prison, Sarah didn't shower; she threw her clothes on and left the house in a hurry. She called Megan on the way to the correctional facility but didn't get an answer.

"Megan, Dylan's a match. Can you believe it? He's a match. I'm on my way to tell him now. Call me back."

Sarah was not nervous this time. She was smiling as she put her things into the locker and was patted down by the guard. Her heart was racing in anticipation of giving Dylan the good news. She reached for the phone on the wall as soon as she saw Dylan enter the room on the other side of the glass.

"You're a match!" she announced before Dylan had a chance to take his seat and put the phone to his ear.

"Okay," he said with no emotion.

"What do you mean, okay? That's great news!" She grinned.

"Did you get me a lawyer?"

21

"Yes, my cousin Ryan is a great lawyer. He is looking over your case now."

"Oh yeah? When is he coming to see me?" He leaned back in his chair and studied her.

Sarah dropped her shoulders and sighed. "I don't know. I will check with him and let you know. Dr. Knolls said Michael will be ready for the transplant in two days. I'll have to make arrangements with the warden, but I wanted to tell you first."

Dylan's eyes narrowed and fixated on her, "Remember our deal, Sarah. I want to speak with the lawyer before I agree to the transplant."

"I gave you my word. Don't you trust me?"

"No, I don't! I don't even know you, but I'm sure you love your husband very much and will do anything to help him get better. If you want me to do the transplant in two days, I suggest you get a move on with my lawyer."

This isn't going to be as easy as I thought. "Okay, I will speak to Ryan right after I leave here."

"Don't even think about double-crossing me," Dylan said, glaring at her.

Chills ran down her spine. "No, of course not," she said and looked away. "I'd better be going. I have a lot of details to work out."

"Yes, you do. You better get moving."

Refusing to allow herself to be discouraged, Sarah hung the phone up and walked over to the guard standing beside the door.

"I need to speak to the warden."

"I will have someone escort you to his office," the guard said, then reached for his radio and requested an escort. The warden was waiting for her when she reached his office.

"Nice to see you again, Mrs. Evans. Please have a seat." Sarah smiled and took her seat. "I guess you have some good news to report."

"Yes, Dylan is a match. The doctor wants to do the transplant in two days."

"That is great news! Wow, two days. I'll need to make the arrangements to have him transported. Which hospital will the transplant be taking place at?"

"Columbus Springs Hospital. I'll have Dr. Knolls reach out to you with all the details."

"Alright."

Sarah stared at him a minute, spinning her wedding ring around on her finger. "Can I ask you a question?"

"Sure."

"Do you think Dylan killed that woman? He claims he's innocent."

"I don't know, Sarah. Every inmate here says he is innocent. Let me give you some advice. Don't get involved. You don't want to get yourself mixed up with him. He's trouble. Let him donate his stem cells, get your husband better, and move on with your life."

He's right; don't get involved, Sarah. But what if he's innocent? Don't you want to know, for sure? "But what kind of inmate is he?"

"He's had his share of problems with other inmates. He certainly isn't a commendable prisoner. Why?"

"I was just wondering what kind of person he is. I don't know much about him." She looked down at her wedding ring and wondered why Michael kept his brother a secret. "I didn't even know my husband had a brother until just recently."

"If he wants to donate his stem cells, let him do it and say thank you but don't get sucked into feeling sorry for him. Dylan is dangerous; he will blackmail and manipulate you to get what he wants. Please be careful when dealing with him. Don't let his good looks make you feel sorry for him."

Sarah squirmed in her chair and then sat up straighter when she caught the warden gazing at her. "Is he blackmailing you?"

Sarah blushed. "No, no. I'm just curious about him. I wanted to know about the man who is going to save my husband's life." Sarah stood up, "I better be going. I need to get to the hospital. Thank you for meeting with me."

"You're welcome. I hope your husband gets better."

"Thank you. Me too." She left, and the guard standing on the other side of the office door escorted her out of the prison.

chapter 5

The receptionist looked up from her computer and rolled her eyes as soon as Sarah entered the Goldstein & Finch Law Firm. "Mr. Finch is in a meeting. He can't be disturbed," she said, coming around her desk and planting herself in front of Ryan's office door.

"I just need a minute of his time. It's important."

"I'm sure it is, but you need to make an appointment. You can't keep barging in here and expecting to see him any time you want. He is a busy man."

Sarah tried to get around the woman to enter the office, but she refused to move. "Ryan! Ryan! I need to talk to you; it's important."

Two seconds later, Ryan came out of his office. Julie gave Sarah a dirty look, then returned to her desk. "Sarah, what is it this time? I'm with a client." He grabbed her by the arm and guided her away from his door and out of earshot of his client.

"Dylan is a match. He has agreed to do the transplant, but he wants to speak to you first."

"So, what's the emergency? Just make an appointment with my secretary, and I will go and see him."

"You don't understand. Michael needs the transplant right away.

Dr. Knolls wants to do it in two days. I need you to meet with him right away."

"Okay, okay. I'll go and see him tomorrow. Now, please leave. I'm in the middle of a meeting."

Relief washed through her. This was going to happen. Michael was going to get his donation. He was going to live. Sarah hugged her cousin tightly, "Thank you so much!"

Ryan wiggled out of the hug and said, "I got to get back to my client."

After finishing up with his client, Ryan pulled the records for Dylan Hogan's case up on his computer and started reading the documents. From what he could tell, the prosecutor had a solid case against Dylan. Ryan dragged a hand over his balding head. What was he getting into with this? He printed out the court records and wrote himself a note on it to request a copy of the police files, then put the papers into a folder and into his briefcase.

The next day, Ryan went to visit with Dylan. He reviewed the court records as he waited for Dylan in the visitation room. Two minutes later, Dylan came shuffling into the room wearing an orange jumpsuit, his hands and feet shackled. Ryan looked him over; he was a good-looking man, physically fit, and in the prime of his life. He could see how Sarah wanted to believe in his innocence.

The guard removed the handcuffs from Dylan's wrists and then went outside and stood by the door. Ryan offered Dylan his hand and said, "Good afternoon, Dylan. My name is Ryan Finch, and I have been retained by Sarah Evans to represent you for your appeal."

Dylan shook Ryan's hand. "It's nice to meet you, Mr. Finch. Thank you for taking my case."

"Please, call me Ryan. First, things first, I need you to sign this if I am going to represent you." He slid a form and pen in front of Dylan. Dylan looked it over, then signed it and slid it back to Ryan.

"I read your file, so I know the details of your case, but I'm going to need you to tell me in your own words exactly what happened the night Stacy Richards was killed. Start from the beginning, tell me how you met and how long you knew each other before she died." Ryan pulled a pad and paper out of his briefcase and wrote notes as Dylan began to explain.

"Stacy and I had been seeing each other for several months. We met at a party on campus. My buddy, Sam, introduced us, and we hit it off. I walked her home from the party that night. I asked for her phone number, she gave it to me, and I kissed her goodnight. I called her the next day and asked her out on a date. We had been seeing each other a couple of times a week since the party."

Ryan sat back in his chair and raised an eyebrow. "Were you exclusive?"

"I'm not sure. I think so. We didn't have that conversation; I can only speak for myself. I wasn't seeing anyone else."

Ryan huffed and crossed his arms over his chest. "So, you don't know if she was seeing anyone else?"

"No, I guess I don't. But I really don't think she was seeing anyone else."

Ryan placed his hand under his chin and rested his elbow on the table. "Alright, so, tell me what happened the night she was murdered."

"I called her around 6 p.m. and asked her if she wanted to grab some dinner with me. She said yes, and I met her at La Cucina around seven. We had dinner then went back to her place. We had sex, and I left her apartment around 10:30."

Ryan was writing all this down on a pad. When he finished, he looked up at Dylan and asked, "Did you kill Stacy?"

Dylan's face turned red with anger. "No, absolutely not!"

Ryan's gut told him Dylan was telling the truth. "Do you have any idea who might have?"

"No, I thought about it a lot, and I can't think of anyone. Maybe someone tried to rape her, and she fought back, and he killed her."

"I'm glad you brought that up. Did you rape her? Maybe she said no, and things got out of control?"

Dylan slammed his fist on the table. "No, I already told you. It was consensual. We were dating. There were plenty of girls I could have had sex with that night. I would never rape a woman."

Ryan got up and paced the room. "If I am going to represent you, I need you to be completely honest with me. If there is anything you are hiding, now is the time to tell me. I don't want any surprises once we go to court." Ryan leaned over Dylan and spoke into his ear, "Do we understand each other?"

Dylan turned to face Ryan. "I'm not hiding anything. I didn't kill her. You've got to believe me."

Ryan went back around to the other side of the table and took his seat. "Okay, let's talk about your alibi. Is there anyone who can testify that you left her apartment around 10:30?"

Dylan dropped his head down, "No, I went straight home and went to sleep."

"Did you have a roommate?"

"Yes, but he wasn't home when I got there. The police already interviewed him; he didn't get home until 1 a.m."

"Do you know if the police had any other suspects?"

"I don't know. They had me guilty right from the start. I doubt they even looked for any other suspect."

"I will find out. I requested a copy of the police file."

"What are my chances of getting a new trial?"

"First, we have to find a reason for an appeal. That's why I need to know if there were any other suspects. I'm also going to need to do some investigating into Stacy's past. Are you prepared for that? We may have to question her character."

Dylan leaned back in his chair and sighed. "Stacy was a nice girl. I don't think you will find anything in her past."

"You'd be surprised what people can hide. What about you? Is there anything in your past I need to know about?"

"No, I have nothing to hide. Look, I don't know what Sarah or Michael told you about me, but I'm not a bad person. Michael hates me because his dad had an affair with my mother. He's mad at the wrong person."

Ryan put his pen down. "I think I have enough to get started. Give me a week to get the police file and do some research, and I will come back to see you and let you know if I think we have a chance at getting an appeal."

Dylan looked directly into Ryan's eyes. "Thank you, Ryan. I didn't kill her; I can't spend the best years of my life behind bars for a murder I didn't commit."

"I'll be in touch." He placed his notepad into his briefcase, then knocked on the door and told the guard waiting on the other side of the door. "We're done here."

chapter

6

When Sarah got to the hospital on Wednesday morning, Dylan was being prepped for his blood donation. He was lying in bed next to a large machine, wearing a hospital gown and a disposable bouffant cap as a nurse explained the procedure to him. She was surprised to see that he didn't seem nearly as tough to her as he did when he was in prison. She thought he looked somewhat vulnerable and maybe even a little scared.

"Dr. Knolls will use a small catheter to draw your blood. It will go directly into this machine to separate the stem cells out of it, and then the blood will be returned to your body. This whole process will take anywhere from one to two hours and will need to be done anywhere from two to four times, depending on how many stem cells the patient needs. Some common side effects you may experience are chills, numbness or tingling around your mouth, and cramping in your hands. You will be given a medication to help your body replace the stem cells. This medicine can cause bone pain, muscle aches, headache, fatigue, nausea, and vomiting. You will remain in the hospital for recovery anywhere from a few days up to a week. Do you have any questions?"

"Yes, what are the risks of complications?"

"There is less than a 1% chance of severe risks and complications, such as heart-related issues." His forehead beaded with sweat.

"Can Sarah stay with me during the procedure?" He turned to look at her for solace.

"Yes, of course she can."

Sarah walked closer to his bed and gave him a reassuring smile.

Dylan reached his hand out, and Sarah hesitated before she accepted it. Just then, Dr. Knolls entered the room.

"Hello, Mr. Hogan, Sarah. How is everyone feeling today?"

"I'm a little nervous," Dylan said.

"That's understandable. You are doing a good thing for your brother. You have the chance to become a hero today." Dr. Knolls smiled at Sarah.

"Would you like something to calm your nerves?"

"No, thank you. I'll be alright."

"Okay. If you are ready, we will get started. All I need you to do is lie back and try to relax. Just let me know if you are experiencing any of the side effects the nurse went over with you. If you need to stop, we can take a break if necessary."

"Ready."

Dylan looked nervous for the first several minutes. Sarah wanted to distract him to help get his mind off the procedure and was eager to learn more about her husband's past that he kept from her.

"So, tell me, Dylan. How did you and Michael meet?"

"We met when we were nine years old. Michael and I were on the same soccer team. We hit it off right away. Our parents would sit together and talk to each other at our games. Before we knew it, they had become good friends, and we were having picnics together and going on vacations together. We didn't know it at the time, but my mother and his father had an affair ten years earlier, which produced a baby. My mom was married to my father at the time, so she just passed it off as his. When Michael and I became friends, the two reconnected, and the affair started up all over again."

Sarah swallows, pushing down the lump in her throat so she can get her words out. "You must have been sad when you and Michael were no longer friends."

"Yes, I missed him a lot at first, but then he attacked me, and I hated him. You know what is funny? Michael and I wanted to be brothers so bad that when we were eleven years old, we pricked our fingers and mixed our blood together so that we could become blood brothers. Then, one day, we found out that we actually were brothers, and we didn't want to be brothers anymore. What is it they say, be careful what you wish for because you just might get it?"

Dylan was sweating profusely; his forehead and hair were soaked. "Do you feel okay? You don't look too good," Sarah asked Dylan, then she looked over at the nurse. "Is this normal?"

The nurse moved closer to Dylan and asked, "How are you holding up? Do you need to take a break?" then she wiped his forehead with a towel.

"No, I'll be alright. Please continue."

"Okay, you just let me know if you need a break."

"I will."

Still trying to figure out what she had gotten herself into, she asked, "So, what did Ryan have to say about your case?"

"He is looking into reasons for an appeal. He's going to request the police files and get back to me in a week."

"Oh, that's good. Ryan is an excellent criminal lawyer. Don't worry; he will find something."

"I hope you're right." Dylan began to shiver. The nurse went to get him a heated blanket and laid it on top of him.

"I'm sorry, it's so hard on you. I can't thank you enough for doing this for Michael."

Dylan nodded, then closed his eyes and laid his head back on the pillow.

Sarah and Dylan didn't talk for the remainder of the procedure. It was quiet except for the sound of Dylan's blood whirling through the machine next to them. Finally, after another forty-five minutes, Dr. Knolls returned, looked at a reading on the machine, and announced they were done for today.

"Great job, Dylan. How are you feeling?"

"Tired."

"That's to be expected." He turned the machine off and then disconnected the catheter. I'm going to need you to get some rest. We are going to need to repeat the procedure tomorrow to get more stem cells."

"Okay, doctor. I'll try."

Sarah said, "I'll go now, so you can get some rest."

"Okay, but you'll be back tomorrow, right?"

"Yes, I'll see you tomorrow."

Sarah and Dr. Knolls left the room and walked together to Michael's room.

"How many times do you think he will need to go through that?" Sarah asked the doctor.

"Hopefully, just twice. Once we give Michael the healthy stem cells through an IV transfusion, we must wait and see how his body reacts to them. You never know if the cancer will fight them. Michael has undergone a massive dose of chemotherapy and radiation, so I am optimistic his body will accept them."

When they got to Michael's room, the doctor checked the chart hanging at the end of his bed.

Sarah went to Michael's bedside, "Hi, honey. How are you today?" Sarah put her hand to his forehead. He was still unresponsive but was no longer burning up.

"His fever is down. That is a good sign, right?" Sarah asked the doctor.

"Yes, we can't give him the transfusion if he has an infection. If he continues to keep the fever down, we can do the transfusion in a couple of days."

"Did you hear that, Michael? You need to keep fighting the infection so that you can get the transfusion and get better."

Dr. Knolls returned the chart to the end of Michael's bed and then said, "Okay, I will check on Michael later."

"Thank you, doctor."

The next day, when Sarah arrived at the hospital, Dylan's procedure had already started. He was lying in his bed with his eyes closed, sweating profusely.

"Good morning, everyone," Sarah said when she entered his room.

"Good morning," the nurse from yesterday said with a smile.

Dylan slowly opened his eyes and barely whispered, "Good morning."

"You okay?" Sarah asked.

"I've been better." He was shaking uncontrollably.

"Do you want another heated blanket?" Sarah asked.

"He already has two," the nurse answered.

"I just can't get warm." As soon as Dylan said the words, he fell back against his pillow and started convulsing.

"Blood pressure dropping!" yelled the nurse. "Get Dr. Knolls!"

Seconds later, Dr. Knolls came rushing into the room with a crash cart. Sarah backed away from Dylan's bed and watched as the doctor placed the electric paddles from the defibrillator to his chest and yelled, "Clear," before shocking his heart.

Another nurse came into the room and grabbed Sarah by the elbow, pulling her out of the room, "I'm going to need you to wait in the waiting area. Dr. Knolls will come and speak with you as soon as he can."

Sarah anxiously paced the waiting room and worried if Dylan was going to make it. If Dylan were to die, would Michael's chance of surviving die as well? It seemed like an eternity before Dr. Knolls finally came to see her.

"We were able to stabilize him, but his heart is weak."

"What happened?"

"He suffered a heart attack."

"I don't understand. He's so young. He doesn't have any known heart problems."

"It can happen. Sometimes the body has trouble dealing with the amount of stress the procedure can put on the organs."

"Will he be okay?"

"We have to wait and see. I wish I had better news. We really don't know what will happen. He is stable but unresponsive. We are moving him to the intensive care unit."

"Can I see him before you move him?"

"Yes, come with me."

Sarah stood next to Dylan's bedside with tears in her eyes for a man she had not even known a week ago. "Dylan, I'm so sorry. Please, you have to be strong and fight hard." *Michael's life depends on it,* she thought but didn't say.

chapter

7

Despite Dylan's health concerns, Dr. Knolls said that he had enough stem cells to move forward with Michael's transplant. Just like with Dylan, Sarah was sitting by her husband's bedside, but this time, she was praying for a miracle.

Dr. Knolls explained, "Dylan's stem cells will be infused into Michael intravenously. The procedure will take several hours to perform. We will be monitoring his vitals and blood count throughout the day. The side effects are much of the same as they were for Dylan; nausea, drop in blood pressure, sweating and pain."

Sarah's jaw tensed, and Dr. Knolls must have noticed because his next words were reassuring. "There is no reason to presume that Michael will experience a heart attack like Dylan did. But, Sarah, there are other things to worry about, such as graft versus host disease and graft failure."

"What is that?"

"Graft versus host is when the body identifies the new cells as foreign and attacks them. Graft failure is when the transplanted cells fail to function and produce new cells. And of course, there is always the risk of infection. It's going to be a rough couple of days, and it will take anywhere from two to six weeks before his blood cell counts will return to normal levels."

Refusing to give up hope, Sarah said, "I understand."

As far as Sarah could tell, Michael did not seem to be experiencing the same symptoms as Dylan had. He wasn't sweating and didn't seem to be in any discomfort. She watched the blood pressure monitor intensely and was relieved to see that his pressure remained at a normal level. When the procedure was finally over, Sarah let out a sigh of relief and stopped wringing her hands. She wiped her sweaty palms on her pants and went closer to his bedside.

"It's all done, honey. Now all you need to do is rest and let the stem cells do their thing. I'm exhausted. I'm going to go home and get some rest now, but I'll be back tomorrow."

She kissed Michael on his forehead and left. Before leaving the hospital, she went to the ICU to get an update on Dylan's condition. When she got to Dylan's room, she was surprised to see a woman visiting him because she was told that prisoners were not allowed visitors.

She looked at the guard at the door, he gave her a nod, and she cautiously entered the room and approached the woman, curious as to what Dylan meant to her. The young woman turned and looked up at Sarah; her puffy eyes and blotchy red face told Sarah that Dylan was important to her. "Oh, hello. I'm Sarah. Who are you?"

The woman gave her a warm smile, "I'm Jenna. Dylan and I are friends. Actually, we used to date back in high school."

"Oh, nice to meet you, Jenna. If you don't mind if I ask, how did you know Dylan was here?"

"I'm friends with his sister, Lori. The hospital called her to notify her of his situation." Jenna hesitated a moment, "I don't know why I'm here. I haven't talked to Dylan in years, not since he went to prison. I just felt that I needed to come. How is he doing?"

"No change yet. I was hoping to catch Dr. Knolls to get an update. He usually makes his rounds sometime after five."

"Do you mind if I wait with you?" Jenna asked.

"Of course not. I would love the company. The last couple of days have been crazy. I've been doing a lot of sitting around and waiting. It would be nice to have a distraction." Being a journalist, Sarah couldn't let the opportunity pass without finding out more about Dylan. "I don't really know Dylan that well. What was he like in high school?"

"Oh, Dylan was such a hunk; all the girls wanted to date him, and all the boys wanted to be him. He was quite popular, but he never let it get to his head. Everyone liked him because he was a really nice guy."

"Did you date long?"

"Yes, we started dating in tenth grade and dated all through high school. We only broke up because we both went off to college and didn't want to do a long-distance relationship. I never really got over him. I always thought we would get back together someday, but then he was sent to prison."

Still unsure of whether Dylan was guilty or innocent, Sarah wanted to know more about his case so she could make her mind up. "About that, what can you tell me about his case? Did you go to his trial?"

"I can't tell you much. I didn't go to the trial because I was in college at the time. But I can tell you this. Dylan didn't kill that girl. He would never hurt anyone."

"How do you know that? You weren't there," Sarah said accusatorily.

Jenna's eyes narrowed, and she shot her a curt answer. "Because I know Dylan, and I know that he isn't capable of murder."

"Did anyone ever ask you to speak at his trial as a character witness when he was sentenced?"

Jenna huffed, still clearly annoyed with Sarah. "No. Why are you so curious about his trial?"

"Because I hired a lawyer to file an appeal for him."

She raised an eyebrow at Sarah, "Why did you do that? You said you don't really know him."

"I promised Dylan I would help him if he did the stem cell transplant for my husband. At first, I was curious about his case, but now, I feel responsible for him being here. I will do everything in my power to find the truth. If it turns out that Dylan is innocent, he will be set free, and justice will be served."

Unsure of Sarah's intentions, Jenna asked, "Are you some kind of journalist or something?"

"Yes, but it's more than just that. If Dylan is a good person, like you say, then I want to help him like he helped Michael."

Just then, Dr. Knolls arrived to check on Dylan's status. "Good evening, ladies."

"Hi, doctor. How is Dylan doing?"

"I just came from a meeting with several of Dylan's doctors. If you would like to join me in the conference room across the hall, after I am done examining Dylan, I will give you an update on status and plan of care."

"Okay, thank you, doctor." The two ladies left Dylan's room and went to wait in the conference room. Several minutes later, a tired Dr. Knolls came to see them with a look of concern on his face. He took a seat on the bench across from the ladies, then took a deep breath.

"Dylan has been experiencing several mild heart attacks since his first attack. His white blood cells count is not coming back to where we would like them to be by now. We are increasing his medication to help produce more of them. After much consideration, the best course of action recommended by his team of doctors is to put Dylan into a medically-induced coma until we can get his white blood cells to stabilize and stop putting a strain on his heart."

Sarah put her hand on her forehead as her head started to throb. "That sounds dangerous. Isn't there anything else you can do?"

"Unfortunately, no. This is the best chance for a full recovery. Any one of these heart attacks can be fatal. We need to stop them; this is the best way we know how."

Sarah asked, "How long will he have to be in a coma?"

"We don't know for sure. Just until we can get his blood count back to where it should be."

"I did this to him. I'm so sorry." She turned to look at Jenna with tears in her eyes and started shaking uncontrollably.

Jenna hugged her, "It's okay. He's going to be okay."

"I'm sorry, but I have some more patients to see. I'll see you tomorrow, Sarah," Dr. Knolls placed his hand on Sarah's shoulder and said, "I'm sorry," before leaving.

"Come on. It's late. Let's get you home." Jenna walked Sarah to her car, then said, "Give me your phone."

Sarah handed Jenna her phone, and Jenna put her phone number into it.

"Here's my number. Text me when you get home, so I know you made it home okay."

"Thank you, Jenna. I will."

When Sarah got home, she settled into bed after texting Jenna to let her know she was home. She called Megan and gave her an update on Michael and Dylan and filled her in on her encounter with Jenna.

"I don't know, Megan. She is really confident that Dylan is innocent."

"Of course she is. She loves him. She doesn't want to believe that she is in love with a monster."

chapter

8

The next day, before going back to the hospital, Sarah called the Goldstein & Finch Law firm and made an appointment to see Ryan later in the day. She was anxious to get to the hospital to see if there was an improvement in Michael and Dylan's conditions. The nurse was taking Michael's vital signs when she got there.

"How is he doing?" Sarah asked.

"His vitals are good. We have been monitoring his blood count, and his white blood cells are increasing. That is a really good sign." Sarah smiled and let out a sigh of relief.

"Did you hear that, Michael? The stem cells are working."

"When do you think he will be waking up?" Sarah asked the nurse.

"I don't know. That would be a question for Dr. Knolls."

"Okay, I will ask him."

Sarah sat with Michael for close to an hour before leaving to go and visit Dylan. When she exited the elevator onto the ICU floor, she found herself face to face with Jenna, who was just leaving.

"Oh, hi, Jenna. How is Dylan today?" Sarah asked.

"He looks peaceful. The nurse said he hasn't had any heart attacks in the past six hours, which is a really good sign."

"What about his blood count?"

"It's still the same. It hasn't improved. Come on; I'll sit with you," Jenna said and put her arm around her, then walked her towards Dylan's room. When they got there, Sarah was not prepared for the emotions she felt towards this man. She wanted to hug him but didn't know if it would be appropriate. He looked so peaceful; it was as if he were sleeping. She touched his hand and spoke softly to him.

"Hi, Dylan. It's Sarah. I'm meeting with Ryan today to go over your case with him. Hopefully, I will have some good news for you tomorrow. But you don't need to worry about that right now. You just focus on getting better, and I will take care of your appeal."

"Do you mind if I go with you to the meeting?" Jenna asked Sarah.

Relieved to have another person's perspective on the matter, Sarah responded, "No, not at all. I would love it if you did."

Sarah and Jenna sat by Dylan's bedside as Jenna shared funny stories and memories of Dylan for over an hour. The two women laughed and smiled, and Sarah felt that she was finally getting to know and understand the man lying before her.

"We need to get going if we don't want to be late for our meeting with Ryan," Sarah said.

She touched Dylan's hand, "I'll be back tomorrow."

The two of them left the hospital and rode together to Ryan's office.

"I really hope Ryan has some good news for us," Sarah said.

"Me too."

When they got to the office, Sarah approached Julie's desk and said, "Good afternoon, Julie. We have a three o'clock appointment with Ryan."

Julie called Ryan on the phone and announced they were there, then said, "Please have a seat, and he will be with you in a minute." Apparently, when Sarah wasn't pushing past her, the woman could be quite pleasant.

A few minutes later, Ryan's door opened, and he and a client walked

Blood Brothers

out of the office. They shook hands and said their goodbyes, then Ryan turned to Sarah and Jenna, "Hi, Sarah, please come in."

The two ladies followed Ryan into the office, and he shut his door behind them then took his seat.

"Ryan, this is Jenna. She is a friend of Dylan's since high school," Sarah said.

"It's nice to meet you, Jenna. How is Michael doing?"

The two women took a seat, and Sarah said, "So far, so good. His white blood cell count is going up. Dr. Knolls is extremely optimistic about his recovery."

"That's great news."

Anxious to hear what Ryan had to say, Sarah got right to business, "So, what did you find out? Do we have a case for an appeal?"

"So, Dylan said he left Stacy's apartment around 10:30 p.m. and that she was still alive when he left. According to the coroner, Stacy's time of death was anytime between 11:30 p.m. to 1:30 a.m. If we can prove that Dylan left at 10:30 and did not return to her apartment at any time that night, I think we have a good chance at filing an appeal."

Sarah hung on to his every word as she visualized the night in her head.

Ryan continued, "I did some digging, and I found out that the apartment building where she lived had video security cameras. I checked the trial records, and there were no security tapes presented as evidence. I need to find out why that was the case. If there were tapes, where are they, and why weren't they presented as evidence? I plan on making a visit to the apartment complex after our meeting today."

She clapped her hands together, realizing that this was big. "That's great news!"

"Don't get too excited, Sarah. Maybe the reason the tapes weren't presented is because they don't exist. Also, even if there were tapes, they may have been destroyed by now. It has been several years since her murder."

43

Sarah shrugged her shoulders in response to what he had just said, "Okay, what else do we have?"

"I pulled the police files. There were two other persons of interest besides Dylan. One was a guy by the name of Mark Gordon. He was dating Stacy just before she started dating Dylan. Stacy's friends said that she broke up with him because he was jealous and possessive. His alibi was that he was home sleeping. The only person to confirm his alibi was his mother, which is a flimsy alibi if you ask me. I'm going to have a private investigator check him out. See what kind of guy he is."

"That's good. What about the other suspect?"

"It was a guy named Paul Nelson. Apparently, he was stalking Stacy. She filed a restraining order on him two months before she was murdered. He was removed from the suspect list because several people attested that he was at a party the night of her murder and didn't leave until close to 2:00 a.m. I'm going to check it out, anyway. How is Dylan doing? I'd like to pay him a visit to talk to him about his case."

A look of realization passed over Sarah's face, "Oh, I didn't tell you? Dylan was placed in a medically induced coma to stabilize his heart. You're not going to be able to speak with him. Will this have any effect on his appeal?"

"Sorry to hear that. No, if I get enough evidence to substantiate an appeal, I can file it on his behalf. He doesn't even need to be there for a trial."

"That's good."

"Okay, if there isn't anything else, I'd like to finish up here and pay a visit to Stacy's apartment complex."

"Just one question," Sarah shot a look at Jenna before she asked, "Do you think that Dylan is innocent?"

"I haven't made my mind up yet. I'll let you know after I see this tape, if it even exists."

Jenna spoke up for the first time. "I'm telling you; Dylan is innocent. He didn't hurt anyone. You'll see."

Sarah placed a hand on Jenna's arm then got up to leave, "We better let you get going. Thank you, Ryan. Good luck."

After the two women left, Ryan shut down his computer and left his office. He walked by his secretary's desk and said, "Good night, Julie. I'm leaving for the rest of the day."

"Good night, Ryan."

Ryan drove to the Cardinal Pointe high-rise apartment complex and walked inside, taking note of where the security cameras were located as he did. He went to the security desk and said to the guard, "Hello, I would like to speak to the superintendent."

"Is he expecting you?"

"No."

"What may I tell him this is regarding?"

"I am a lawyer representing Dylan Hogan. I'd like to speak to him about the murder of Stacy Richards. She was a tenant here four years ago."

"Just a minute." The guard called the superintendent on the phone, and several minutes later, a chubby man wearing work clothes and carrying a wrench came out to greet him. He pulled a rag out of his back pocket, cleaned his hands, then offered one to Ryan.

"I'm Jim. I'm the superintendent here. You asked to speak to me?"

"Hi, Jim. I'm Ryan Finch. I represent Dylan Hogan regarding the death of Stacy Richards. Is there somewhere we can talk in private?"

"Sure, right this way." Ryan followed Jim into his cluttered apartment. "Can I get you something to drink? I have water and lemonade."

"No, thank you. I'm fine. I just need to ask you a couple of questions if that is alright?"

"Yeah, sure." Jim cleared a pile of newspapers off a chair. "Please have a seat." Ryan took a seat at the kitchen table and tried not to touch any of the stuff piled in front of him.

"How long have you been working here?" Ryan looked around the apartment. Judging by the amount of clutter he had accumulated, he suspected that Jim had lived there for many years.

"Almost ten years now."

"So, you were here when Stacy Richards was murdered?"

"Yes, that was terrible. Such as sweet girl, and so young too."

"Did you know Dylan?"

"Not too well. I did see him coming and going from the building. He was a friend of Stacy's, right?"

"Yes, they were dating. What did you think of him? Were you surprised to hear he was arrested for her murder?"

"He seemed nice. He always went out of his way to say hello when he saw me. He held the door open for everyone. I thought he was a good guy, which is why I was surprised to find out he murdered that young girl."

"How long have they had the security cameras?"

"I don't know. They've been here since I have been here."

"Have they always worked? I'm curious because the security tapes never came up as evidence in Dylan's trial."

"I know." Jim got up and went over to a bookshelf and retrieved a tape. Despite the chaos of the apartment, Jim knew exactly where everything was. He walked back and placed the tape on the table. "The tapes are recorded over after seven days. Once I heard about the murder, I removed the tape so it wouldn't be recorded over. I thought it might be needed as evidence. I was expecting the police to ask for it, but they never did."

Surprised, Ryan raised an eyebrow and asked, "Did you tell them you had it?"

"Yes, when they didn't ask for it. I called them and told them I had it. They asked me what time it showed Dylan left that night, and I told them. They said they would come and get it, but they never did."

"May I have it?" Ryan could see some hesitation on Jim's face. "I can get a court order if necessary?"

"No, that's not necessary. I guess it will be okay."

"Did you happen to look at it?"

"Yes."

"Do you recall what time Dylan left the building that night?"

"It's been so long. If my memory is correct, I think it was around 10:30, but let's take a look."

Jim and Ryan went into Jim's office and put the tape into the player and rewound it back to 10:15 p.m. then fast-forwarded it until Dylan exited the elevator and walked into the lobby. He froze the screen just as Dylan pulled the door open, about to exit the building. The timestamp read 10:25 p.m.

"According to the coroner, Stacy was murdered somewhere between 11:30 p.m. and 1:30 a.m. I need to see everyone who came and went during that time period. Would that be on this tape as well?"

"Yes. I didn't remove the tape until 7:00 a.m. the next day."

"Thank you so much, Jim. You have been very helpful. I may need you to testify about this evidence if we end up going back to trial."

"You're welcome. Whatever I can do to help."

chapter

Sarah rounded the corner of the hospital floor and heard her husband say, "Where is Sarah?" when she was right outside of his room. She rushed into the room and found Michael sitting up in bed, talking to his sister Megan.

"You're awake!" She hurried to his side and gave him a big hug. "I can't believe you're awake. How do you feel?"

"I feel okay," he smiled at his wife. "Dr. Knolls says my blood count is going up, and if it continues to go up, I will feel better and better every day. How long was I out of it?"

"A week. Your organs started to shut down. I was so scared. I thought I was going to lose you." She hugged him again.

"Yeah, Dr. Knolls said I was really close to dying. It's a good thing you found a donor when you did. Was it someone we know?"

Sarah took a deep breath. "Michael, your donor was your brother Dylan."

Michael's eyes widened, and his nostril flared, "What? Who told you about Dylan?"

Megan spoke up, "I did. She found a picture of the two of you and asked who he was. Don't be mad at her. She saved your life."

"I don't want anything from him. You knew that Megan. What now? I suppose everyone expects me to forgive him?" He clenched his jaw and pouted his lips.

Sarah raised her voice in anger, "Forgive him for what? He didn't do anything wrong. It was your father who had the affair, not Dylan. He saved your life, Michael. You have no idea what he has been through for you. You should be grateful to him."

"Grateful for what? I bet he blackmailed you into doing it. Dylan doesn't do anything for nothing." He saw the look on her face and knew that it was true. "I knew it. What does he want, Sarah?"

"He wants me to help him with his appeal. I hired my cousin, Ryan."

Michael threw his hands into the air. "You did what? Forget it, Sarah. You don't even know what you are getting yourself into. Do you even know what he was charged with? Murder, Sarah. He is a murderer, and you are going to help set him free."

"You don't know that. Have you ever even researched his case?" She placed her hands on her hips and raised her voice. "Do you hate him so much that you never even considered he might be innocent?"

"He's not," Michael crossed his arms in anger and turned away from Sarah.

"He's in a coma, Michael. He's in a coma because he helped you. He may die. You think about that while you lie here hating him." She left the room in a huff, tears swelling up in her eyes.

Michael turned to Megan, "Is that true?"

"Yes, he had a heart attack when he was donating his stem cells. His body isn't making white blood cells to replace the ones he gave you. The doctor put him into a medically-induced coma to relieve the strain on his organs."

Michael got quiet for a moment, then he said, "Well, I didn't ask him to do this for me."

"No, your wife who loves you very much did. She couldn't bear the thought of losing you. She would do anything to help you. You need to think about that when you are sitting here being mad at the people who saved your life."

Michael grit his teeth. "So, you think he is innocent too?"

"I don't know. We never even considered it. Maybe he is innocent. Let the lawyers figure it out. You owe him that much, Michael. He saved your life."

Michael turned away and looked out the window in disgust.

"I'm going to go check on Sarah. I'll see you later." She leaned in to give her brother a kiss, and he turned his cheek away from her.

Megan found Sarah sitting in the waiting room down the hall, her hands covering her face as she cried. Megan sat down beside her and put her arm around her. "You okay?"

"Can you believe him? He is being so ungrateful."

"Yeah, I expected this reaction. Just give him time. He'll come around. He's not heartless. This is just a shock for him."

"Dylan is in a coma because he helped him, because I asked him to. I won't rest until I make things right."

"Come on," Megan stood and put her hand out to Sarah. "It's been a long day. Let's get out of here. Why don't you come to my house and have dinner with Jake and me?"

"Okay, I just want to visit Dylan for a while, then I'll come over."

"That's fine. It will give me time to start dinner."

Sarah went to Dylan's room to visit him and update him on his case.

"I had a meeting with Ryan today. He has some good leads on your case. If he gets enough evidence, he can move forward with your appeal, even if you can't be there."

She touched Dylan's hand, "Michael woke up today. Your stem cells are working. You did a good thing, Dylan. I'm going to repay you for this one day, I promise."

Sarah sat with Dylan for another twenty minutes and then said, "I'll see you tomorrow, Dylan," then left.

When she got to Megan and Jake's house, she rang the bell and waited for someone to answer. It was only a matter of seconds before Jake opened the door and greeted her.

"Sarah, come on in. It's so nice to see you. How is Michael doing? I've been meaning to go and visit him." He leaned in and gave her a kiss on the cheek.

"Hi, Jake. He's doing okay. He woke up today. Dr. Knolls said his blood count is improving." Sarah removed her coat and handed it to Jake.

"That's great. Megan is in the kitchen. Would you like a glass of wine or something else to drink?"

"Wine would be great." They walked into the kitchen and joined Megan, then Jake went to the wine cooler to get a bottle of wine.

"Something smells good," Sarah said.

"I hope you like chili," Megan said, using a ladle to scoop chili out of a pot and into a serving bowl.

"I love it, especially on a cold night like tonight. Thank you for having me over for dinner. I haven't had a home-cooked meal in weeks."

"You're welcome. I hope things can go back to normal soon now that Michael is doing better."

"Me too. But now I'm worried about Dylan too."

"Why are you worried about him?" Jake asked.

Sarah looked at Jake with a confused expression, "What do you mean, why? Because I asked him to help Michael, and now, he's in a coma."

Jake shrugged his shoulders, "You don't owe him anything."

Sarah shook her head, and her eyes got big. "Not you too. What is wrong with all of you? I owe him everything; he saved my husband's life."

"Let's eat!" Megan said, carrying the serving bowl of chili to the kitchen table and giving her husband a stern look.

During dinner, Jake asked, "What is Ryan saying about Dylan's chances of getting an appeal?"

"He's looking into it. He has a couple of leads he is following up on. There were two other suspects the police investigated. He's going to check into them."

"Did he say who they were?" Jake asked.

Sarah buttered a piece of bread and said, "Yes, one of the suspects was someone Stacy dated before Dylan, and the other was a guy who was stalking her. Ryan is running a background check on them, but it may be nothing. The police did rule them out."

"Yeah, don't get your hopes up. I'm sure it's nothing," Jake put a spoonful of chili in his mouth and ate it.

"You're probably right. It's just that Jenna is so sure that Dylan could not have killed anyone, and the more time I spend with her and learn about Dylan, the more I feel it in my gut that he didn't do it."

"Are you sure you just don't want to believe that he did it because you are grateful to him for saving Michael's life?" Jake asked.

Sarah sat back in her chair, "I don't know. Maybe."

"Can we please talk about something else? I invited Sarah to dinner to help get her mind off her problems for a little while," Megan said.

Jake said, "Sure, I'm sorry. How are things going at the store?"

"Great. Sales are really starting to pick up, but it always does right before the holidays."

After dinner, the three of them sat by the fire in the living room and enjoyed a cup of cocoa while Megan shared stories about their childhood.

"What was Dylan like as a child?" Sarah asked.

"He was smart and funny and athletic. He loved all kinds of sports. If he wasn't playing them, he was watching them on tv. I loved having him around the house all the time. I missed him so much after every-thing happened."

"Do you think he and Michael can ever mend their relationship?"

Megan said, "I don't know. If they don't repair their relationship after this, I don't think they ever will. I think it all depends on whether or not Dylan is innocent."

"Yeah, you're probably right. Well, it's getting late. I better go." Megan and Jake walked Sarah to the door. When they opened the door for her to leave, they saw that it had snowed while Sarah was there. Jake got his coat and said, "Give me your keys. I'll start your car and clean it off for you."

Sarah bent down and put her boots on. "That's okay. You don't have to do that."

"Don't be silly, I insist." He took her keys from her then grabbed his coat out of the closet. "It will only take a minute." He went outside to clean her car. When he was done, he came back and said, "You're good to go."

"Thank you both for everything. I don't know what I would do without you, guys," Sarah said, then she gave each of them a kiss good night.

chapter 10

hase Templeton, the retired cop/private investigator Ryan hired, was having trouble locating Stacy's ex-boyfriend, Mark Gordon. Mark's last known address was from four years ago. When he moved out of that apartment, it was as if he fell off the face of the earth. There were no credit card transactions, no bank statements, and no driver's licenses renewals.

Wondering if he was deceased, Chase did a search for a death certificate and found nothing. *Okay, I'll have to come back to him*, he thought. Next, he did a search for the stalker, Paul Nelson. He found that Paul had a history of harassing women. There were multiple restraining orders filed against him over the years by women he was obsessed with. Stacy was not the first woman to file a complaint against him.

He had multiple arrests for breaking his restraining orders and stealing personal items from woman's homes. He was currently being held at the county jail for breaking a restraining order. *Okay, he will be easy to locate. I'll pay him a visit later today.*

Chase wrote down the names of the three people who attested to seeing Paul at the party the night of the murder. Then he did searches for their home addresses and places of employment. Two of the people were still in Ohio, but one had moved to Arizona. He would have to call her. He wrote her phone number next to her name then immediately dialed the number. After several rings, a woman answered the phone, "Hello."

"Hello, I would like to speak to Margie Culligan."

"This is she."

"Hello, Margie. My name is Chase Templeton. I work for Goldstein & Finch Law Firm on behalf of Dylan Hogan."

Sounding a little annoyed, she said, "I don't know a Dylan Hogan. What is this about?"

"It is about the death of Stacy Richards. Dylan Hogan is the man currently serving time for her murder."

"Oh, but I don't know him. I still don't know how I can help you."

"Please, let me explain. I am not calling to speak to you about Dylan. I would like to ask you a few questions about Paul Nelson. Do you know him?"

"Yes, I know Paul." She hesitated, "He's a real creep."

"I understand that you attested to seeing him at a party the night Stacy was murdered. Is that correct?"

"Yes, he was there."

"And you are absolutely sure the party was on the night of the murder?"

"Yes. If she was murdered on September 12th, then I'm sure. It was my boyfriend's birthday, and I threw him a party that night."

"Okay, that's good. You said that he left the party around 2 a.m., correct?"

"Yes, he was one of the last to leave."

"Approximately how many people were in attendance at this party?"

"I don't know; fifty or sixty."

"Good, good. Is it possible that he left the party and came back, and you didn't notice?"

"Sure, I guess it's possible."

"You called him a creep. Would you care to elaborate on that?"

"Yeah, the way he stares at women. It creeps me out. I didn't know it at the time, but it came out later that he was a stalker. I'm not surprised, after seeing the way he obsesses over women. Listen, I'm late for work. Is there anything else I can help you with?"

"No, that's it. Thank you for your help Margie. Have a good day."

"You too, bye."

Chase made notes about his phone call next to Margie's name, then closed the folder and headed to the county jail to pay a visit to Paul Nelson. He sat in an interrogation room and waited for Paul. When the door opened, a tall, scrawny, tattooed-covered man entered the room and took a seat at the table.

Paul looked Chase over, "Who are you?" he asked in a rude manner.

"My name is Chase Templeton. I am a private investigator. I'd like to have a word with you about Stacy Richards."

"Oh, no way. I'm not talking to you. You're just trying to pin her death on me. I didn't have nothing to do with her death."

"Then help me exclude you."

"Look, man, I was at a party the night she was murdered. There were plenty of eyewitnesses who saw me there." A look of confusion came over Paul's face. "They already got the guy who killed her. He's in prison. Why are you here?"

"I was hired by a law firm that is representing his appeal."

Paul got up from the table and said, "We're done here." He went over to the door and yelled, "Guard!" Then the guard took him back to his cell.

After leaving the jail, Chase paid a visit to Sampson's Fish Factory and went straight to the office. He waited several minutes for two men in a heated conversation to acknowledge him. When they didn't, he cleared his throat to get their attention. Finally, the two men turned around and looked at him. "Can I help you?" The one man asked, sounding annoyed.

"Yes, I was wondering if I could have a word with one of your employees by the name of John Townson?"

"What is this about? He in trouble?"

"No, no trouble. It's not about him. I want to talk to him about someone's whereabouts on the night of a murder."

The man gave him a questionable look. "Are you sure he's not in trouble?"

"Yes, I'm sure. It's not him who's in trouble."

The manager turned back to the man he was just arguing with and said, "We are done here. Can you send John in?"

"Sure." The man left the office.

"Have a seat. You want a cup of coffee?" the manager asked Chase.

"No, thank you." He took a seat as requested.

Several minutes passed, then the door to the office opened. A man stuck his head into the room, "You wanted to see me, boss?"

"Yes, there is a private investigator here to speak to you."

John turned to look at Chase with concern. Chase got up out of his chair and extended his hand to John.

"Nice to meet you, John. My name is Chase Templeton. I would like to ask you a few questions about Paul Nelson. If that's okay with you."

John shook his hand and then responded, "Sure. I guess that would be alright," he said, clearly uncomfortable with the idea.

"First off, how well do you know Paul Nelson?"

"Pretty well. We've been friends for several years."

"Would you say that you have the same circle of friends?"

He nodded his head, "Yes."

"I know this may be hard to remember, but did you attend a birthday party for Todd Sampson four years ago?

"Yes."

"Do you remember the date of the party?"

"Yes, it was September 12th."

"You are positive that was the date of his party?"

"Yes, it was his actual birthday. He is a good friend of mine."

"Okay, on the night of September 12th, where was the party held?"

"Margie's apartment."

"And where was Margie's apartment located?"

"Downtown on 7ᵗʰ street."

"Good, good. Was Paul Nelson in attendance at this party?"

"Yes, he was there."

"You're sure of it?"

"Yes, we had a conversation at the party. He was telling me about this new girl he liked."

"Did he tell you her name?"

"Yes, it was Stacy."

"After the night of the party, did you and Paul ever have another conversation about Stacy?"

"No."

Chase wrote something down in his notebook, then looked up at John and asked, "Why is that?"

"At the time, I didn't know, but later, I heard that Stacy had been murdered that night."

"Did you have a discussion with him about her death?"

"No."

"Did you see Paul again after the party?"

"Yeah, sure."

"And you didn't think it was weird that he didn't mention the girl he liked was murdered?"

"No, and I didn't want to bring it up and make him upset."

"Did the police ask you about Paul's whereabouts on the night of the murder?"

"Yes, I told them I saw him at the party that night."

"What time did you leave the party?"

"Around midnight."

"Was Paul still there?"

"I guess so."

"What do you mean, I guess so? Didn't you say goodbye to him before you left the party?"

"No. My girl and I had a fight. She stormed out, and I went after her. I didn't say goodbye to anyone."

"So, you can't be sure that he was still there?"

"No, I guess not."

"One last question. Do you think Paul had anything to do with Stacy's murder?"

John hesitated a moment, looked away from Chase, and said, "No."

"Thank you, John. You have been a great help."

John stood up and shook his hand, "You're welcome."

The manager said, "You can go back to work now."

After John left, Chase turned to the manager and said, "Thank you for letting me speak with John."

"You're welcome. Let me walk you out."

Chase made one last stop at Baker Technologies and interviewed Greg Mason before he headed over to the Goldstein and Finch Law Firm to update Ryan.

"What were you able to find out about the two other suspects?" Ryan asked Chase.

"I was unable to locate the ex-boyfriend, Mark Gordon. He seems to have gone off the radar. I couldn't find a death certificate, so he's not deceased. The other suspect, Paul Nelson, the stalker guy, is currently being held at the county jail. He wasn't very cooperative; he thinks I'm trying to put the murder on him. I was able to interview the three eye-witnesses who saw him at the party that night. They all confirmed that he was there but can't swear that he was there the entire time. He could have left the party and came back." Ryan placed his hands together and stared at Chase, hanging onto his every word.

Chase continued, "The party was held at an apartment on 7th street, which was only five minutes away from Stacy's apartment. With so many people in attendance, he could very easily have slipped out and returned to the party unnoticed."

"That's great. Can you get me a picture of Paul Nelson? I would like to check the security tape to see if he paid Stacy a visit the night she was killed."

"Not a problem. I'll send it over to you right away." Chase stood up and made his way to the door.

"Thank you." Ryan sent him a look of approval, "Good work, Chase."

chapter

11

Sarah was relieved to see Megan and Jake were visiting Michael when she got to the hospital. Things had been strained between them ever since she told him about Dylan.

"Hi, everyone." Unsure of where they stood, she didn't give Michael a kiss like she normally would. "How are you feeling today?" she asked with a sense of coolness evident in her tone.

"I'm feeling good." He reached for her hand, "Sorry about yesterday. I shouldn't have gotten mad at you. You only did what was best for me. Please accept my apology." He pulled her into his chest and hugged her.

Emotions overcame her, and Sarah began to cry. She was relieved to have her husband back. Michael could hear her cries; he pulled her away from himself and looked at her. "Hey, I'm okay. We're okay. Don't cry, baby. Everything's going to be okay."

"What about Dylan?" Sarah asked, wiping the tears from her face.

"Dylan's going to be okay too. He's a fighter; he has Evans' blood in him. I can't tell you we will be friends after this, but I'll keep an open mind. He saved my life; I owe him that much. If he didn't murder that girl, I will stand by him."

"Oh, Michael. I don't think he did it. I can't explain why, but I feel so strongly about it. You'll see."

Michael asked curiously, "So what is Ryan saying?"

"He is having a private investigator checking out the two other suspects the police had. One was a guy Stacy dated before Dylan, and the other was a guy that was stalking her. Either one of them could have been the murderer. He was able to retrieve the security tape from Stacy's apartment building the night she was killed. He thinks it will prove that Dylan left the building before Stacy was killed and that he never returned. Ryan says with the tape, Dylan has a good chance of getting an appeal."

"That's great news!" Megan said.

"How is Dylan doing?" Michael asked.

"His blood count isn't coming up, but it's not dropping either, so the coma seems to be working. He's not experiencing any more heart attacks."

"Is there anything the doctor can do to increase his white blood cells?"

"No, he already increased his medicine. Dr. Knolls said we just have to give him time. Once his body isn't in stress mode any longer, it will start producing more white blood cells."

"Okay, I want to see him if Dr. Knolls says it's okay."

"If I say what is okay?" Dr. Knolls asked, walking into the room.

"Michael wants to visit Dylan. Would that be alright?"

The doctor smiled, "I think we can make arrangements for that."

"Thank you, doctor."

"Now, I'm going to need you all to take a walk for a minute so I can examine Michael."

"Come on, let's get a cup of coffee," Sarah said to Megan and Jake, and the three of them left and headed to the cafeteria.

"Well, it looks like you are making progress," Megan said to Sarah on their way to the elevator. "Michael is really coming around to the idea of forgiving Dylan."

"Yeah, can you believe it?"

Jake said, "Don't get your hopes up, Sarah. If Dylan killed that girl, nothing is going to change. Michael won't forgive him, and he will be going back to jail."

Determined not to allow Jake to ruin her mood, Sarah said, "I'll worry about that when the time comes. All I know is, right now, things are looking up. Ryan is making progress with the appeal, and Michael wants to visit Dylan."

After having coffee, Megan and Jake left, and Sarah went back to Michael's room. When she got there, he was sitting in a wheelchair waiting for her return.

"Wow! Look at you. How does it feel to be out of bed?"

"It feels great. Are you ready to go?"

"Go where?"

"To see Dylan."

"Sure. Let's go." She got behind the wheelchair and started pushing Michael out of the room. Before they got to the ICU, Sarah asked, "Are you sure you want to do this?"

"Yes, I'm sure."

"Dr. Knolls said that Dylan can hear us, so please don't say anything to distress him."

"I won't."

Sarah rolled Michael into Dylan's room next to his bedside and then lowered the foot locks on the wheelchair. Michael stared at the man he hadn't seen in years and was forced to come to terms with his feelings towards him. As childhood memories they shared flashed through his mind, he realized that he no longer hated him, and he felt responsible for his medical condition.

"Hey, Dylan. It's me, Michael. I came to say thank you for what you did for me." Not knowing what else to say, Michael looked over at Sarah.

"Hi, Dylan. It's Sarah. Things are going good with your appeal. I think Ryan will be filing it any day now. Jenna sends her love. She said she will come and visit you this weekend. She's really worried about you."

Sarah and Michael sat with Dylan for several minutes, and then a nurse came in and said, "We need to change his sheets now. Would you mind coming back in a little while?"

Michael tapped Dylan's hand and said, "I'll see you later, Dylan," and Sarah smiled as she rolled her husband out of the room.

chapter 12

On Wednesday, Ryan filed the papers for Dylan's court appeal on the basis that there was new evidence to support Dylan's claim that Stacy was alive when he left her apartment the night she was murdered. After filing the appeal electronically, he turned his computer off and locked the office up for the night.

He headed out into the cold, dark night and walked towards the only car in the dimly lit parking lot. Feeling as if someone was watching him, he quickly turned and looked behind him, but no one was there. He sped up his pace and pressed the unlock button on his car remote. When he finally got into his car, he locked the doors and breathed a sigh of relief.

He stopped at the local bar for a drink and a bite to eat before heading home. After taking a seat, the bartender asked, "What can I get you?"

"A scotch and a menu."

"You got it."

A minute later, the bartender placed a glass of scotch in front of Ryan, and he quickly chugged it down then slammed the glass back onto the bar. The bartender refilled it, "Bad day?"

"No, not really. Just got spooked a little. You know?"

"Yeah. Can I get you something to eat?"

"I'll have a burger and fries and a glass of water, please."

"Sure thing."

By the time Ryan finished his burger and fries, he had calmed down and felt foolish, like he may have overreacted. The bartender came over, took his empty plate away, and asked, "Can I get you anything else?"

"No, just the check, please."

Ryan's cell phone rang. He glanced at his phone lying on the bar and recognized his partner's name displaying on it.

"Hey, Bob. What's up?"

"I'm at the office. You need to get over here. Your office has been robbed." The hair on Ryan's neck stood up as a chill ran down his spine.

"Did they take anything?"

"Who can tell? Your whole office is trashed. You're going to have to go through everything. The police are here. You need to file a report."

"I'll be right there." Ryan disconnected the call and threw some money on the bar, then left.

When Ryan pulled into the office parking lot, there were two police cars there, with lights flashing, along with his partner's car. He pulled his car directly in front of the building and ran into the office.

"Bob!" He yelled, running towards his office.

"In here," Bob shouted back at him.

When Ryan got to his office, he was shaking his head in disbelief; the entire office was trashed. Filing cabinets were dumped over; files were scattered everywhere. All the cabinets were open.

"How will I ever know what is missing? It will take days to go through all of this."

Suddenly, Ryan had a thought and ran to open his desk drawer. It was empty.

"Oh, no."

"What is it?" Bob asked. "What's missing?"

"The security tape for Dylan's appeal. It's gone."

"Are you sure? Maybe it's somewhere in this mess." Bob said, looking around the office.

Ryan looked around as well but knew it was gone. Fury burned in his chest. "I just filed his appeal. We don't have a case without that tape."

A police officer approached Ryan and said, "Mr. Finch, I need to ask you a few questions."

He sunk into his chair and sighed. "Okay."

"What time did you leave the office tonight?"

"Around 6:30. I stayed late because I was working on Dylan's appeal. I was the last one to leave. I felt like someone was watching me when I was walking to the parking lot, but I didn't see anyone, so I just dismissed it. They must have broken in right after I left."

"Do you have any idea who might have wanted that tape?"

"I don't know, but I would imagine it was the person who murdered Stacy Richards."

"Okay, I put down the tape as stolen property. Is there anything else you notice that is missing?"

"No, but I'll have to go through everything first."

"Your office was the only office vandalized, and they didn't take the computer or anything else of value, so they probably came for the tape."

The officer handed Ryan his business card. "If you find that anything else was taken, please give me a call, and I will add it to the report."

He took his card and said, "I will."

Ryan started cleaning up the mess and could not find anything else missing. He called Sarah to give her the bad news.

"Hi, Ryan. How are things going?"

"Terrible, Sarah. I'm sorry, but I have some bad news."

Sarah paced the room, "Oh, no. What is it?"

"Someone broke into my office. They stole the tape."

Her heart sank. "No! What does that mean for his appeal?"

"It's the whole basis for our appeal. I don't think we have a chance at getting an appeal without it. Sarah, I need you to think. Who knew about the tape? Did you tell anyone?"

"Just Megan and Jenna."

"Is it possible they told someone, or someone overheard you?"

"I don't know. I guess it's possible."

"I'm sorry, Sarah. Without that tape, we are back to square one."

"Damn. Who do you think could have taken the tape?"

"There is no need to change our original thinking. Our primary suspects are still Mark Gordon and Paul Nelson until we have reason to believe it is someone else."

"But Paul is in jail, and we don't even know where Mark is."

"That doesn't mean they weren't involved. They could have hired someone to steal the tape."

"Yeah, that's possible."

"Sarah, I really believe that Dylan didn't commit the murder. I think the answer to who did is on that tape, and we were very close to figuring it out. I need you to be careful. I don't want you to talk to anyone about the case. Don't tell anyone the tape is missing. That way, we will have some leverage. Do you understand?"

"Yes, I understand."

"Okay, let me go. I need to call Chase and give him an update."

"Thank you, Ryan. I'm sorry I got you into this mess."

"It's okay, Sarah. Just be careful."

"I will."

Ryan called Chase next. "Hi, it's me. I'm going to need you to step things up. Someone broke into my office tonight and stole the security tape. I need you to put pressure on Paul and find Mark. We need to get that tape back."

"I understand. I'll get right on it."

chapter

13

Chase returned to the county jail to put some pressure on Paul. Having worked there for many years, he advanced to the desk with confidence and said to the officer he knew well, "I need to speak with a detainee, Paul Nelson."

The officer grabbed a clipboard hanging on the wall next to him, looked it over, and said, "Mr. Nelson made bail yesterday."

Chase tapped the counter with his fist. "He did. How much was his bail?"

"Hold on, I'll check." He walked back to his desk and punched a few keys on his computer. A few seconds later, he said, "$5,000."

"Really? Did he use a bail bondsman?"

"Yes, his bail was posted by Powell Bail Bonds, Inc."

"Thank you."

Chase had already checked Paul's finances and knew that he was broke. He needed to find out how he posted bail, so he left the county jail and went straight to Powell Bail Bonds, Inc.

A middle-aged woman wearing too much makeup looked up from her computer when she heard someone entered the office. She observed a self-assured, good-looking man walking towards her and straightened her posture; she glanced at his ring finger to see if he was married, then smiled at him and asked, "Can I help you?"

"Yes, a friend of mine got himself into a bit of trouble. I would like to bail him out of jail. Can you help me?"

"Sure, what is your friend's name?"

"Paul Nelson."

"Okay, and where is he being held?"

"Franklin County jail."

She checked the computer then said, "It looks like you are too late. Mr. Nelson has already posted bail."

"He has. By whom? He just asked me to bail him out yesterday."

"I'm afraid that information is confidential. Maybe you can ask your friend."

"Yeah, I'll do that. Were you here yesterday when the down payment was given?"

"Yes, I was here."

"Do you remember what time it was?"

"Yeah, it was around noon. Look, I really think you should be asking your friend these questions. I'm sure he will be happy to tell you all the details."

"Yeah, I will. Just one more thing. Was it a male or female?"

"It was a male."

Chase looked at her name tag and said, "How old would you say he was, Mary?"

"He was in his late twenties, early thirties."

"Oh, it must have been his brother, Stan. Brown hair, right?"

"Yes. He was good looking too."

"Yeah, that's Stan. Thank you, Mary. Have a nice day."

"You're welcome."

Chase left the bail bondsman company, went to his car, and called Ryan.

Ryan was waiting for his call. "Hi, Chase. What do you got for me?"

"It seems our friend Paul Nelson posted bail around noon yesterday. Do you think he has the tape?"

"It's possible. Can you check his house?"

"Sure thing."

Chase parked his car outside of Paul's rental house and watched and waited. Around 5 p.m., a car pulled up in front of his house and honked the horn. Seconds later, Paul came out of the house and jumped in the car, and they sped off. Chase waited a minute to be sure they were not coming back, then sprang into action.

He put gloves on his hands, looked up and down the street, making sure no one was watching, then went around to the back of the house. He tried the door, but it was locked. He used a small manual glass cutter to cut a circle into the glass pane on the door, then put his hand through it and unlocked the door.

Once inside, he immediately started his search for the tape. He rummaged through the living room, opening cabinets, and checking drawers but didn't find it. After coming up empty-handed, he headed upstairs to the bedroom. The room was a mess, with dirty clothes and trash everywhere. He checked under the bed, but it wasn't there. Then he went to the closet; he found a shoebox on the shelf, pulled it down, and opened it. Bingo! There was the tape. It had Cardinal Point written across it.

Chase grabbed the tape and got out of there as fast as he could. He rushed over to the Goldstein & Finch Law Firm and flew into Ryan's office before Julie could even say a word. Ryan was sitting alone, reading files as Chase came in and threw the tape on his desk, "You need to give me a raise!"

"You got it! I can't believe it, Chase. So, we were on the right track. It seems that Mr. Nelson didn't want us to have this tape. Let's see what he has to hide. Come with me."

The two men left the office and went down the hall to a conference room where there was a television and a video recorder on a shelf. He popped the tape into the player, and the two men watched from the time stamp of 10:25 when Dylan left the apartment complex until 2:30 am, but they didn't see Paul on the tape."

"I don't understand," Chase said. "I didn't see him."

"Me either. But he had something to do with it. Why else would he steal the tape?"

"Let me keep investigating. We'll figure it out."

"Yes. In the meantime, I'm going to put this tape in a safety deposit box at my bank. But first, I need to make a phone call. Come with me."

Ryan and Chase returned to the office, and Ryan opened his desk drawer and shuffled things around, then pulled out the business card the detective gave him the night of the robbery. He called the number on the card.

"Detective Hansen, please."

"This is he."

"Hi, this is Ryan Finch. You gave me your card the other night when my office was robbed."

"Oh, yes. How are you doing, Mr. Finch? Did you find anything else was taken from your office?"

"No, actually. I'm calling to let you know that I found the tape when I was cleaning up the mess. It appears that nothing was taken after all. I think it was just a case of vandalism."

"Oh, I'm glad to hear that. I will make a note of it in the file. If you find anything else is missing, feel free to give me a call and let me know."

"I will. Thank you, Detective."

chapter 14

Around ten p.m., Paul was dropped off at his house. He staggered his drunken self to the porch, then turned and waved to his friends, "Good night, guys. I'll see you later."

He was so intoxicated; he struggled to unlock the door and tripped on the carpet runner as he entered the house. He stumbled his way to the couch, then fell forward and passed out. The next morning, he felt someone push his shoulder, "Wake up."

He opened his eyes to find a man standing over him. "Get up. I need the tape."

Still hungover from the night before, Paul was slow to sit up. His head was pounding. He put his hand to his head and said, "How did you get in here?"

"The door was unlocked. Pull yourself together and go get me the tape."

"Okay, okay. It's upstairs in a shoebox in my closet."

The man ran upstairs and came back a minute later, holding the shoebox in his hand. "It's not here!" He pushed the box in Paul's face.

"What do you mean it's not here?" Paul looked in the box filled with tissue paper. He shuffled the paper around. "It has to be here."

The man pushed Paul, "Stop playing games with me! Where's the tape?"

"I don't know. I put it in the box and put it in my closet."

"Have you been home the entire time since you put the tape in the box?"

"No, I went out with some of my buddies to have a drink to celebrate getting out of jail."

"You fool! Someone must have broken in and taken it. I can't believe you didn't lock it up. You're an idiot!" Then the man slapped Paul across the face, leaving a red handprint on his cheek. He wrapped both hands around Paul's neck and began to squeeze. Paul tried to pull the man's hands off his neck. His face turned red as he struggled to breathe. A minute later, Paul's lifeless body fell back into the couch, his bulging eyes staring at the man.

Paul's dead body lay on the couch unnoticed for weeks until his landlord stopped by to pick up the rent. When he got to the front door, he smelled a horrific stench even before he knocked. "Paul, are you okay? What is that awful smell?"

He tested the door; it was unlocked. He opened the door and could see the decaying body from the doorway. He gasped and quickly slammed the door shut and paced on the porch as he called the police.

"911. What's your emergency?"

"My tenant is dead."

"Okay, are you sure he's dead? Did you check for a pulse?"

"No, he's dead. He is gray, and he smells awful. Looks like he has been dead for some time."

"Okay, sir. Just remain calm. What is your address?"

"700 Pond Road."

"The police are on the way. Is there anyone else in the house?"

"I don't know. I found him on the couch and ran back outside."

"Okay, just stay on the porch and wait for the police. They will be there shortly."

The police and ambulance arrived minutes later and removed the body and searched the house for clues. The preliminary cause of death was thought to be strangulation. They found that the back door was broken into, and they dusted the house for fingerprints. It didn't appear to them that it was a robbery, so at the time, they didn't have a motive for his death.

Ryan saw the story of Paul's death on the eleven o'clock news later that night and called Chase.

"Hey, Chase. Did you see the news?"

"Yeah. What do you make of it?"

"Well, we didn't see Paul on the tape, so maybe he was working with someone, and they did him in."

"That's a possibility. What do you want me to do now?"

"See if you can find out who might have killed him?"

"Okay. What about Mark Gordon? Do you still want me to see if I can find him?"

"Yeah, but finding out who killed Paul is the priority."

"Got it. Do you want me to give my buddy, Rick, over at the police station a call to see if they lifted any prints from the crime scene?"

"Yeah, maybe we'll get lucky, and they will be in the database. Let me know what you find out."

chapter 15

"How are you feeling today?" Dr. Knolls asked Michael when he made his morning rounds.

"I feel great! When do you think I can go home?"

Dr. Knolls looked at Michael's chart and smiled, "I am incredibly pleased with your progress. If your blood count continues to rise, I see no reason why you can't go home tomorrow."

"Yes!" Michael smiled and clapped his hands in excitement. "I can't wait to get out of this place."

Dr. Knolls put up one finger, "Now, wait a minute. If I send you home, you have to promise me that you will take it easy and you will come in every other day to have your blood checked."

"I promise. Thank you, doctor."

"You're welcome." He patted Michael's arm. "I'll be back later to check on you."

Michael called Sarah to give her the good news.

"Good morning, honey. Guess what?"

"What?"

"Dr. Knolls said I can go home tomorrow."

"Really? That's awesome. There is so much I need to do before you come home. The house is a mess. I need to go grocery shopping. Let me get going. I'll be up later to visit. Do you need me to bring you anything?"

"No, just get here as soon as you can. I miss you."

Sarah smiled, "I miss you too."

She hung up with Michael and immediately called Megan.

"Megan, Michael is coming home tomorrow. Can you believe it? After months of being in the hospital, he is finally coming home. I was thinking we could have a little homecoming celebration at the house. Nothing big, Michael will be tired, just a few people. Could you help me?"

"Of course. What do you need me to do?"

"Could you stay at the house and let people in when I go to the hospital and pick him up tomorrow?"

"Yes, I can do that. What else do you need? How about I get the cake and make a welcome home sign?"

Sarah grabbed a piece of paper out of the junk drawer and started making a list of things she needed. "That would be perfect. I don't know what time he is coming home yet. As soon as I know, I'll let you know. I got to go. I have so much to do."

"Okay, Sarah. Let me know if you need anything else."

"I will. Thank you."

The next day, Sarah buzzed around the house in excitement, cooking and cleaning in preparation for Michael's return. Around 2 p.m., Michael called and told her he was getting discharged around 5:30. She quickly called Megan to let her know the time.

"Megan, I need to go to the hospital around five. Can you be here before five?"

"Yes, I'm on my way to pick the cake up now. I'll be there well before that."

When Sarah got to the hospital, Michael was dressed and sitting in a chair next to his bed, waiting for her. He had good color in his face and was excited to see her.

"Wow! You look so good. How are you feeling?" Sarah asked him, then gave him a kiss.

"I feel like a million bucks. I'm ready to fly this coop." As soon as he said the words, a nurse came through the door pushing a wheelchair. "Dr. Knolls signed your discharge papers. You're free to go."

"Great! Let's go." Michael said, then got up and moved over to the wheelchair.

"Do you mind if we visit Dylan first?" Sarah asked her husband.

"No, I was thinking the same thing."

When they got to Dylan's room, Jenna was visiting him again.

"Oh, hi, Jenna. This is my husband, Michael."

"It's nice to meet you, Michael," Jenna said.

"Nice to meet you too," Michael replied.

"Michael is being discharged; we are going home, but I wanted to check on Dylan first."

"Oh, that's great news. I'm so happy for you both." Sarah could see the look of worry on Jenna's face and felt a little guilty.

"How is he doing today?" she asked Jenna.

"His nurse said that his blood count is improving a little."

"Did you hear that, Dylan? Your blood count is coming up. You're getting better."

"How is the appeal going?" Jenna asked.

"Ryan filed it. It's in the court's hands now." She didn't tell Jenna about the tape being stolen. "We just have to wait and see if they grant him the appeal."

"How long does that take?" Jenna asked.

"Ryan said it can take anywhere from a couple of weeks to a couple of months."

Jenna's shoulders dropped, "Oh, that's such a long time."

"Yeah, I know." Sarah reached for her hand. "Hey, would you like to come over tonight and join us for dinner?"

"Oh, no. I wouldn't want to put you out. It's Michael's first night home."

"You're not putting me out. I already made dinner. We would love to have the company, right, Michael?"

"Yes, please join us. That way, Sarah won't be fussing over me so much."

"If you're sure."

"We're sure." Sarah and Michael said in unison.

"Great, I'll text you our address." Sarah pulled her phone out of her purse and sent Megan a text.

The three of them stayed with Dylan for a little while longer then left together. Sarah and Michael gave each other a surprised look when Jenna leaned over and kissed Dylan on the lips. "Bye, Dylan. I'll be back tomorrow."

As they were leaving the hospital, Sarah was rattling on about nothing, when suddenly, she noticed that Jenna was quietly crying.

She stopped walking and put her hand on Jenna's shoulder, "Oh, Jenna. What is it? What's wrong?"

"I love him so much. I thought I was over him, but I'm not. I can't lose him."

"Oh, honey. You're not going to lose him. Dylan is strong. This is just the beginning; he's going to get better, and Ryan's going to clear his name. He's going to have his whole future ahead of him. You'll see."

"Do you really believe that?" Jenna asked, wiping the tears from her cheeks.

"Yes. I do."

When they got to the parking lot, Jenna went her own way to her car, and Michael and Sarah went to theirs. On the car ride home, Michael said, "You shouldn't have gotten her hopes up like that, Sarah. You don't know that he is going to get better, and even if he does, he's probably going back to prison."

"Yes, I do. I know it just like I knew he was going to be a match for you. All of this happened for a reason, Michael. I know it in my heart."

Not wanting to argue with his wife, he said, "Okay, if you say so."

Sarah parked the car in the garage, then helped Michael into the house. When she opened the door from the garage, everyone yelled, "Welcome home!"

The kitchen was decorated with balloons and a welcome home sign and smelled of many delicious foods. Megan and Jake greeted them first. "Welcome home, brother," Megan said, giving him a hug and a kiss. Jake patted him on the back. "Looking good, man."

Ryan stepped forward next. "Welcome home, buddy. You look good."

"Thank you, everyone. It's so nice to see all of you."

Two of Michael's college buddies came up and gave him a big bear hug. "We got an extra ticket to the Dolphins game on Sunday. If you are up to it, we would love to have you."

Sarah stepped forward, "I don't think he will be up to going to the game on Sunday, but you are always welcome to watch the game here."

Michael rolled his eyes and laughed, "You heard the boss, guys."

The doorbell rang, "I'll get it. I'm sure it's Jenna."

When she answered the door, she said, "So glad you could make it. I couldn't tell you in front of Michael that we were having a homecoming celebration. Come in, and I'll introduce you to everyone."

"Everyone, this is Jenna. She is a friend of Dylan's. This is my sister-in-law, Megan, and her husband, Jake."

"It's nice to meet you, Jenna," Megan said, extending her hand to her.

"Jake, do I know you?" Jenna asked. "You look so familiar."

"I don't think so."

"Jenna, these are Michael's college buddies, Glen and Dan."

"It's nice to meet you both."

"Who's hungry?" Sarah asked. "I have enough food for an army."

Everyone helped themselves to the buffet and took seats in the dining room. Sarah took a seat next to Megan and Jake and asked, "What are we talking about?"

"Jake wants to take me away for our anniversary next week. I told him it's really busy at the store right now. I can't get away for a week. We can celebrate our anniversary at another time."

"Talk some sense into her, Sarah. She works too hard. She needs a break, and I need some alone time with my wife." His eyes traveled up and down Megan's body.

"I agree with Jake. Why don't you compromise? Go up to the cabin for a long weekend."

"I'll think about it," Megan said.

After dinner, they cut the cake and had coffee, then everyone started to leave so that Michael could get some rest. Sarah walked Ryan to the door and asked, "Anything new with Dylan's case?"

"Paul Nelson was murdered."

"What does that mean for his case?"

"I think everything is connected. I just don't know how yet. Paul wasn't on the tape; I don't think he visited Stacy the night of her death, but I can't help but feel like his death is related to hers somehow. It may have even been the same person who killed them both. I'll keep you posted. Goodnight, Sarah."

chapter 16

Jenna left the party and couldn't get Jake out of her head. She was positive she had met him before but just couldn't remember where it was. She went to bed that night, thinking about him and willing her mind to remember.

After several hours of sleep, she was tossing and turning in bed as a nightmare disrupted her slumber. She was running away from him; he was chasing her with a knife. Finally, just as he was about to stab her, Jenna forced herself to wake up and sprang up in her bed. She was sweating and shaking as she remembered where she had met Jake before. It took several minutes for her to calm herself down.

She looked over at the clock; it was 3 a.m. Afraid to go back to sleep in fear of continuing her nightmare, she turned on the television and flipped through the channels settling on an episode of Friends she had seen many times before. She thought about what she needed to do the next day and wasn't looking forward to doing it.

She overslept the next morning and reached for her cell phone when she realized she was due at work in five minutes. She called the office.

"Hi, Greg. It's me, Jenna. I'm not feeling well today. I'm going to take a sick day today."

"Okay. Feel better, Jenna."

"Thank you."

She called the Goldstein & Finch Law Firm next, and Julie answered right away.

"Goldstein & Finch. How may I help you?"

"I need to speak with Ryan."

"He hasn't come in yet. I can take a message and have him call you when he comes in."

"Okay, can you please have him call Jenna? You know what, never mind. Is it possible for me to come in and see him today? It's really important."

"Hold on, and I'll check his schedule."

A minute later, she said, "He has an opening at ten. What can I tell him it is regarding?"

"It's about Dylan Hogan's appeal."

"Okay, I'll put you down for ten o'clock."

"Thank you. I'll see you in a little while."

Jenna struggled with the thought of what she was about to do and considered whether she should call Sarah to let her know what was going on. In the end, she decided that it would be best to talk to Ryan first.

She took a shower and dressed for her meeting with Ryan, then headed to the local coffee shop for a quick cup of coffee and breakfast. She ordered a cup of coffee and blueberry muffin, then took a seat and looked at her phone as she ate her food and drank her coffee.

She could feel the presence of someone standing next to her, "Hi, it's Jenna, right?"

She looked up from her phone and saw Jake standing over her. Caught off guard, she fumbled and spilled her coffee as she lowered it back to the table.

"Oh, let me help you," Jake said, grabbing some napkins from the napkin holder.

"That's okay. I got it," she said, grabbing the napkin next to her. The two of them wiped the spilled coffee at the same time, and she pulled her hand away as his hand touched hers.

"Are you okay?" he asked. "You seem a little jumpy." He stared at her, his eyes penetrating through her, straight into her soul.

"I'm fine. I'm late for a meeting. I got to get going," she said, getting up from her table and rushing to the garbage with her trash.

Jake watched her leave the coffee shop then called Megan as he waited in line to place his order.

"Hey, baby. Just checking in to see what time you want to leave today?"

"I just have a few things I need to do here. I should be done around noon, and then we can get on the road."

"That's great, baby. I can't wait to get away with you. I'll meet you at home."

Jenna got to Ryan's office a few minutes early, and Julie was expecting her. When she entered the office, Julie said, "Hi, Jenna. If you'll just have a seat, I'll let Ryan know you are here."

Julie let Ryan know that Jenna was here for his meeting, and he immediately came out of the office.

"Jenna, hi. How are you?" He looked around the room and said, "Sarah's not with you today?"

"No, it's just me."

"Come on in. What can I do for you today?"

"It's about Jake."

"Jake? What about Jake?'

"When I met him at the party yesterday, I knew that I met him before, but I couldn't remember where. I couldn't remember because he didn't go by the name Jake when I met him."

His brows perched low, "I don't understand. What name did he go by, and what does this have to do with Dylan's case?"

"I met him at a bar several years back. A mutual friend introduced us. He went by the name Mark Gordon."

She could tell by the look on Ryan's face that this perked his interest. "Mark Gordon, are you sure?"

"Yes. I'm positive."

"Okay. Does he know that you know who he is?"

She clenched her hands together to stop them from trembling, "I don't know, maybe. I just ran into him at the coffee shop. I was so nervous; I spilled my coffee."

"Okay, Jenna. Don't do anything. I will have Chase look into it. Whatever you do, don't tell anyone, especially Sarah. I don't want anyone acting different around him. It could tip him off. Stay away from him until I have a chance to check it out and call the police. I'll let you know once I have proof that he is Mark Gordon."

She got on her feet. "Okay. Thank you, Ryan."

Ryan sent her a reassuring smile, "Don't worry, Jenna. We'll get to the bottom of this."

Jenna left the office still shaken up. She needed to see Dylan. She got in her car and headed in the direction of the hospital. She only went a few miles when she saw smoke coming from her engine. She pulled to the side of the road and opened her hood. She called Triple A Roadside assistance and then got back in the car to wait.

When Triple A arrived thirty minutes later, Jenna was nowhere in sight. The tow truck driver called the number on file and left a message when no one answered.

"Hi, this is Pete from Triple A. I'm here to tow your car. I'll wait ten minutes, but if I don't hear from you, I'm going to have to leave." Ten minutes later, Pete left the car on the side of the road and went to his next call.

chapter

17

Jenna knew the minute he pulled up behind her that her car trouble wasn't random. She quickly locked her doors and reached for her cell phone. She was only able to dial 9-1 when he slammed a hammer against her window. Glass shattered everywhere, hitting her in the face. She dropped her phone and threw her hands over her face, shielding her eyes from the broken shards.

He reached through the window and grabbed her by the neck and lifted her out of her seat. "Let's go!"

She reached for the door handle and pulled it. The door unlocked and opened in one motion.

"You couldn't leave things alone. I told you I didn't know you, but you couldn't leave things at that," he said as he dragged her to his car. It was broad daylight, but no one paid any notice as the cars whipped past them.

"What am I going to do with you?"

"I already told Ryan. He's calling the police. If I were you, I would let me go and get out of town as soon as possible. You can get a head start."

"I have a wife, remember? You expect me to leave her? I love her; I'm not leaving without her."

"She won't want to be with you after she finds out what you did. You should leave now."

"I can't."

Jake drove a short distance, then pulled onto an old dirt road that led to an old, abandoned factory. "Come on." He put the car in park, then grabbed her elbow and pulled her across his seat and out of the car. He pushed her forward, and she stumbled and fell. He kicked her with his foot, "Get up!"

She grabbed a handful of dirt and stones and threw them in his eyes and ran. He squinted and yelled out, "Damn it, get back here." He rubbed the dirt out of his eyes, then once he was able to see again, he ran after her and grabbed her by the hair.

"We can do this the easy way or the hard way. The choice is yours." He pushed her forward again and guided her into the factory. Once inside, he leaned her against a large metal pipe. Then, he reached into his back pocket and retrieved a rope and tied her to the pipe.

"What are you going to do to me?"

"Shut up, and let me think."

He paced back and forth, then took his phone out of his pocket. The time was 11:32 a.m. "I don't have time for this. Megan is expecting me. I'll be back later."

"You can't just leave me here," she yelled at him as he walked out of the factory.

Jenna waited until she heard his car pull away, then looked around for something to help her escape. There was nothing within her reach. She pulled and tugged on the rope, trying to loosen it, but only managed to give herself rope burns. She yelled for help, but no one heard her. She wasn't due anywhere until work the next day. She prayed that someone would look for her before then.

chapter 18

Sarah and Michael were sitting at the breakfast bar, eating lunch, when Sarah said, "I need to head out to run a couple of errands. Will you be okay if I leave you alone for a while? I could call Megan and ask her to come sit with you?"

Michael shot her a look of annoyance. "Don't be ridiculous. I'll be fine, now stop fussing over me."

"Okay, I won't be long," she gave him a kiss goodbye and left.

Sarah was at the pharmacy picking up Michael's prescriptions when her cell phone rang.

"Hi, Ryan. What's up?"

"Sarah, I don't know how to tell you this, so I'll just say it. I found out why we couldn't find Mark Gordon."

"Oh yeah, why?"

"Because he changed his name."

"Okay, so did you find him under his new name?"

He sighed, "Yeah. He changed his name to Jake Harbor."

"That can't be our Jake."

"I'm afraid it is. I checked the security tape, Sarah. Jake visited Stacy's apartment the night she was killed."

"Oh my God! Poor Megan. I've got to warn her."

"Sarah, please don't do that. Jake is dangerous. Let the police handle it." The phone went dead. "Sarah, do you hear me? Sarah!"

She disconnected the call and ran out of the pharmacy without getting the prescription. She raced through the parking lot and plowed into a woman, practically knocking her over in the process.

The woman gave her a dirty look. "Hey, watch where you're going."

"Sorry. I'm so sorry," she said without slowing down.

When she got to her car, she jumped in, started it up, and pulled out of her parking space in a moment's time. She only went a couple of blocks down the road when she was forced to stop at a red light. She reached for her phone and called Megan.

When she didn't answer, Sarah left her a message. "Megan, it's Sarah. Call me back; it's an emergency."

The light turned green, and Sarah impatiently honked her horn at the driver in front of her. "Come on, go!"

She used the passing lane and sped past the car, giving the driver an angry look as she did. Several minutes later, she pulled in front of the antique store, threw the car into park, and left it running as she ran into the store.

"Megan!" she yelled, running through the store and up to the counter.

"She's not here," Mary, the woman behind the counter, said.

"Where is she?"

"She and Jake went away for the weekend."

"Damn! Did they say where they were going?"

"Yeah, they went up to her parents' cabin."

"What time did they leave?" Sarah asked, already making her way to the door.

"Around noon," Mary yelled to her.

"If she checks in, tell her to call me. It's an emergency," she said and pulled the door open and left.

Sarah jumped back into the car and called Ryan. "Ryan, I can't get a hold of Megan. Jake took her to the cabin. I'm heading there now. I have to warn her."

"He won't hurt her. He loves her, Sarah. He doesn't even know that we are onto him. Don't go up there. I'm calling the police. Let them handle it."

"I have to. I have a bad feeling about this. Just call the police and have them meet me up at the cabin."

"Okay, please be careful. Don't provoke him."

"I won't."

Ryan got off the phone with Sarah and dialed Detective Hansen's number.

"Detective Hansen speaking."

"Hello, detective. This is Ryan Finch again."

"Oh, yes, Ryan. Did you find something else was stolen?"

"No, I'm actually calling about something else."

"Okay, what can I help you with?"

"I'm representing a client by the name of Dylan Hogan. He is serving thirty years for rape and murder, but I have reason to believe he is innocent. I have some evidence that implicates a man by the name of Jake Harbor. I'm worried that Jake has taken a hostage up to a cabin by the lake. I was wondering if you could go up there and check things out?"

"Who is it that he has taken hostage?"

"His wife, Megan."

"Wait a minute. His wife? Is it his estranged wife?"

"No. She went with him willingly, but she doesn't know he's a murderer. Look, I know how this sounds; you have to trust me. Her life and possibly another woman's life is in danger. Can you please check it out?"

"I'll tell you what. Why don't you come into the station with your evidence, and I'll take a look at what you have and decide whether or not I need to check things out. How does that sound?"

"We don't have time," Ryan said, then hung up and called Chase.

"We got a situation. I need you to do something for me."

"I'm listening," Chase replied.

chapter 19

When Detective Hansen got off the phone with Ryan, he looked up to see a dispatcher standing next to his desk. "Would you mind taking this one?" She held out a small piece of paper. "We got an abandoned car found on the highway over on Route 17. The tow driver said he got a call that a woman needed a tow. When he got there, she wasn't there."

"Just have it towed." He shook his head and went back to focusing on his computer.

"I would, but the tow driver said something wasn't right. He wanted someone to check it out."

Detective Hansen snatched the paper out of her hand in a huff, "Alright."

She smiled at him, "Thank you. I owe you one."

It was getting dark when Detective Hansen pulled up behind Jenna's car. He got out of the car and left his headlights on as he walked to the car. He shined his flashlight into the front seat and saw the broken glass from the driver's window all over the front seat. He moved the flashlight around and saw a cell phone and purse were lying on the passenger side floor.

He opened the car door, reached in, and retrieved the purse. Then he removed the wallet and checked the ID. The name on the driver's license read Jenna Morris. He called the station to have the car towed and processed for evidence.

The factory was total blackness now, the temperature had dropped to twenty degrees, and Jenna could hear rats scurrying all around her. Her stomach growled. She licked her dry, cracked lips, then slid her body down the pipe and took a seat on the cold, dirty floor and closed her eyes. She had been tied up for over eight hours. She was exhausted and scared and no longer had any fight in her. She slowly drifted off to sleep.

Jenna was standing barefoot on a beach, the ocean breeze blowing through her hair as she looked out at the red and orange rays radiating the sky as the sun vanished behind the turquoise water.

"So beautiful."

Jenna turned to see who was speaking and smiled as she saw Dylan walking up to her. "Yes, it is."

"I wasn't talking about the sunset. I was talking about you." he said, then came up beside her and wrapped his arm around her.

"Oh, Dylan. I've missed you so much." She pressed her head against his shoulder.

"I've missed you too. I never stopped loving you."

She started to cry, "I love you too. How did everything go so wrong?"

"I don't know. I only wish we had time to make things right between us."

"Me too."

"Can you do something for me?"

"Anything."

"I need you to wake up, now."

"But I'm so tired, and I want to stay here with you."

"No. Wake up, honey. Open your eyes. I'll find you. I promise."

Jenna tried to open her eyes, but they were so heavy. "That's it, open your eyes, baby." Then he was gone.

She slowly opened her eyes and saw the red and blue police lights flashing outside of the factory window. She pulled her broken body up onto her feet and started yelling, "In here. I'm in here."

Detective Hansen and his partner were searching the grounds of the old factory with flashlights. "It's dark. Let's come back in the morning when it's daylight," his partner said.

Detective Hansen put a finger to his lips. "Shhh, did you hear that?"

He heard something again. "Help, I'm in here."

"Come on." The two policemen ran into the factory and followed the sound of her voice, then found Jenna tied to a pole.

"Oh, thank heavens. Please help me."

Detective Hansen untied her and asked, "Who did this to you?"

"Jake Harbor."

After taking Jenna to the hospital to be checked out, Detective Hansen called Ryan to tell him the news.

"Ryan, it's Detective Hansen. I'm going to need the address for that cabin. We have a woman in custody who says she was kidnapped by Jake Harbor."

"Oh my God. Is it Sarah?"

"No, a woman named Jenna Morris. Do you know her?"

"Yes, she is the one who figured out Jake was dangerous."

chapter

20

Sarah called Megan for the third time in the last half-hour, then threw her phone on the seat in frustration when she got no answer. When she finally pulled the car onto the dirt road leading to the cabin, she started to question whether she should have waited for the police. She let out a sigh of relief when she saw Jake's car parked in front of the cabin. *Thank God, they're still here.*

She jumped out of the car and called out to Megan as she rushed to the porch, "Megan, Megan. Are you there?"

Megan opened the door with a confused look on her face, and Jake followed her to the door. "I'm here. What's the matter?"

Sarah looked over at Jake and said, "It's Michael. I need you to come with me. He's back in the hospital. He's asking for you."

"Oh my God. Okay, just let me get my things." She turned and ran to get her purse, and Sarah stepped into the foyer.

"What happened?" Jake asked.

"I don't know. His blood count must have dropped. I found him on the floor."

"Why didn't you call us? We would have met you at the hospital."

"I did, but no one answered." Jake pulled his phone out of his pocket and looked at it. There were no calls. "You didn't call me."

"I know, I don't know what I was thinking. I should have called you."

Megan came running back into the living room carrying her purse. "Okay, I'm ready." She stopped in her tracks at the sight of Jake and Sarah.

All the color drained from her face, "Jake, what are you doing?"

Jake stood behind Sarah; his arm was wrapped tightly around her neck as she struggled to free herself.

"Michael is not sick. She came here to get you."

"Okay, but you are hurting her. Let her go, Jake."

Jake dragged Sarah to the bedroom, pushed her inside, and slammed the door shut. "I have so much to explain to you, Megan, but we don't have time." He ran outside to the shed. When he returned, Megan was in the bedroom with Sarah.

"Get away from her," he yelled at Megan.

"Jake, this is crazy. You're acting nuts. This has to stop."

Jake came up behind Megan and put a chemically saturated rag over her nose and mouth. She fought in vain to remove his hand until she eventually passed out.

"What are you doing?" Sarah asked, backing up and moving away from him.

Sarah was next. Her vision went black just before she passed out. Jake tied the two women up and put them on the bed, then left the bedroom and put a kitchen chair under the door handle, locking them in. He needed to act quickly; he knew he didn't have much time.

He drove back to his house and retrieved his gun from the safe along with Megan and his passports. He headed over to the antique store next. Mary just closed the store up for the night and was counting the money in the office when she heard someone banging on the door.

"We're closed," Mary yelled, coming out of the office and walking towards the door, "We open tomorrow at nine."

She saw that it was Jake, "What are you doing here? I thought you and Megan went away for the weekend?" she said, unlocking the front door.

"We did. I just need to get some money." Jake flew through the door and rushed to the office. It took Mary a minute to lock the door again, and then she followed him into the office.

"What are you doing?" she asked as she watched Jake grab all the money out of the register drawer lying on the table. "I didn't count that yet."

"It's okay. Megan will count it later and adjust the books," he said, stuffing the money into a gym bag.

Knowing how particular Megan was about the books, Mary said, "I better call Megan and see if she is okay with this." She grabbed the phone off the desk and started to dial Megan's number.

Click! Jake pressed his finger on the disconnect button. "I told you I would take care of it."

Mary stopped dialing and turned to look at Jake, who was pointing a gun at her. "Put it down," he said.

She put the receiver down, "Jake, what are you doing? Are you in some kind of trouble? Maybe I can help?"

She moved towards him, intending to touch his arm, and Jake shot, hitting her in the stomach. Mary grabbed her abdomen, then fell to her knees. "Why?"

Jake grabbed the rest of the money, ripped the phone cord out of the wall, and left Mary bleeding on the floor. Mary waited until she heard the front door slam, then she dragged herself to the cabinet where she kept her purse. She opened the cabinet door, reached up, and snatched her purse off the shelf, spilling the contents of it all over the floor. She retrieved her cell phone, leaned her body against the wall, and called for help.

There is just one last loose end I need to tie up before we leave, Jake thought. He was about half a mile away from the factory when he saw the police barricade. *Damn it!* He slammed his fist against the steering wheel, then made a U-turn and went back the way he came.

Sarah woke up first. Her hands and feet were bound, her head was foggy, it was hard to think. She looked around the room as her memory came back to her, then looked to her left and saw Megan lying unconscious next to her. She pushed her with her shoulder.

"Megan, wake up. We need to get out of here before he comes back."

Megan's eyes began to flutter, then slowly open. "What is going on, Sarah? I don't understand any of this."

"Megan, Jake is the one who killed Stacy."

She shook her head in disbelief, "No, no way. You're crazy!"

"It's true. We have proof. Jake went to her apartment that night."

"I don't understand. Jake didn't even know Stacy."

"Jake used to date Stacy right before she started dating Dylan. I mean, Mark used to date Stacy."

"Do you hear yourself, Sarah? You're not making any sense. Who is Mark?"

"Jake is Mark. He changed his name. His real name is Mark Gordon, and he dated Stacy. After her death, he changed his name to Jake Harbor. Ryan has the documents to prove it. I'm so sorry, Megan, but it's true. It's all true."

Megan started to cry. "I'm married to a monster. How did I not see it?"

"None of us saw it. I think he tried to change. When I contacted Dylan, I think he got scared that the truth would come out."

"Oh my God, poor Dylan. He spent three years in jail for something he didn't do. We have to help him."

"I know. We will. But first, we need to get out of here. Put your back against mine, and I will try to untie you."

Megan put her back to Sarah's. Sarah tugged and pulled at the knot, and it started to loosen. Several minutes later, the rope fell off Megan's wrists.

"I got it! Hurry up, untie me."

Megan untied Sarah's wrists, and then the two women untied the rope around their feet. "Let's go," Sarah said, then ran to the door.

She tried to push it open, but it didn't budge. She put all her weight into it, but still, it didn't open. "There's something against it. Try the window."

The two ladies ran to the window, and Sarah was unlocking it when she saw headlights approaching the cabin.

"Hurry, he's coming back." Sarah lifted the window and pushed Megan out of it. "Run, I'm right behind you."

Megan made a dash for the woods, running as fast as she could. She stopped when she heard a gunshot.

"Sarah!" She turned and ran back towards the cabin.

chapter

21

Michael looked at the clock again and knew in his gut that something was wrong. He called Sarah again and left another message.

"It's me, again. Where are you? Please call me back as soon as you get this. I'm really starting to worry."

He paced the living room and imagined all kinds of terrible things that could have happened to her, but the truth was worse than anything he could have envisioned. He called Megan, hoping she would know where Sarah was.

"Megan, it's Michael. I was wondering if you heard from Sarah. She left a couple of hours ago to run some errands. She's not back yet, and she's not answering her phone. Okay, call me when you get this message."

"Where is everybody?" Michael said out loud to himself.

He tried Jake's number but didn't leave a message. Then called Ryan as a last resort.

"Hello."

"Finally, someone answers the phone. I'm sorry to bother you, Ryan, but I don't know who else to call. Have you seen or heard from Sarah? I can't get a hold of her."

"Oh no, when was the last time you spoke to her?"

"Three hours ago." His heart sank. "What do you mean, oh no?"

"There is so much I need to catch you up on, but right now, we need to find Sarah. I think I know where she may be."

"What do you mean? Is Sarah in trouble?"

"Yes, I think Jake is going to hurt her."

"Jake? No, don't be silly. Jake loves Sarah."

"I know you don't understand right now, but Jake isn't who you think he is. I think he is holding her hostage at the cabin. The police are on their way there now. Look, Michael, just stay put and keep your phone on. I'll let you know as soon as I know anything." He hung up.

Michael grabbed his coat and car keys and flew out of the house, then jumped into his car and sped away. *Sarah needs me.*

chapter
22

Sarah climbed out of the window and ran toward the woods, in the direction of Megan. The night was cold and dark, the only light coming from the moon above. The snow-covered ground was slippery, making it hard for her to get traction as she ran. Jake was chasing her, his gun pointing straight for her. He fired a shot, hitting Sarah in the leg. She cried out in pain and fell to the ground.

Infuriated, he walked up to her and pointed his gun at her head. Megan came running out of the woods, waving her arms and yelling, "No! Jake, please no!"

He turned his attention to Megan and listened to her pleads. "Please don't kill her. I'll come with you if you let her go."

Sarah said, "No, Megan. You don't have to do this. He's dangerous."

Megan walked up to Jake and grabbed him by the elbow. "Come on, let's go," she said and pulled him in the direction of the car. "The police are on their way."

Sarah applied pressure to her gunshot wound to try and slow the bleeding. She lay on the cold, wet ground, shivering and bleeding, and watched the car drive away.

She wasn't wearing a coat and knew she needed to get inside before she froze to death. She forced herself onto her feet and whined in pain with every step she took. She dragged her injured leg behind her, leaving a trail of blood as she staggered her way back to the cabin. When she finally got to the front door, she stumbled inside, slammed the door closed behind her, and collapsed on the floor.

After having some trouble locating the cabin, Chase finally found it and prayed he was not too late. He drew his gun and pointed it at the cabin as he made his way to the porch.

"It's over, Jake. You need to turn yourself in."

Seconds later, "I'm coming in." He kept his gun pointed in front of him as he kicked the front door open and found Sarah lying on the floor in a puddle of blood.

"Sarah," he fell on his knees and felt for a pulse, then let out a sigh of relief when he got one.

He took out his cell phone and called the police. "Hold on, Sarah. Help is on the way." He touched her face; she was ice cold. He grabbed an afghan off the couch and put it over her. Then he applied pressure to her wound and called Ryan while he waited for the police and paramedics to arrive.

"Ryan, I'm at the cabin. Sarah's been shot. Jake and Megan aren't here. The police are on the way."

"Oh my God! Is she alright?"

"She was shot in the leg. I think she's going to be okay."

"Thank you, Chase. You saved her life."

"You're welcome."

Just then, Chase could hear sirens coming toward the cabin. The paramedics quickly attended to Sarah, putting her on a gurney, starting an IV, and assessing her injured leg while the police interrogated Chase.

"What is the victim's name?"

"Sarah Evans."

"Okay, and do you have any idea what happened tonight?"

"Sarah came to the cabin to warn Megan about her husband, Jake. He must have shot her and fled with Megan. He kidnapped another woman tonight. He needs to be stopped before anyone else gets hurt. They couldn't have gotten far."

"Okay. What is his full name?"

"It's Jake Harbor."

"Do you know what he is driving?"

"I'm not sure; he may be driving a black Ford Explorer."

The detective wrote some notes on his notepad, then removed the police radio from his shoulder and spoke into it, "Townes – 25. I have an 13-88 and a possible 10-22 in process. Suspect's name is Jake Harbor, possibly driving a black Ford Explorer. The kidnap victim is his wife, Megan Harbor."

"Copy that. 13-88 and possible 10-22. Will notify all units."

The detective put his radio back on his shoulder, then turned back to Chase. "What is your name?"

"Chase Templeton."

"What brought you up to the cabin tonight, Chase?"

"I'm a private investigator. I was hired by the Goldstein & Finch Law Firm, and I was tracking Jake Harbor. We believe he murdered Stacy Richards."

"What time did you get here?"

"Twenty minutes ago. I found Sarah unconscious, and I called the police right away."

After several more minutes of interrogation, Chase asked, "Are we done here?"

"Yes. We're done. Don't go out of town, in case we have any more questions for you."

"Okay. Thanks, officer."

Detective Hansen had just watched the ambulance pull away, taking Jenna Morris to the hospital, when a call came over the radio. Any available unit, please respond, 13-88 at the Evans Antique Shop. He walked over to a woman from the crime scene unit and asked, "You okay here?"

"Yes, we got this."

"Okay, good." Then he retrieved his radio and responded to the call. "Hansen – 33, 10-4."

Detective Hansen was the first to arrive at the antique shop. He drew his gun and cautiously entered the store.

"Police, hands up!"

"I'm in here," Mary yelled. "He's not here."

Hansen kept his gun drawn and headed to the back of the store. When he got to the office, he found Mary propped against the wall. She was holding her stomach, her hands covered in blood.

The detective quickly put his gun back into his holster, rushed to her side, and applied pressure to the wound.

"He took all the money and shot me," Mary said, panting between words.

"Who? Do you know who did this to you?"

She shook her head. "Jake Harbor."

chapter

23

Michael ran into the emergency room and raced up to the reception desk. "My wife has been shot." He leaned on the counter, panting, and tried to catch his breath.

"What is your wife's name?"

"Sarah Evans."

The receptionist punched some buttons on the computer and then picked up the phone and pressed one button. A second later, she said, "Sarah Evans' husband is here."

When she got off the phone, she said, "You can have a seat, and the doctor will be right out to speak with you."

Several minutes later, a doctor approached Michael. "Mr. Evans?"

"Yes."

The doctor put his hand on Michael's shoulder. "I'm Dr. Stevens. We removed the bullet from your wife's leg, and we are in the process of trying to stabilize her."

"Is she going to be, okay?"

"Yes, she's lost a lot of blood. She's going to need a couple of pints of blood, but she is going to be fine."

Michael let out his breath that he hadn't realized he was holding, "Thank you, doctor. Can I see her?"

"Yes, I'll take you to her."

Michael followed the doctor back into the emergency department and into the bay, where Sarah was resting.

"Hey, baby," Michael said as he approached her bed and then touched her hand. "I love you!" A tear fell down his cheek, and he realized what it must have been like for Sarah when he was close to death.

Sarah was weak, but she heard him and turned her head in the direction of his voice. She tried to open her eyes, but they were too heavy.

"It's okay, baby. Just rest. I will be here when you wake up."

When Sarah woke up, she saw that Michael was asleep in the chair next to her. She reached over and gently touched his hand. Michael's eyes shot open, "You're awake."

"Dylan didn't do it," were the first words Sarah whispered.

"I know, baby. It was Jake."

"We have to help Dylan."

"We will. The police are looking for Jake as we speak. They know everything."

"He has Megan."

"I know. Don't worry; the police will find them and bring her back. But I really wish you didn't go after him yourself. You could have been killed."

"I'm sorry. I had to warn Megan."

"You are always trying to help everyone. That's what I love about you. You can't save the world, Sarah. Sometimes, you have to let the police handle things. Promise me you will stay out of this from now on."

"I promise."

"How do you feel?"

"Like I got run over by a truck. My leg is killing me."

The nurse came in and administered some more pain medication into Sarah's IV bag, and she drifted back to sleep. Michael stayed with her until he could hear her softly snoring, then he left to visit Dylan.

Dr. Knolls was behind the desk on the ICU floor. "Michael, what are you doing here? You're not due for bloodwork until tomorrow."

"You won't believe it if I told you, but Sarah is in the hospital."

"Sarah?" He looked surprised, "Is she okay?"

"She was shot. The doctor says she is going to be okay. She's resting now, so I thought I would stop in and check on Dylan. How is he doing?"

"He's doing the same. No better, but no worse either. There's a new experimental drug on the market that I think might help him. It's still too early to know, but it seems promising. My colleagues are looking into it for me. I'll let you know as soon as we have enough data to determine if it can help him."

"Thank you, Dr. Knolls."

"Now, what about you? You are supposed to be resting. Are you taking your medicine?"

"Who can rest with all this going on? No, I haven't taken my medicine. Sarah went out to get my prescriptions, and that is when she got shot. She never got a chance to fill them."

"Well, that's not good. You need your medications." Dr. Knolls removed his prescription pad from his white overcoat and scribbled Michael's prescriptions on it, then he ripped the top sheet off the pad. He handed the paper to a nurse sitting at the desk and said, "Can you please send this down to the pharmacy department and have it delivered to Michael Evans once it is filled? He will be in Dylan Hogan's room."

"Yes, doctor."

Dr. Knolls turned back to Michael, "As soon as you get your medications, I want you to go straight home and rest. And don't forget to come back tomorrow for your blood work."

"Thank you, doctor. I will, I promise."

Michael went into Dylan's room and pulled a chair up to his bed. He stared at Dylan and saw him differently than he had before. He saw the young boy he played soccer with, the boy who used to be his best friend.

"I know you didn't kill Stacy. It was Jake. I'm sorry I didn't believe you. I'm sorry for a lot of things. I hope that you can find it in your heart to forgive me one day. You need to get better. There are so many things I need to make right between us. Dr. Knolls says there is a new medication on the market that might help you. Hang in there, Dylan."

chapter

24

A black Ford Explorer pulled up to the Mexican border patrol, and the driver handed two passports to the guard at the gate. "Good evening, sir," Jake said to the man at the gate.

"What's your business for traveling to Mexico?"

"Pleasure. My wife and I came here on our honeymoon. We loved it so much we wanted to come back."

The guard lowered his head and looked at Megan through the window. "Good evening, mam."

Jake pressed the knife he had hidden under the jacket between them into Megan's side. Megan sat up straighter to alleviate some of the pressure and responded, "Evening, sir."

The guard opened a passport, and two one-hundred-dollar bills fell to the ground. He placed his foot over the money and stared at Jake. The two men silently faced off for several seconds, then the guard handed Jake the passports, "Enjoy your stay in Mexico."

"Thank you, sir."

Jake drove away from the gate and watched the guard bend down and pick up the money through his rear-view mirror, then said to

Megan, "I'm sorry about that. I don't want to hurt you. Are you tired? I'm tired. We need to find a motel for the night."

Megan said nothing and gazed out of the window. Jake reached for her hand and acted like nothing was wrong, "I know you're mad at me. Everything is going to be okay; you'll see."

Megan turned and looked at him like he was crazy. *He can't be serious*, she thought.

They found a motel a short way down the road and pulled into a parking spot in front of the office. Jake turned the car off and said, "Come on."

"I'm tired. Can't you just get the key?"

"No, you're coming with me. I'm not going to have you running away on me."

The two of them got out of the car and entered the office. "We'd like a room for the night," Jake said to the clerk behind the desk.

"I need an ID and credit card, please."

Jake handed the woman his ID and credit card and said, "I am going to pay cash."

"That's fine. I just need to make a photocopy of your card in case there are any damages to the room. We won't process it unless necessary."

"Okay."

"How many nights will you be staying with us?"

"Just one."

"And how many keys would you like?"

"Just one," Jake replied.

The clerk looked at Megan to see if she agreed, and Megan responded by looking away. The woman printed out one room card and handed it to Jake.

"Here you are. You are in room 405."

Jake looked at her name tag and said, "Thank you, Leslie."

On the way out of the office, Jake grabbed some takeout flyers off the shelf and then held the door open for Megan, "After you, darling."

The clerk smiled and thought, *Why can't I find a nice guy like that?*

When they got to their room, Jake said, "Why don't you take a shower, and I'll order us something to eat? Is there anything special you want? Pizza, Chinese, Italian?"

Megan threw her hands in the air, "I can't do this, Jake."

"Do what?"

"Pretend like nothing is wrong. You just shot Sarah. She could be dead for all we know."

"I'm sure she is fine. But, if it will make you feel better, I'll check and see." He pulled out his phone and did a Google search, and minutes later, he found what he was looking for. "She's fine, see." He handed her his phone and showed her the article covering the story. "She's at the hospital and is expected to make a full recovery."

Megan scanned the article, then said, "Thank God."

"I think I want Chinese. Is that alright with you?"

She shook her head in disgust, "That's fine." Then, she went into the bathroom and slammed the door behind her. She locked the door and searched the bathroom for a weapon, but there was nothing. She went to the window, unlocked it, opened it, then stuck her head out and looked around. They were on the fourth floor, too high for her to jump. There was no one in sight.

She closed the toilet lid and took a seat on it. She sat there for a long time, contemplating what she could do. After coming up with no ideas, she turned the water on in the shower and started to undress.

She stood in the shower, closed her eyes, and let the hot water run down her face and body and cried. *How did this day go so wrong? I am in Mexico with my husband, and I have never been so scared in my life.*

There was a pounding on the bathroom door, "Megan, dinner is here. Come and eat while it's hot."

She came out of the bathroom in her shirt and panties, with her hair wrapped in a towel. "I don't have any clothes."

"I know, I'm sorry about that. We'll go shopping tomorrow. Now, come eat."

The small table under the window was all set up with Chinese food, paper plates, cups, and napkins. "I got all your favorites."

She took her seat at the table and said, "I don't understand how you can act like nothing has happened."

He ignored her comment and dug into his food. "Mmm, this is so good!"

After dinner, Jake went into the bathroom and left the door open while he peed and undressed, keeping his eyes on Megan the whole time. When he was done, he slid the bed up against the door, so there was no way for her to leave, flicked the light switch off, and then climbed into bed and said, "It's been a long day. Let's get some sleep."

Megan stood in the dark for several minutes, then she inevitably climbed into bed and lay as far away from her husband as she could, making sure that she didn't touch him.

The next morning, when she awoke, Jake had already showered and dressed and was sitting at the table, looking at his phone.

"Good morning, sleepyhead. You better get up. It's almost checkout time."

Megan gazed at her husband smiling at her, and then looked around the room and remembered where she was and what had transpired the day before.

"There's an IHOP just down the road. I figured we could grab some breakfast and then go shopping. We'll need to find a place to stay. We could travel a little farther into town if you like. I know you love to stay in town."

Megan said nothing as she got out of bed, walked to the bathroom, and slammed the door. Several minutes later, when she came out, the bed was moved back into place, and Jake was gone. She searched the room for a pen and paper and scribbled a note, then she flung the door open to leave and found Jake sitting in a chair waiting for her right outside the door.

"Ready to go?" He smiled at her and got up from his chair.

While they were having breakfast, Megan said to him. "We need to talk about this."

"Talk about what?"

"Jake don't play games with me. About everything." She lowered her voice, leaned into him, and spoke with conviction, "You killed a woman, for God's sake. How about we start there?"

He ignored her, "I was thinking we will need to get an apartment until we are able to sell the house. Do you want a one-bedroom? Maybe we should get a two-bedroom in case people want to come and visit."

Megan slammed her fist against the table and yelled, "I don't want an apartment! I want to go home!"

Several people in the restaurant turned and looked at her. "Keep your voice down. You're making a scene," Jake said.

She lowered her voice a little, "I don't care. I want to go home."

Jake raised his hand and got the waitress' attention, "We'll take the check, please."

Jake paid the bill, and they left. When they got in the car, he turned to Megan and said, "Look, we can do this the hard way or the easy way. The choice is yours, but we're not going home. Get that through your head. The next time you make a scene like that, there will be consequences." He started the car, then drove away.

chapter
25

The housekeeper knocked on the door of room 405, then used her master key to let herself in to clean. She started by stripping the bed, she removed the comforter and sheets, then her eye caught a handwritten note on the nightstand. Unable to read English, she picked up the note, stared at the words, and contemplated what she should do with it, then folded it and placed it in the pocket of her apron and went back to work.

Six hours later, when she finished cleaning all her rooms, she headed back to the office to clock out for the day. She punched her timecard into the clock, then said, "Buenas noches," to the woman behind the desk and handed her the note.

"What is this?" The receptionist asked, unfolding the note and reading it.

> HELP! I'm being held hostage by Jake Harbor. He is wanted for murder in Ohio. Call the Franklin County Police.

The receptionist shot the housekeeper a confused look and asked, "Is this a joke?"

The housekeeper shook her head and walked out. "Buenas noches."

The receptionist Googled Jake Harbor on her computer, read the results, then went to find her manager. She tapped on his office door, opened it, and poked her head in.

"Excuse me, sir. I think this is something you need to see." She handed her boss the note along with Jake's driver's license. "I Googled Jake Harbor and found a couple of articles. He is wanted for kidnapping and shooting a woman. I didn't see anything about murder, but that doesn't mean it isn't true. What should we do?"

"You can go back to the desk now; I'll call the police."

"Franklin County Police, how can I direct your call?"

"I need to talk to the person in charge of the Jake Harbor case."

"Okay, one minute, please."

A few minutes later, Detective Hansen got on the phone. "Detective Hansen speaking."

"Hello, detective. My name is Jose Rodriguez. I'm the manager of the Hideaway Motel here in Tijuana, Mexico."

"Yes, Mr. Rodriguez, what can I help you with?"

"I think the man you are looking for was just here."

"Who might that be?"

"Jake Harbor."

"Is he there now?"

"No, they checked out. The housekeeper found a note in their room when she was cleaning. It says, HELP! I'm being held hostage by Jake Harbor. He is wanted for murder in Ohio. Call the Franklin County Police."

"Are you sure it was him? Did you get a picture ID?"

"Yes, we got his driver's license."

"Okay, I'm going to need you to fax me a copy of his license and a copy of the note. My fax number is 614-755-3539. Thank you so much for calling us. You did the right thing."

"You're welcome. I'll send the fax right away."

Detective Hansen got off the phone and called his buddy Chase right away.

"Hey, I just got a call. There's been a Jake sighting in Mexico."

"Mexico? I thought you had the borders covered?"

"Do you know how easy it is to bride the Mexican border patrol?"

"Okay, okay. So, where's he at?"

"He rented a room at the Hideaway Motel in Tijuana. They're not there now, but they couldn't have gone far."

"Are you sending someone to find them?"

"I'd have to get permission. With resources the way they are, I doubt it will be approved. I'll notify the Tijuana police, but I don't know if it will do any good. They won't extradite unless we guarantee no death penalty. Again, I would have to get permission for that."

"Okay, thanks for letting me know. I'll take care of it myself."

"Good luck!"

When Chase got off the phone, he called Ryan to give him an update.

"Jake is in Mexico. He was spotted at a motel in Tijuana. What do you want me to do?"

"Are the police going after him?"

"No."

"I guess you better go then."

"Okay, I'll keep you posted."

After their phone call, Chase packed a bag and hit the road while Ryan headed over to the hospital.

Ryan entered Sarah's hospital room carrying a large, colorful flower arrangement, and she smiled when she saw it. "Wow! They're so beautiful. Thank you."

"You're welcome. How are you feeling?"

"I'm feeling stronger today. The transfusion really helped."

He placed the flowers on the windowsill, then gave Sarah a kiss on the cheek before taking a seat next to her bed. "I have some news."

She raised her eyebrows and showed excitement on her face. "Did you find Megan?"

"Not yet, but they've been spotted in Mexico. Chase is on his way to Mexico as we speak."

"Chase? What about the police? Why aren't they going after him?"

"It's a jurisdiction thing. They may go after him, but they need permission first. It will be much faster if Chase goes after them. We don't want them to get away while we are waiting on approval."

She shifted her position in the bed. "Megan is okay, right?"

"As far as we know, yes."

"Good. So, what does this mean for Dylan? You have proof that Jake murdered Stacy. Can you get him released?"

Ryan raised both hands in the air, "Whoa, whoa! Slow down there. Jake hasn't been trialed yet. There is a process we must go through. The police know that Jake kidnapped Jenna and shot you and Mary, that's all they know for sure, and even then, he hasn't been trialed yet. After I leave here, I'm going to pay Detective Hansen a visit and present him with the evidence."

Clearly frustrated, Sarah said, "How long will that take?"

"As long as it takes. Look, Sarah, Dylan's still in the hospital; he isn't going anywhere soon. All we really have on Jake is that he dated Stacy and he went to her apartment the night she died. We still have to prove that he murdered her."

Sarah snapped at him, "Awe come on! He kidnapped Jenna to cover it up. He shot Mary, for heaven's sake."

"I agree with you, but you never know what a jury will think. We need to build a solid case against Jake. Are you prepared for that? He is your brother-in-law. Is this going to cause problems between you and Megan?"

"No, she watched him shoot me. She knows he's bad."

"There's my beautiful wife," Michael said, coming into her hospital room. "Hi, Ryan. How are you?"

"I'm good. How are you? You're looking great."

Michael smiled, "Thanks, I feel good. I'm getting better every day."

"That's good." Ryan looked at the clock on the wall. "I would love to stay and catch up with you, but there is someplace I need to be. I just gave Sarah an update on the case. I'll let her fill you in." He tapped Sarah on the leg. "Make sure she gets some rest."

Michael rolled his eyes, "I'll try. Take care, Ryan."

chapter

26

Jake and Megan stood in the empty two-bedroom apartment and looked out the massive bay window at the beautiful sun setting over the crystal blue water.

Jake placed his arm around his wife's waist, "Look at this view, Megan. It's amazing!"

"I'll give the two of you a minute to discuss," the landlord said and went into another room.

"What do you think?" Jake asked Megan.

Megan turned away from the window to face Jake. "It's a great apartment, but I want to go home."

"We already discussed this. We are not going home. You can help me pick out an apartment or not, but either way, I will be picking a place for us to live."

She shot him a glare. "We didn't discuss it at all. You made the decision. I had no say in it?"

Jake wrapped his arms around Megan, "I'm sorry, baby. Don't be mad at me. Of course, you have a say. I want to make you happy. That's all I've ever wanted."

Megan wiggled out of his arms. "I don't understand how you can just act like nothing has happened. How can you expect me to up and leave our life back home?"

"It will be a fresh start for us." He pointed out the window. "Look how beautiful it is here."

The landlord walked back into the room. "So, what do we think? Do you want the apartment?"

Jake looked at Megan, and she turned away from him, "We'll take it. Is it possible to move in right away?"

She shook her head. "I'll have to run a credit check and wait for your check to clear before you can move in."

Jake said, "We can pay cash if that will make it faster."

"Okay, I will need the first and last month's rent for security. If you pass the credit check, you can have the key today. There are some applications over on the kitchen counter. If you will give me your names and social security numbers, I will run the credit check while you fill out the application." She handed Jake a pen and a piece of paper.

Jake jotted down their names and social security numbers and handed the paper back to her, then she left to run the credit check.

"Jake don't do this. I'm going home. You are just wasting money."

He gave her a confused look, "You would leave me? Don't you love me?"

"Love you? I feel like I don't even know you."

Jake turned away so Megan wouldn't see the tears in his eyes, then went to the kitchen counter to fill out the application. The two of them remained silent as he filled out the paperwork. Several minutes later, the landlord returned to the apartment.

"You both have excellent credit. The apartment is yours."

"Great!"

"I'm going to need the $3,200 deposit."

"Sure." Jake placed his gym bag on the counter and counted out $3,200, then handed it to the landlord. She counted it for herself, then handed him the key to the apartment.

"Here you go. I hope the two of you are very happy here."

Jake's face beamed as he looked at his wife across the room. "Thank you."

The landlord left and closed the door behind her. Jake smiled at Megan, exhilaration radiating off his face, "I think we better go shopping if we want to have something to sleep on tonight."

Megan was finding it hard not to get caught up in the excitement of furnishing and decorating the new apartment with the man she still loved very much. *Don't do this. He shot Sarah, or did you forget? He may have even murdered Stacy.*

Jake and Megan went to the furniture store and purchased a bedroom set and living room set and paid for it with a credit card. Next, they went to a mattress store and bought a mattress and box spring and scheduled to have it delivered later that day.

"Let's stop at Kohl's on the way home. We need to get sheets and a comforter," Megan said to Jake.

Jake smiled and said, "Okay." *She's coming around*, he thought.

After an exhausting day of shopping, Jake and Megan picked up a pizza and a bottle of wine and headed back to the apartment to wait for the mattress to be delivered. When they got to the porch, Jake unlocked the apartment, then took the bottle of wine from Megan and said, "Wait here." He took the pizza and wine into the apartment, then ran back to the porch and said, "Let's do this right." Then he picked her up and carried her into the apartment.

"Put me down!" Megan squirmed and tried to get out of his arms. He quieted her with a kiss and carried her into the living room before he put her down.

"I'm starving," she said, then grabbed the paper plates and handed one to him.

"Me too. Did we buy a corkscrew?"

"Yes, it should be in one of the bags from Kohl's. They're still in the car."

"I'll get them." Jake ran back to the car to get the bags. When he came back, he dug through the bags, found the corkscrew, and opened the bottle of wine.

During dinner, Jake said, "This is just like old times. Remember when we were first dating, and I used to visit you at your studio apartment?"

Megan looked around the apartment, "This place is so much nicer than that. We've come a long way since then."

"I know, but do you remember how happy we were? I couldn't keep my hands off you." He placed a hand on her neck and then ran it down her chest and cupped her breast, sending all kinds of emotions through her body and mind.

She closed her eyes, "I remember."

"I feel like this could be a fresh new start for us." He kissed her neck tenderly.

There was a knock on the door. "That must be the bed." She sprang up to answer the door, happy for the distraction.

"Where do you want this?" the delivery guy said as he and another man carried the box spring into the living room.

"The first bedroom on the left." Megan pointed to the hallway leading to the bedrooms.

The men carried the box spring into the bedroom, then went to the truck to get the mattress. Jake handed the man a tip, and the two men left. He poured a second glass of wine into their plastic cups and handed one to Megan.

"Thank you," Megan said, taking her cup. She walked over to the window and stared out at the horizon. Jake came up behind her and wrapped his arms around her and kissed her neck. Unable to resist him, Megan closed her eyes and melted into his body. After a few minutes, she pulled away and said, "I need to make the bed."

She went into the bedroom and removed the plastic covering from the box spring and mattress, then started making the bed. After the bed was made, she went into the bathroom to take a shower. When she came out of the bathroom, Jake was lying in bed wearing only a pair of boxer shorts.

The sight of his masculine body had an amorous effect on her, and she suddenly became aware of how much alcohol she had consumed.

He smiled, tapped the area of the bed next to him, and said, "Come here."

Determined to be strong, she climbed into bed and kept her distance from him. "It's been a long day. I'm tired. Goodnight, Jake."

Jake grabbed her by the waist and pulled her against him. "Oh, no, you don't. We need to christen our new place." He turned her onto her back and gave her a slow, intimate kiss. When he kissed her, somehow, everything bad in the world went away for a moment. He was no longer a murderer; they were merely a husband and wife showing the love they had for each other.

No, you need to be strong. He ran his hand down her body, taking extra time in the areas he knew brought her to her breaking point. She arched her back off the bed and grabbed the sheet in her fists when his hand caressed her mid-point, sending a tingling sensation throughout her body. She tried to push him off, but her body could no longer resist his touch, and she no longer wanted to.

He's your husband. Maybe just one last time, to say goodbye. She gave in to her desires and lifted her arms as he raised her nightgown over her head and threw it on the floor. He ran his mouth along her chest and kissed each breast, and she ran her fingers through his hair and pressed his head firmly to her breast.

After their tender lovemaking session, Megan laid her head on Jake's chest as he fell asleep. She listened to his rhythmic breathing and cried because she knew it would be the last time he would ever make love to her.

chapter 27

hase interviewed the manager of the Hideaway Motel, then got a room for the night. Exhausted from the long drive, he dropped his bag by the door, removed his shoes, then threw himself across the bed and fell right to sleep, clothes and all. He slept for eight hours and only woke up because housekeeping was knocking on his door.

He opened his eyes and looked at the clock; the time was 9:10 a.m. He answered the door and said, "Can you come back later?"

"Si."

The housekeeper left, and Chase grabbed his cell phone and took it with him into the bathroom. He checked his text messages. There was a text from Detective Hansen. "Call me."

After using the bathroom and washing his hands, he called Detective Hansen.

"Detective Hansen, speaking."

"It's Chase. What's up?'

"We got a hit on Jake's credit card. He ordered furniture to be delivered to 310 Kiernan Way, Apartment B."

"Thanks. I'm on my way." He was already reaching for his shoes.

"You're welcome. Bring this guy in."

"I will."

Megan rolled over and touched the empty bed beside her as guilty thoughts ran through her head. She could hear the shower running; Jake was already up. She got out of bed and headed to the kitchen. She unpacked the coffeemaker she bought at Kohl's the day before and was setting it up when there was a knock at the door. *Who could that be?* she wondered.

She opened the door, and Chase was standing in front of her, a gun pointing at her face. "Hands up!" She raised her hands in the air.

"Where's Jake?" He asked, making his way into the apartment and looking in every direction.

Megan backed away from him, "He's in the shower."

"Are you okay?"

"Yes, I'm fine."

Chase made his way down the hallway, keeping his gun drawn in front of him. He followed the sound of the shower running and waited. Several seconds later, Jake came out of the bathroom with a towel wrapped around his waist, "Hands up!" Chase yelled, pointing the gun in his face.

Jake raised his hands in the air and locked eyes with Megan as she stood there trembling and crying and watched Chase handcuff her husband.

Jake's only concern was Megan. "It's okay, baby. I'll get this straighten out."

After a day and a half of traveling non-stop, Chase delivered Jake to the Franklin County Police Department. He pushed Jake forward and up to the front desk.

"We're here to see Detective Hansen," Chase said to the officer behind the desk.

"Just a minute." He called Detective Hansen, and two minutes later, the detective came out. When he got to the lobby and saw Jake with Chase, he said, "I knew you would find him." Detective Hansen patted Chase on the back.

"Was there ever any doubt?"

"No, good work." He took Jake by the elbow and said, "Come with me." He turned to face Megan and said, "You can't come back here. We have to book him."

"Can I post his bail?"

Detective Hansen shook his head, "He has to go before the judge first. That won't be until tomorrow. Why don't you go home and get some rest?"

Jake gave her a sympathetic look, "It's okay, baby. Go home and get some sleep."

Detective Hansen started reading Jake his Miranda rights as he walked him to the back of the police station.

Chase turned to the sobbing Megan. "Come on. I'll take you home."

Once they were back in his car, Megan said, "I don't want to go home. Can you take me to see Sarah?"

"Sure. She's still in the hospital. I'll take you there."

Megan studied Chase for a minute, then said, "He wasn't going to hurt me, you know."

Chase shrugged his shoulders. "If you say so."

"He loves me. He would never hurt me."

"Megan, he's hurt a lot of people. I don't think you ever really knew him at all. You can't deny what he has done. You saw him shoot Sarah. He shot Mary, too."

She quickly turned her head to face him, "Mary? Is she okay?"

"She's in critical condition. She's fighting for her life." After a pause, Chase said, "Then there's Jenna."

"Oh my God. What about Jenna?" The reality of the situation was finally setting in for her.

"Jake kidnapped her. The police found her at the old, abandoned tire factory." He looked over at Megan and could see how distressed she was becoming. "I'm sorry to lay all of this on you, but it's true. He's crazy, Megan. I think he killed Stacy too. He's going away for a long time. You're going to have to accept that and move on with your life."

Megan became quiet, and they rode the rest of the way in silence. They arrived at the hospital and went straight to Sarah's room.

"Oh my God, Megan. You're okay!" Sarah exclaimed as she held her arms out to Megan.

"Yes, I'm fine." She rushed to Sarah's bed and into her arms.

"We were so worried about you," Michael said.

Sarah turned to Chase and said, "Thank you for bringing her back."

"You're welcome."

"Did you get Jake?" Sarah asked.

"Yes," Chase replied.

"Oh, thank heavens. He won't be hurting anyone else."

"How are you feeling?" Megan asked Sarah.

"I feel good. I'm getting released tomorrow."

"That's good." Megan dropped her head to her chest and said, "I'm so sorry, Sarah."

Sarah shook her head. "Don't do that. It's not your fault. I should be apologizing to you. I brought all this about. I didn't mean to ruin your life."

"No, it's better I know. I just don't understand how I didn't see it."

Sarah took Megan's hand and said, "We'll get through this together. We're family. I love you."

"I love you too."

"You look exhausted. When was the last time you slept?" Sarah asked Megan.

"It's been over twenty-four hours," Chase replied.

"I'll go home soon, I promise. I need to check on Mary and Dylan first."

"Okay, then you better get going. Visiting hours are almost over."

Megan gave Sarah another hug, "Bye. I'm so happy you're okay."

"Bye, Megan."

They went to Mary's ICU room next. Mary's husband was sitting by his wife's bedside and looked up to see who had entered the room.

Her husband jumped to his feet. "What are you doing here? Did you come to finish off the job?"

"No! I didn't have anything to do with this. You have to believe me."

"I don't have to do anything! I want you to leave." He pointed to the door. "You are not welcome here."

"Please, if you'll just let me explain." Then Megan realized there was nothing she could say that would make any difference. "Okay, I'll go." She turned and left.

Chase stayed behind for a minute longer and said, "She had nothing to do with this. She didn't even know Mary was shot until I told her twenty minutes ago."

Megan stopped at the nurses' station on her way to Dylan's room, "How is Mary Preston doing?"

"She's hanging in there. The surgery went well. She just needs time to recover."

"Thank you," Megan said in barely a whisper, then headed towards Dylan's room.

When she got to his room, she walked up to his bed and laid her upper body across his and said, "Dylan, I'm so sorry. I should have been there for you. Please forgive me." She lay there sobbing until Chase came into the room and pulled her off him.

"Come on. It's time I get you home."

When Chase took Megan home, he helped her into the house and then said, "You must be hungry. We haven't eaten since breakfast. I can make us something to eat. I'm a pretty good cook."

Megan went upstairs to her bedroom while Chase went into the kitchen to cook. When she came back downstairs, she had showered and changed into sweats.

Chase smiled at her and said, "I made burgers."

She took a seat at the table and said, "That's fine," then started to cry.

Chase put the plate he was carrying on the table and wrapped his arm around her, "That's good, let it out." She put her head on his shoulder and cried.

After she finished crying, she said, "I'm sorry. I'm so embarrassed."

"Don't be, it's fine. You've been through a lot. Why don't you try to eat a little?" He pushed her plate closer to her.

She took a couple of bites from her burger, and Chase devoured his, then he said, "Why don't you go lie down on the couch? I'll clean up."

After Chase washed the dishes and cleaned up the kitchen, he went into the living room and found Megan asleep on the couch. He removed the throw from the back of the couch, placed it over her, and left the house, locking the door behind him.

chapter

28

Jake had been up all night; he was exhausted and on the verge of having a breakdown. He reached for his third cup of coffee with shaking hands and spilled it all over the table.

Detective Hansen jumped out of his chair to avoid coffee flowing into his lap and shouted, "Can we get some napkins in here?"

A minute later, another officer entered the interrogation room, carrying a handful of napkins. He wiped up the spilled coffee on the table and then the puddle on the floor.

"Thank you," Hansen said to the officer as he left the room, then he turned back to face Jake, "Now, let's go over this again. Why did you shoot Mary?"

Jake put his hand to his head and rested his elbow on the table. "I told you before, I didn't shoot anyone."

Detective Hansen slammed his fist against the table. "Both women said it was you. Are you telling me it was a mistaken identity? That your sister-in-law doesn't know what you look like?"

"No, she obviously knows what I look like, but maybe someone looks like me. I don't know. All I know is I didn't shoot anyone. Give me a lie detector test; I'll prove it."

"And what about Jenna Morris? I suppose you didn't kidnap her either?" He pushed his chair away from the table and got up and paced.

Jake dropped his head in weariness, "I didn't."

"Okay, we'll see about that." Hansen left the room, and Jake folded his arms on the table, placed his head in between them, and closed his eyes.

Thirty minutes later, the door opened, "Wake up!" Detective Hansen shouted at him and poked his shoulder. A man followed Hansen into the interrogation room carrying a polygraph machine. He didn't even look at Jake or acknowledge him before going right to work, setting up the machine and then connecting Jake to it.

"This is Richard West; he will be administering your polygraph test today."

"Just relax. If you are ready, we will get started," Richard said to Jake.

"I'm ready."

"Okay, great. Is your name Jake Harbor?"

"Yes." The needle on the polygraph machine rose and fell very minimal.

"Is your name Mark Gordon?"

Jake didn't even flinch, "No."

"Was your name ever Mark Gordon?"

"No." The needle rose slightly.

"Did you shoot Sarah Evans?"

"No."

"Did you shoot Mary Rosen?"

He gave an adamant, "No."

"Did you kidnap Jenna Morris?"

"No." Again, the needle barely moved.

"Did you kidnap your wife, Megan?"

Jake sighs, "No, my wife and I went away for our anniversary."

"Did you murder Stacy Richards?"

"No."

The questioning went on for twenty minutes, then Richard said, "Thank you. I think we are done here."

"Did I pass?" Jake asked.

"Detective Hansen will go over the results with you." He disconnected Jake from the machine and started packing it up, then left the room.

Detective Hansen was waiting for Richard in the hallway outside of the interrogation room. "Well, he failed, right?"

"No, he passed with flying colors," Richard said, walking away from the detective.

"What? No way. He must have found a way to beat the test. How is that possible?" Detective Hansen said, following Richard down the hall and back to his office.

"I don't know. People who lie and beat the test usually have some spikes in their heart rate; he had none. If he is lying, he doesn't know it."

"Great," Detective Hansen said and watched Richard enter his office. He stood in the hallway dumbfounded for several minutes, then he turned and headed back to the interrogation room.

Jake saw Detective Hansen's face when he entered the room and said, "I told you I wasn't lying."

He shook his head, "I don't know how you beat the system, but I will figure it out." The detective grabbed Jake by the elbow and pulled him up. "Come on. We're done for now."

Jake dropped his head to his chest as Detective Hansen pulled his arms behind his back and placed him in handcuffs.

chapter 29

When Megan awoke the next day, she was surprised to realize it was morning and she slept the entire night on the couch. She slowly sat up and stretched, then reached for her cell phone on the coffee table. She called Ryan and pleaded for his help.

"Will you represent Jake?"

"Oh, I don't know if I can do that. I am personally involved. Maybe he would be better off with someone else."

"No, you're the best! He needs you."

"Megan, I need to ask you something."

"Okay."

"What exactly do you expect me to do for him? He shot two people and kidnapped another. There is no doubt of that. He may have killed a woman. I don't know if anyone can help him."

"I know he is guilty, and I have accepted the fact that he is going to prison. I'm asking for your help to keep him from getting the death penalty. Please, Ryan, I'm begging you."

Several seconds passed, and then Ryan let out a sigh, "Okay, Megan. I'll help you."

Megan started to cry, "Thank you, Ryan."

"I'll call the police station and see what time his arraignment is today. After everything he's done, I don't expect the judge to release him on bail."

Megan swallowed to make way for her words, "I understand."

"I'll call you when I know the time."

"Thank you, bye."

Ryan called the Franklin County Police station and asked to speak to Detective Hansen.

"Hello, this is Ryan Finch. I need to meet with a client you have in custody. His name is Jake Harbor."

"Okay, please hold while I check on his status."

Ryan pranced around his office with the phone to his ear as he waited for the man to return to the phone. Finally, the man spoke, "Mr. Harbor is due in court for his arraignment at 1:00 p.m. If you go to the courthouse at 12:30, we will arrange for you to counsel your client before his indictment."

"Okay. Also, I'm going to need your case records before the arraignment. Could you please have Detective Hansen fax them over to me?"

"Sure. What is your fax number?"

"He has it."

"Okay, thank you."

As soon as Ryan got off the phone with the police station, he called Megan to give her the time. Then he left his office and walked up to Julie's desk.

"I'm going to need you to clear my schedule from 12:00-3:00 p.m. I'm needed in court. Also, I'm expecting an urgent fax. Please bring it to me as soon as it comes in." He turned and headed back to his office.

"Yes, sir."

Thirty minutes later, Ryan was working on a case when Julie knocked on his door and entered. She handed him some papers and said, "Here's the fax you were waiting for."

"Thank you."

Ryan read the report and was not surprised to see the two kidnapping charges of Jenna and Megan, as well as the attempted murder charge of Sarah. However, he was not aware of the attempted murder charge of Mary.

He took a deep breath and sighed, then went back to reading the report. He was shocked to learn that Jake passed a polygraph test. His mind raced with ideas of how he could use this information to benefit his case. Ryan remained in this office strategizing his case until it was time to go to the courthouse.

He entered the courthouse and placed his briefcase and the contents of his pockets into the bin, then walked through the metal detector.

"Hi, Sam. How are you today?" Ryan said to the courthouse guard.

"I'm good." Sam shook his head, "You're here again. Don't you ever rest?"

"Nope," Ryan said and picked up his watch, placed it on his wrist, and snapped the clasp shut. He picked up the rest of his stuff and headed to the conference room. When he got there, Jake and a guard were already waiting for him. Jake looked like he hadn't slept in days; he had dark circles under his eyes, and stress was apparent on his face.

"Hi, Jake," Ryan said and took a seat across from him.

"How's Megan?" Jake blurted out.

"She's doing the best she can. She's worried about you. She asked me to represent you. Is that okay?"

"Yes, of course."

"Okay, we don't have much time before you are due in court. Are you aware of the charges against you?"

"Yes, two counts of attempted murder and two counts of kidnapping."

"Okay, so obviously we will plead guilty. But I need to know what this rampage was all about. Did something happen to make you snap?"

"What? No! I'm not pleading guilty. I didn't do anything. I took a lie detector test. It will prove that I'm innocent."

Ryan tipped his head and looked at Jake over his glasses, "I don't know what kind of game you are playing, but this is serious. The victims have identified you. Mary's assault was recorded on the security cameras."

Jake got a confused look on his face, "I don't understand. I didn't do any of it."

"You need to trust me. It will be best if we plead guilty. I was thinking we should plead not guilty by reason of insanity."

Jake raised his voice, "I'm not crazy."

"Jake, if the prosecutor thinks you have no remorse and are a cold-blooded killer, they are going to ask for the death penalty. I need you to trust me on this."

"But that would be admitting that I did it. I won't plead guilty to something I didn't do."

"You're making a mistake." Frustrated, Ryan got up and left the conference room. When he went into the hallway, Megan was sitting on a bench waiting for him.

She jumped up and approached Ryan as soon as he came out of the room. "How is he?"

"He's tired. He's not thinking clearly. He keeps insisting he isn't guilty. I don't know how I am going to be able to help him if he won't agree to the insanity plea."

"I know. He told me he's not guilty too. It's so weird, but I almost believe him. I know he's guilty. I saw him shoot Sarah with my own eyes, but he's so convincing."

Ryan placed a hand on Megan's arm. "Maybe you can convince him?"

"I'll give it a try."

"Come on. We don't have much time." The two went back into the conference room, and Jake was sitting with his head down and didn't look up when the door opened.

"Hi, Jake." Jake looked up when he heard Megan's voice.

"Megan, oh, baby, are you okay?"

"I'm okay. I need you to do something for me."

"Yes, anything."

"I need you to plead guilty."

Jake's eyes filled with tears. "Megan, they'll send me to prison. We won't be able to be together. Is that what you really want?"

"No, it's not what I want, but I would rather you go to prison than be put to death."

"But I didn't do it, Megan. Why won't you believe me?"

"Because I watched you shoot Sarah, that's why! Jake, I don't understand what is going on with you, but I can tell you this. You did those terrible things. You are guilty!"

Just then, there was a knock on the door, and the door opened. A man poked his head into the room and said, "It's time."

Megan got on her feet first. She leaned across the table and hugged Jake and said, "I love you," then left the room. The guard took Jake by the arm and led him out of the room, and Ryan sat there for a minute with a sick feeling in his stomach as he slowly packed up his papers and put them into his briefcase.

Megan took her seat in the courtroom and watched as Jake was led into the room through the side entrance and took his seat next to Ryan at the defense table. The court was called into session, and the prosecutor presented the charges against Jake. The judge turned to look at Ryan and asked, "How does your client plea?"

Ryan got on his feet and turned to look at Jake, unsure of what he would say. Jake turned around and looked at Megan, and then nodded his head in approval as a tear ran down his cheek, then Ryan said, "Not guilty by reason of insanity."

The prosecutor immediately jumped to his feet. "Your Honor. This is the first we have heard of this. Jake Harbor is clearly sane. This is just a tactic to avoid the death penalty."

"I hear your concern, counselor. However, this is a court of law, and we must give the client the benefit of the doubt. I will hereby order that Jake Harbor receive a psychiatric evaluation to determine his sanity at the time of his rampage."

The prosecutor then said, "If we are to believe that Jake Harbor is unstable, and also given the fact that he is pleading insanity today, the prosecution asks that he be held without bail until his trial."

The judge looked over at Ryan, who said nothing, then said, "Jake Harbor is to be held without bail at the Franklin County Correctional Facility for Men until his trial." The judge slammed the gavel against the sounding block, and the court was adjourned.

Megan watched as the guard removed Jake from his chair and led him out of the courtroom, his head down. He didn't even look her way, and her heart shattered into a million pieces.

chapter

30

On Thursday, just one day after being discharged, Sarah was back at the hospital visiting Dylan. She sat by his bedside and updated him on the Jake situation.

"Jake is pleading guilty by reason of insanity. The judge is holding him without bail until his trial," Sarah told Dylan.

Dr. Knolls walked into the room and said, "Oh, hello, Sarah. How are you feeling today?"

"I feel great," she smiled.

"That's good," he said, checking Dylan's IV bag and then looking at the beeping monitor.

"How much longer do you think he will need to be in a coma?"

"Well, I just received the preliminary case study on the new neutropenia drug, and it looks really good. I think it might help Dylan."

"That's great! When can you start giving it to him?"

"Whoa, slow down! I will need to get permission from his health-care proxy since he doesn't have one. I would need approval from his next of kin. It is a new drug, so it's still in the experimental stage. You must know that not all family members are willing to experiment with their loved one. What do you know about his family? Are his parents still alive?"

"No, they are both deceased."

"What about siblings?"

"He has a sister, Lori, and two half-siblings, Michael and Megan. I don't know if he has any other siblings. How does that work if he does?"

"The oldest sibling would be the next of kin."

"Michael is older than Lori. If there are no other siblings, he would be the next of kin."

"Okay, I will find out if there are any other siblings and let you know as soon as I figure it out. In the meantime, you might want to have a discussion with Michael about the experimental drug."

"Thank you, doctor. I will."

"Okay, Sarah. You need to get home. You shouldn't be on your feet too long; you're still recovering," Dr. Knolls patted Sarah on the shoulder and left.

Sarah left Dylan's room and walked down the way to Mary's room. She peeked her head into the room, saw that Mary's husband and daughter were there, and kept walking, since ICU only permitted two visitors at a time. *I'll try again later*, she thought, then went back to Dylan's room to wait for Michael.

After Michael finished his bloodwork, he came to Dylan's room to get Sarah.

"Hey, babe. Are you ready?"

"Yes." Sarah got up from her chair.

"Hey, Dylan," Michael tapped Dylan's arm. "It's Michael. Hang in there, bud. Things are going to work out real soon. We're going to get you better and get you out of here."

"It's funny you should bring that up. There is something I need to talk to you about."

"Yeah, what is it?"

"I was talking to Dr. Knolls, and he thinks the new drug might help

Dylan, but he will need to get permission before administering it to him because it's considered experimental. He doesn't have a healthcare proxy, so it is up to his next of kin. Does Dylan have any other siblings besides Lori and you and Megan?"

"No, not that I know of, but it's possible because we lost touch."

"Okay, well, even if there was another child, it wouldn't matter because the oldest sibling would be the next of kin. That would be you, Michael."

"Me? Are you sure?"

"That's what Dr. Knolls said."

"Okay, well, I need to know more about this drug. What are the side effects?"

"I don't know. I'm sure Dr. Knolls will go over everything with you once he determines if you are the next of kin."

Michael stared at Dylan, and Sarah could see he was deep in thought. "Come on, let's go, I'm hungry," Sarah said.

Michael said, "Bye, Dylan. We'll be back tomorrow."

chapter

31

Dylan was in a state of bliss as Jenna came to him once more. They were back in high school again. They had just finished lunch, and Dylan was holding her hand as he carried her books and walked her to her next class. They reached the door of her classroom, and Dylan leaned in and stole a kiss, not caring that her history teacher was watching. Jenna blushed, then rushed to her seat.

Suddenly, it was prom night, and Dylan and Jenna's father were standing at the bottom of the stairs, waiting for Jenna. Dylan let out a soft whine when Jenna appeared at the top of the steps; she took his breath away. She was so beautiful in her white sequence gown, with her long blond hair curled in loose ringlets.

Jenna smiled at Dylan when she got sight of him in his tuxedo, with his fresh new haircut and dazzling blue eyes. Next, they were at the prom, and he was holding her in his arms. The two were dancing to one of their favorite songs, and Dylan never wanted it to end. When the song ended, the lights were turned up, and the principal announced they were going to crown the king and queen.

The principal introduced the nominations for prom king, and Dylan Hogan's name was announced along with three other boys' names.

The four candidates stood on the stage, and Dylan stared out at Jenna, smiling just for her. Jenna clapped her hands, jumped up and down, and cheered when the principal declared Dylan the winner. He placed the crown on Dylan's head as the others left the stage.

Next, it was time to introduce the nominations for prom queen. Jenna Morris' name was called as one of the nominations. She took her place on the stage on the opposite side of the principal and Dylan, along with the other three candidates, and held her breath as she waited for the winner to be announced. Unfortunately, her name was not called. Disappointed, she left the stage and was forced to watch as Tracy Sampson was crowned and took her place next to Dylan.

The principal announced the prom king and queen would have their first dance, and Jenna tried her best to hold back her tears as she watched Dylan smile at Tracy as he held her in his arms. When the song was halfway over, Dylan said something to Tracy and left her on the dance floor. He walked over to Jenna and put out his hand, "May I have this dance?"

Jenna smiled and took his hand and let him lead her onto the dance floor. He removed his crown, placed it on her head, and said, "You will always be my queen."

Then it was summer, and Jenna and Dylan were having a picnic under a shady tree at the park. Dylan had just carved their initials inside of a heart into the tree, and he told her that he loved her for the first time and then went in for a kiss. She returned his kiss and then rested her head on his shoulder. The two were perfectly content sitting in silence as Jenna ran her hand up and down his arm.

Jenna was sitting in Dylan's hospital room and talking to him nonstop. When she ran out of things to talk about, she pulled her chair up closer to his bed, placed her head on his shoulder, and ran her hand up and down his arm. She closed her eyes and wished he would wake up.

Suddenly, she felt his hand on her back. She jumped up and stared at him, knocking his hand back in place on the bed.

She ran to the nurses' station. "Someone page Dr. Knolls. Dylan is waking up. He moved. He put his hand on my shoulder."

The nurse ran into Dylan's room to check things out. When she got there, she looked at the monitor and saw there was no change. Jenna followed her back into Dylan's room and said, "He moved. I swear. Check the monitor. He put his hand on my back. You need to call the doctor."

"It is not uncommon for a comatose patient to experience involuntary movements. It doesn't necessarily mean that he is waking up. I will let Dr. Knolls know that he moved when he makes his rounds. He should be coming in shortly if you would like to speak to him yourself." Then she left the room, unfazed.

Jenna turned to Dylan and took his hand in hers. "You heard me; I know it. I'm right here, Dylan. I'll be right here for you when you wake up. Come back to me."

Jenna stayed by Dylan's bedside and updated him on what she had been up to since high school as she waited for the doctor to make his rounds. She jumped out of her chair and blurted out, "Dylan is waking up," as soon as Dr. Knolls entered the room.

"Yes, I heard he moved his arm."

"He put it on my back."

"I highly doubt he is waking up. We have him in an induced coma. It was just an involuntary movement. Let me remind you, we don't want him to wake up until we can get his blood count to a healthy level. Otherwise, he could have another heart attack."

Jenna frowned, "When will that be?"

"Hopefully, very soon. There is a new drug I want to try on Dylan. I just need to get Michael's approval first. I'm meeting with him today to go over all of the details with him and answer any of his questions."

Jenna's face lit up. "That's great! Thank you, doctor."

"You're welcome. Just remember. It is a new drug. There are no guarantees it will work."

"I know." Jenna was already on the phone calling Sarah.

"Sarah. What time is Michael meeting with Dr. Knolls today? I'd like to sit in and hear what he has to say about the new drug, if that's okay with him."

"Hold on, and I'll check." Jenna could hear Sarah asking Michael what time he was meeting with Dr. Knolls and if it would be okay if Jenna attended the meeting. A minute later, Sarah got back on the phone.

"He's meeting the doctor at three o'clock. He said it's fine if you want to attend. Meet us at the doctor's office at three."

"Okay, I'll be there. Please tell Michael I said thank you."

"I will. I'll see you later, Jenna."

chapter 32

Jake was lying on his cot thinking about Megan and trying to block out his cellmate, Sonny, who wouldn't stop talking, when a guard walked up to his cell and unlocked the door and said, "Let's go, Harbor."

Surprised and anxious to get away from Sonny, Jake jumped to his feet and asked, "Where are we going?"

"You're going to the psych house for an evaluation." He took a pair of handcuffs out of his back pocket, and Jake held out his arms. Once his hands and feet were securely bound, Jake looked over his shoulder at his cellmate and said, "See you later."

The inmates hollered and heckled Jake as he was led past their cells. "Hey, pretty boy. You want to come to my cell?"

He was taken on a winding maze through the building, which ended at a pair of open double doors where a prison travel van was waiting for them. There were two other inmates already seated in the van; each gave Jake a dirty look as he climbed into the van and took his seat. The guard attached Jake's handcuffs to a long chain connected to the van wall, which would limit Jake's movement to one foot in each direction. The prisoners were seated so that they couldn't reach each other if they tried.

After a twenty-minute ride, the van pulled up to the circular drive-way of the Ohio Psychiatric Institution, where three guards were waiting to escort the inmates to their psychiatrists. One of the guards looked at his clipboard then called out, "Jake Harbor."

Jake replied by taking a step forward.

"Come with me," the guard said and turned to walk into the building. Jake took quick short steps, which was all the shackles would allow, double-timing it, in an attempt to keep up with the guard. Jake looked around and noticed several of the patients were heavily sedated; they appeared to be in a zombie state. He shook his head in disbelief as he passed a man sitting in a chair drooling on himself.

Eventually, they reached an office with the name Dr. Peter Newcombe on the door. The guard knocked, and seconds later, the door was opened by a chubby, balding, middle-aged man with a friendly face. He smiled at Jake and said, "Please come in."

He swung the door open further and said, "Good afternoon, Jake. My name is Dr. Newcombe. Please have a seat." He pointed to the couch and then closed the door behind them.

Jake took a seat on the couch, and Dr. Newcombe turned to look at the guard. "Could you please uncuff him and wait outside?"

"Sure," the guard removed Jake's handcuffs, then left the office and stood guard on the other side of the door.

Jake rubbed his wrists, then relaxed his body and sank deeper into the couch. Dr. Newcombe took his seat in the chair across from Jake and picked up a manilla folder, opened it, and read for a minute, showing no emotion as he did. When he was finished, he closed the folder, pushed his reading glasses onto the top of his head, and stared at Jake. He seemed to be analyzing him. After a minute, he said, "So tell me, Jake. What happened on February 19th?"

Jake folded his arms across his chest. "Nothing. I didn't do anything."

Dr. Newcombe tilted his head so that his reading glasses dropped down to his nose and opened the folder again to double-check something, then closed it and stared at Jake. "It says that you are pleading not guilty by reason of insanity. Do you know what that means?" The doctor removed his glasses and placed the arm of the glasses into his mouth and bit down on it.

"Yes."

"Well, that means that you know that you committed these crimes, but you were temporarily insane, as if you couldn't control yourself. Is that what you are saying happened?"

"No. I didn't commit those crimes." Jake saw the look of disbelief on the doctor's face. "I can prove it. I took a lie detector test. If you don't believe me, check the results."

The doctor referred to the folder once again and looked for the results of the polygraph test. "Yes, it says here that you passed."

"I know. I told you I didn't do any of the things I am being accused of."

"Then why are you here?"

"I don't know. I don't understand why Mary and Sarah said I committed these crimes." Jake shrugged his shoulders and sighed. "Maybe I am crazy. How could I not remember doing such awful things?"

"It is possible you are intentionally blocking out what you did. I would like to see if that is the case. Have you ever had hypnotherapy?"

"No."

"I would like to put you under hypnosis to determine what might be going on with your mental state of mind. Would that be okay with you?"

Jake shrugged his shoulders, "Yeah, I guess so."

"Okay, please lie down on the sofa and try to relax. This will not hurt at all."

Jake lay down on the couch and closed his eyes. Dr. Newcombe said, "That's good, just relax, Jake. Now, I want you to imagine that you are walking in a field of flowers and the sun is shining down on you. It is a warm day, with a slight breeze blowing the branches of the trees that surround you. You are walking through the field and heading in the direction of a cliff. When you get there, you stand at the top of the cliff and look out at the sky before you. The beautiful blue sky is filled with cottony white clouds. You feel safe as you stand on the cliff taking in the beauty of the world around you. You look down the cliff and want to go to the bottom. You take your first step down the steep rocks, and as you do, you start to go into hypnosis. As you take your second step, you go even deeper. I will count to ten, and each time I say a number, you take another step, and with each step, you will go deeper and deeper under. When I reach the number ten, you will be completely under. One – two – three – four – five – six – seven – eight – nine – ten."

"How do you feel, Jake?"

"Fine."

"Okay. I want you to go back to the morning of February 19th. You are lying in bed, and you have just opened your eyes. What happens next?"

"I hear Megan in the shower. I get out of bed and use the bathroom down the hall. When I return to the bedroom, she comes out of the bathroom wearing a towel. I give her a kiss, and she pushes me away and tells me she is going to be late for work. She tells me I need to wait for tonight. We are going away for our anniversary."

"That's good. Now, what happens after she goes to work?"

"I do some things around the house, then I go to the coffee shop around the corner to get a coffee. Jenna is there; I just met her at Sarah and Michael's house the night before. I walk over to her table to say hello to her. She is acting strange around me, like she is nervous or something. She spills her coffee all over the table and quickly makes an excuse to leave."

"Is she afraid of you?"

"Yes, but I don't know why."

"Okay, what happens next?"

"She leaves, and I follow her."

"Why do you follow her?"

"Because she knows who I am, and I can't have her telling anyone."

"Who are you?"

"Mark."

"Mark who?"

"Mark Gordon."

"Where is Jake?"

"He's not here. It's better if I handle things."

"What do you do after you follow her, Mark?"

"I follow her to Ryan's office. I wait for her to go inside, and then I get out and cut the hose to her radiator. I get back in my car and wait for her to come out. She gets in her car and drives away, and I follow her. Smoke is pouring out of the hood of her car; she pulls over on the side of the road. I pull up behind her."

"What did you do to her, Mark?"

"I broke her window and dragged her out of her car."

"Where did you take her?"

"I took her to an abandoned tire factory."

"What are you going to do to her?"

"Kill her."

"Why?"

"To keep her from telling Megan what I've done."

"What have you done? Up until now, you haven't committed any crimes."

"I killed that bitch."

"Who? Who did you kill?"

"Stacy Richards."

"Why did you kill Stacy? Take me back to the night of her death."

"Stacy and I had been dating for almost a month, and she refused to sleep with me. She said she was a good girl and she needed time before jumping in bed with someone. Then she broke up with me and started dating someone else. I was such a fool; I really believed she was a good girl. I was wrong about her."

"How did that make you feel?"

"I was pissed. I wanted her back. The night she was killed, I went to a bar and got drunk, then I went to her house to try and get her back. When I got there, I went to the door to knock, but I didn't, I just stood there frozen in place as I could hear her moaning on the other side of the door. She was having sex with someone."

"What did you do next?"

"I went down to the lobby and took a seat and waited. I didn't know who she was dating or what he looked like; I just hoped that once I saw him, I would know. I waited for over an hour and watched every guy who came off the elevator and wondered if it was him. When Dylan entered the lobby, I instinctively knew it was him. I could see Stacy falling for a pretty boy like him. I wanted to attack him as I visualized the things that he had just done to Stacy. Things that I wanted to do to her."

Dr. Newcombe was writing all of this down. "Then what happened?"

"I watched Dylan leave, and then I took the elevator up to her apartment. She opened the door as soon as I knocked and said, 'What did you forget?' She thought I was Dylan coming back. She looked disappointed that it was me. She pulled her short silk robe closed and tightened the belt around her waist. 'What are you doing here?' She tried to close the door a little bit, but I pushed it open and let myself in. The room was lit with candles and smelled of sex. She told me I needed to leave. I took a seat on her couch and said, 'Is this where you had sex with him?' She said, 'That's none of your business,' and asked me to leave. I grabbed her arm and pulled her into me. She tried to get out of my grip, but she wasn't strong enough. I pulled her into my lap and ran my hand up her thigh and under her robe. She wasn't wearing any panties. She flinched and moved her thigh away from me. 'Don't pretend to be a nice girl. I know what you did with him. I heard you.' She kneed me in the balls. I doubled over in pain, and she escaped my grasp and ran into the kitchen. It took me a second to catch my breath, then I ran after her. She was fumbling in her purse for her cell phone.

She just got it out and was about to call the police when I grabbed a knife out of the butcher block and put it to her throat. 'Put it down!' I said, and she dropped the phone on the counter. I tightened my grip around her neck and dragged her into the bedroom and threw her on the bed."

"Did you rape her?"

"No, we had sex. She wanted it."

"Are you sure about that?"

"Yeah, I would never hurt her."

"Are you saying you didn't murder her?"

"I didn't have a choice. She was going to kill me."

"You always have a choice. Please tell me what happened."

"After we had sex, I was lying in bed with my eyes closed. I was almost asleep. I felt her get up from the bed. I opened my eyes; she was standing over me, pointing the knife at my heart. I grabbed her wrists; the knife was only inches from my chest. I flipped her over onto the bed and took the knife away from her. She started pounding on my chest and pushed me backward. I pointed the knife at her, and she lunged at me. Before I realized it, I had inserted the knife into her stomach."

"So, it was an accident?"

"Yes."

"Why didn't you call the police?"

"Because they wouldn't see it that way. They would want to know why she had a knife."

"What did you do after you stabbed her?"

"I felt for a pulse; she was dead. So, I cleaned my fingerprints up the best I could, and I got out of there."

"Okay, I think that is enough for today. I am going to count to ten, and when I reach the number ten, you will be fully awake and will have no memory of what just happened. One – two – three – four – five – six – seven – eight – nine." Dr. Newcombe snapped his fingers and said, "Ten."

Jake opened his eyes and looked around the room. "Did it work?"

"Yes."

"Well, did you figure out what's going on?"

"Yes."

chapter 33

ichael flipped through a magazine, trying to kill time as he waited for Dr. Knolls to finish his rounds and return to his office. The doctor came strolling into the office just as Michael finished reading an article on heart disease.

"Hello, Michael. Sorry to keep you waiting. Please come into my office."

Michael placed the journal back into the magazine rack and followed Dr. Knolls into his office as Sarah and Jenna tagged behind. Dr. Knolls led them into his office, then left to get another chair. After everyone was seated, Dr. Knolls said to Michael, "So, I checked, and Dylan has no other brothers and sisters, which makes you his next of kin."

"Yes, I didn't think there were any other siblings besides Lori. No one else has come to visit him."

"So, let's talk about this new neutropenia drug, Plasmaneta. It hasn't been FDA approved yet, but looking at the preliminary test results, I expect it to be approved any day now."

Michael shifted in his seat and wiped his brow. "What are the side effects of the drug?"

"The worst-case scenarios would be spleen rupture, acute respiratory distress syndrome, serious allergic reaction, sickle cell crisis, kidney injury, and inflammation of the aorta." Dr. Knolls saw the reaction on Michael's face and said, "I know this sounds scary, but only a small percentage of people experienced these symptoms. Most people just had minor side effects like difficulty breathing and swelling of the stomach, which went away over time."

Michael shook his head, "I don't know, doctor. You said that the blood donation had a minimal chance of problems too. I already feel responsible for his condition. What if it kills him?"

"I understand. There is no pressure. I just wanted you to know that it was an option. There is one more thing you must consider. Because it hasn't been FDA-approved yet, insurance won't cover it. You will need to pay out of pocket."

Michael sighed. "How much will it cost?"

"It is $10,000."

Michael turned and looked at Sarah and shook his head in disbelief.

Jenna said, "If you decide to go through with it. I could help with the cost. I got some money from my grandmother's inheritance."

Michael said, "Thank you, Jenna. I don't want to make the decision based on money, and that would help." Then he turned back to face the doctor, "I need some time to think it over. Can I give you an answer in a few days?"

"Absolutely, take all the time you need. I can email you the preliminary test results if that will help?"

"Yes, please. I want to look them over."

"I will have my secretary send them to you as soon as possible."

Michael looked like he had the weight of the world on his shoulders as he got up from his seat and extended his hand to the doctor. "Thank you, Dr. Knolls. I will get back to you as soon as I make my decision."

"You're welcome. Please feel free to contact me if you have any other questions."

"Okay, I will."

After the three of them left Dr. Knolls' office, Michael said, "I want to go see Dylan."

"Me too," Jenna said.

Before they entered Dylan's room, Michael stopped and said, "Do you mind if I have a minute alone with him?"

Sarah and Jenna both replied, "Sure."

"Let's go get a cup of coffee," Sarah said to Jenna. The two women turned and headed to the elevator as Michael entered Dylan's room. Michael walked up to the bed and looked down at Dylan.

"Hey, Dylan. It's me, Michael. I just met with Dr. Knolls, and I'm not sure that the new drug he mentioned is a good idea. There are a lot of possible dangerous side effects. I don't know what you would want me to do, and I need to make a decision on whether you should take it. I don't want to do that, so I'm going to need you to fight really hard to get better. You have a whole new life waiting for you when you wake up. You're not going back to jail, and you have people who love you and are waiting to make new memories with you."

Michael's whole body began to shake, and he broke down and started to cry. "Please, Dylan, please get better. I'll never forgive myself if something happens to you. Please give me the opportunity to make things right between us again."

As Dylan lay in a coma, he dreamt of Michael; his memory replayed the good times the two shared together. Their families were together on a camping trip. The two boys just finished kicking a soccer ball around, and then they grabbed their fishing poles and headed down to the lake. As they sat alongside the lake and baited their fishing poles, Dylan said, "Do you think we'll still be friends when we become adults?"

"Of course. Why wouldn't we?"

"I don't know. Sometimes, people lose contact."

"That won't happen to us. You're like a brother to me."

"I wish we were brothers."

"Me too. Hey, I know what we could do. Give me your finger."

Dylan stuck out his hand, and Michael grabbed it, then pricked Dylan's finger with the fishing hook. A drop of blood came to the surface.

Dylan pulled his finger away. "Ouch, what did you do that for?" He was about to put his finger into his mouth when Michael said, "Don't," and grabbed his hand.

"We're going to be blood brothers," Michael said, then pricked his own finger with the hook. He pinched his finger until a drop of blood appeared. Dylan did the same, then the two boys put their fingers together and combined their blood.

"There, now we are brothers forever," Michael said.

"Forever," Dylan repeated, then reached his arm around and placed it over Michael's shoulder.

Michael smiled at him, then forcefully pushed him away. An unexpected Dylan stumbled backward, slid off the embankment, and fell into the lake, then splashed Michael for laughing at him. Michael kicked off his shoes, pulled off his socks and t-shirt, and jumped into the lake, joining his friend.

chapter

34

On Thursday morning, Michael went to the hospital to have his blood count checked again.

"Is Dr. Knolls here?" he asked the lab technician as she inserted the needle into his arm. "Yes, he's in his office. Do you need to speak with him?"

"Yes, please."

"Okay, I'll get him as soon as I am done taking your blood."

"Thank you."

The technician took one vial of blood, removed the needle and rubber band, then covered the insertion point with a cotton ball and applied pressure. "Hold this here, and I'll go get the doctor."

She returned a few minutes later with Dr. Knolls in tow.

"Hi, Michael. How are you doing today?"

"I'm fine. How are you?"

"Good, thank you. I understand you wanted to speak with me?"

"Yes, I've made my decision."

Dr. Knolls took a seat across from Michael and said, "So, what have you decided?"

"I read the preliminary test results, and I think I want to try the medication."

"That's great. I think you are making the right decision. I know that it can be scary when you read the possible side effects, but it has really helped most people in Dylan's situation."

"How soon can you give it to him?"

"We can do it right away since we don't need to get insurance approval. I just need to change his coma medication first. If he doesn't have a heart attack after twenty-four hours on the new medication, I will give him the neutropenia drug."

"What about the payment?"

"The drug company requires fifty percent of it upfront, and then they will bill you for the remainder of it."

"Okay, so you will need that by Saturday."

"No, I won't be here over the weekend. It is my anniversary, and I am going out of town. If it is okay with you, I would like to wait until Monday to give him the new treatment."

"Yes, that's fine."

"Okay. If you will follow me to my office, I need you to sign the consent for treatment form."

"Sure," Michael said and followed Dr. Knolls down the hall.

After Michael signed the form, he asked, "How do I pay the deposit?"

"You will need to get a cashier's check. You can just bring it to the hospital on Monday when we administer the drug. I will have my secretary send you the information of who you need to make it out to."

"Thank you, doctor."

"You're welcome," Dr. Knolls stood up and extended his hand to Michael. "Try not to worry. I will take good care of him."

chapter

35

Jenna cleared off her desk, shut down her computer, then hit the light switch and left her office at the accounting firm. She stopped at her secretary's desk on her way to the elevator, "I'm out of here, Terri."

Her secretary looked up from her computer, "Okay. Any plans for the weekend?"

"No, I'm beat. I'm going straight home to sleep the weekend away."

"I hear you. It's been a long week. See you on Monday."

"See you Monday," Jenna said and raised her hand in a wave as she shuffled her way to the elevator.

She pressed the down button, and the elevator doors opened immediately. She smiled and stepped into the elevator, joining her good friend and lunch buddy, Alyssa.

"Hi, are you heading to the hospital?"

"No, not tonight. I've been there every night this week. I'm really tired. I'm going home and straight to bed."

"Good. You've been running non-stop ever since Dylan was hospitalized."

Jenna put a hand on her neck and applied pressure, "Yeah, I think it's finally catching up with me."

The elevator stopped on the first floor, and the two ladies got off, then walked to the parking lot together.

"Have a good weekend," Alyssa said, then went her separate way to her car.

"You too."

Jenna had to pass the hospital on her way home from work. The closer she got to it, the more tormented she became. *Just go home, Jenna. You need a night off. You can see him tomorrow. Maybe, I should just stop for five minutes. Just to check and see if there is any improvement in his blood count. Come on, Jenna, if there were any improvement, Sarah would have called you. If you don't see him, you will never be able to rest tonight. Just check on him and then you can go home and sleep.*

Jenna sighed, pulled her car into the hospital parking garage, then parked her car and made her way into the building. She was relieved when she got to Dylan's room and saw that no one else was there. She didn't have the energy to hold a conversation with anyone. She just wanted to visit Dylan for a few minutes and go home.

When she got to his room entrance and saw his face, she smiled at him, glad that she had decided to come. "Hi, Dylan. It's Jenna," she took a seat on the edge of his bed and touched his hand.

"I've missed you. It's been a crazy week at work. I'm so glad it's the weekend, and I don't have to work tomorrow."

Dylan could hear Jenna's voice again; he wasn't sure what she was saying, but he knew it was her and sensed that she was there. Her voice was muffled and sounded like she was in a tunnel far away from him. His legs began to wobble as he cautiously took his first step in the direction of her voice. His limbs became stronger with each step he took. Soon, he was running, and her voice became clearer and louder.

"I'm coming," Dylan shouted and ran faster.

Dylan's eyes started to flutter. Jenna stopped babbling, leaned in closer to him, and stared in his face. "I'm here, Dylan. Please come back to me. There is so much I need to tell you."

Dylan slowly opened his eyes and tried to focus on the blurry figure in front of him. It took several seconds for Jenna to come in clearly. She smiled at him in disbelief, "Hi."

Dylan smiled back at her and leaned forward, then took her face into his two hands and kissed her. When he pulled away, he said, "You're really here."

"Yes, I'm here," she whispered and grinned.

"I thought I was dreaming." He pulled her into a kiss again to re-assure himself. They continued to kiss, ignoring the beeping monitor until they heard someone clear their throat. Jenna blushed and turned away from the nurse staring at them in disapproval.

"Take it easy there, big guy. We don't need you having another heart attack. How are you feeling?"

"Good," he smiled at Jenna and held his hand out to her.

Jenna accepted his hand and said, "I don't understand. Why did he wake up?"

"Dr. Knolls changed his coma medication. He may need to increase the dosage. I'll let him know what's going on. I'm sure he will answer all of your questions." She patted Dylan on his shoulder, "No more getting excited, okay?"

He glanced over at Jenna, "Okay."

The nurse checked Dylan's vitals and then said, "I'll be back later to check on you," before leaving the room.

Once Dylan and Jenna were alone, he said to her, "I've written you so many letters."

She raised an eyebrow, "Really? I never got any letters."

"I know. I didn't send them. I wanted you to go on with your life. I didn't think it would be fair to you."

"What did they say?"

"That I loved you and I have always loved you."

"Oh, Dylan. I love you too." She placed a tender kiss on his lips.

"You need to know that I didn't kill Stacy."

"I never thought you did."

They were unable to finish their conversation because Dr. Knolls entered the room.

"Hi, Dylan. How are you feeling?"

"I'm okay. How long was I out?"

"Four weeks. You were in a medically induced coma to reduce the stress on your heart. The nurse told me you got excited earlier. You can't do that; you'll have another heart attack."

"Sorry, I couldn't help myself," he smiled at Jenna.

"Since you are awake, I like to speak to you about your treatment of care."

"Okay."

"There is a new experimental drug I like to try on you. It seems to be having great results increasing white blood counts. I was going to start you on it on Monday. Michael has already agreed to it, but now you can decide for yourself."

"Michael? What does he have to do with it?"

"Well, he is your next of kin."

"Michael would never agree to help me. He hates me."

"You saved his life, Dylan. He doesn't hate you," Jenna said.

Dylan said, "The stem cell transplant worked?"

"Yes, it worked, Dylan. You can see for yourself; I'll call him now." Jenna pulled her cell phone out of her purse and started dialing, then walked out of the room and headed to the waiting area to talk.

"Will you have to put me back into a coma? I don't want that."

"We'll have to see how you do. If you have another heart attack, then yes. That's why it's so important you remain calm and don't get yourself too excited."

"Sorry about that. It's just that I haven't seen Jenna in years."

"I understand. I'm going out of town for the weekend. The nurse will be monitoring your heart and blood count all weekend and keep me updated. If all goes well, we can start the new drug on Monday as planned. There are some side effects you should be aware of and, of course, the price."

"Price? What do you mean price? Doesn't the insurance cover it?"

"No, I told you it was experimental. It hasn't been approved by the FDA yet."

"What is the price? I don't have any money."

"Ten thousand dollars. Michael has agreed to pay for it."

Jenna came back into the room, "I just got off the phone with Sarah. She and Michael are on their way."

Dr. Knolls' beeper went off, "I've got to get this. I'll be back later, and we can talk some more. Remember what I said, don't get excited."

After the doctor left, Dylan asked Jenna. "Did you know that Michael agreed to pay for the experimental drug?"

"Yes. I told you he's not mad at you any longer. He wants to make amends with you."

Dylan was dumbfounded. He leaned back against his pillow and said, "Wow!"

"There is so much you don't know, Dylan. I'll let Sarah and Michael explain everything to you when they get here."

chapter

36

Dr. Newcombe hesitated and then sighed. "Do you know what dissociative identity disorder is, Jake?"

"No, what is it?"

"It is a mental disorder that causes disruptions or breakdowns of memory, awareness, identity and/or perception."

Jake raised his eyebrows, "Like multiple personalities?"

"Yes, like multiple personalities."

Jake stiffened his gaze, "Are you telling me I have multiple personalities?"

Dr. Newcombe nodded, "Yes."

Jake shook his head in shock. "No way. I'm not crazy."

"Think about it, Jake. That would explain how you passed the polygraph test and why you don't remember doing things."

They sat in silence as Jake took a couple of minutes to comprehend what the doctor had just told him. "So, who am I?"

"Your other personality is Mark Gordon, and I'm sorry to tell you that you murdered Stacy Richards."

"No!" Jake got up from the couch and started to pace. He put his hands on his head and tried to think. "I'm not a murderer. I didn't kill anyone."

"You didn't, Jake, but Mark did."

"That's not possible. I would know if I killed someone."

"I'm sorry, Jake. It is possible, and it's true. Your mind split to help you deal with the trauma of what you did. As far as I can tell, you just have the two personalities, but there could be more. I won't know until we dig deeper under hypnosis." He waited for Jake to say something, but Jake remained silent. He went on, "There are some medications I could prescribe to help you deal with the disorder."

"Would it keep Mark from coming back?"

"It's possible, but there is no guarantee. It will help you deal with everything."

"No, thanks. I saw the people when I came in here. They are drugged out of their minds. You're not turning me into a zombie."

For the first time since being arrested, Jake looked scared and no longer confident. Then suddenly, a look of confusion came over his face. "I'll be sent to prison."

A look of compassion came over Dr. Newcombe's face. "I'm sorry, Jake."

Jake walked over to the window and stared out for several seconds. When he turned back around to face the doctor, it was evident that Jake was no longer there, and Mark had taken over.

"This is how it's going to work, doc. You're not going to say a word to anyone about this," Mark said as he started walking towards the doctor's chair.

Dr. Newcombe was quick on his feet. As he rushed to the door, he was able to yell, "Guard, I need help in here."

The guard flung the door open, pulled his gun out of his holster, and rushed into the room to find Mark's arm wrapped tightly around Dr. Newcombe's neck. The doctor was turning red from lack of oxygen.

"Let him go, or I'll shoot!" the guard yelled and pointed the gun in Mark's face.

Mark backed away from the guard, dragging the doctor with him in the process. Dr. Newcombe took the opportunity to grab Mark's arm and loosen the hold on his neck, allowing him to take a gulp of fresh air. Mark struggled to get a tighter hold on the doctor's neck, and the guard leaped forward and tackled the men. Dr. Newcombe scrambled loose, stumbled over to his desk, and pressed the security button as the two men continued to struggle on the ground. A second later, two hospital guards came charging into the room and restrained Mark by using a taser.

Dr. Newcombe watched as a guard placed Mark in handcuffs, then plopped into his chair and rubbed his neck.

"Are you okay?" One of the guards asked Dr. Newcombe.

In shock and unable to speak, the doctor just shook his head.

chapter

37

Sarah got off the phone and rushed downstairs, calling for Michael as she flew down the steps. "Michael, Michael, where are you?"

"I'm in the kitchen. What's wrong?" He closed the refrigerator door and turned to look at her as she entered the room.

"Dylan is awake!"

"What? I don't understand. How?"

"Dr. Knolls changed his medication, remember? Apparently, it had an effect on him, and he woke up. Jenna just called me; he wants to see us."

"Well, let's go." Michael put the leftovers he just took out of the refrigerator back into it and grabbed Sarah by the arm, dragging her out of the kitchen and toward the front door.

"Hold on a minute. I need to get my purse." She went to the living room to retrieve it.

"Okay, I'll wait for you in the car." He grabbed his keys off the keyholder by the backdoor and went into the garage.

A few minutes later, they were on their way to the hospital, and Michael started to worry. "What if he is mad at me? What if he doesn't forgive me for everything, I've done to him?"

"He'll forgive you. You're brothers, remember?" Sarah placed her hand on his thigh to reassure him.

"I hope you're right. I just thought of something. What if he doesn't want to try the new medicine?"

"Well, now that he is awake, I guess that will be up to him. We will just have to try and convince him that it is the right thing to do."

"Is it? What if something happens again?"

"Try not to think about that now. Let's just take things one step at a time."

"Yeah, you're right."

"Jenna said that we can't get Dylan excited because he could have another heart attack."

Michael said, "I don't plan on arguing with him," as he pulled the car into the hospital parking garage.

"Okay, good."

He parked the car and jumped out of it and practically ran to the elevators.

"Will you please slow down?" Sarah picked up her pace and tried to keep up with him. "He's not going anywhere."

He pressed the elevator button, and the door opened. "Come on. The elevator is here."

Sarah ran the rest of the way to the elevator and got in. They rode the elevator from the fourth floor, stopping at every floor on the way down to let people on. Michael sighed in frustration as the people got on too slowly for his liking. Finally, they reached their stop, and Michael bumped into a man as he forced his way out of the elevator.

Sarah smiled at the man and said, "Sorry," as she rushed out of the elevator in pursuit of her husband. "Michael, slow down. He's not going anywhere."

"What if he falls back into a coma?"

"He won't." Sarah followed her husband through the maze of the hospital to a new set of elevators that led to ICU. She had never seen him like this before. They rode the elevator to the ICU without a stop, and when the doors opened, Michael flew out of them and ran to Dylan's room.

Jenna was sitting by Dylan's bedside when Michael suddenly appeared in the doorway and just stared at Dylan for a minute before he entered the room, then rushed up to Dylan and pulled him into a hug. Jenna stepped back to give the two men space just as Sarah reached the entrance of the room. Sarah smiled at what she was seeing and then walked over to Jenna and put her arm around her. They stood in silence as their eyes filled with tears and watched the two men embrace each other.

"Thank you," Michael said, "I owe you my life."

Dylan smiled at Sarah, and she shook her head in confirmation.

When the two men pulled apart, Michael said, "I'm so sorry. Can you ever forgive me?"

"Yes," Dylan replied.

"It was wrong of me to blame you for my mother's death. You had nothing to do with it. It wasn't your fault. It was easier to blame you than to blame Dad. I thought that if you weren't born, my mother could have forgiven my father for the affair. We lost so much time, and it's all my fault. I'll never understand how you agreed to help me after everything I've done to you."

"You have a very persistent wife." Sarah walked up closer to the bedside and placed her hand on Dylan's shoulder.

Michael cast his eyes downward and hesitated, "I don't deserve to have you as a brother. I don't know if I can ever make it up to you, but I'm going to try, even if it takes the rest of my life to do."

Michael drew Dylan into a hug again. After a minute, Dylan pulled away and pushed Michael, causing him to fall off the bed, and everyone laughed. A nurse heard the excitement and came into the room.

"You can't have this many visitors in ICU, and Dylan, you're not supposed to get excited, remember?"

Michael said, "I'm sorry. It's my fault."

"Come on, Jenna, let's go to the cafeteria and get a cup of coffee so Dylan and Michael can catch up."

Once the two women left, Michael pulled a chair closer to the bed and took a seat, then said, "Let me get you up to speed on what's been going on. You're never going to believe it."

"Okay, but first, I want to know how my appeal is going."

"That's what I want to tell you about. I think we know who really killed Stacy."

"Oh, yeah? Who?"

"Megan's husband, Jake."

"What?" Dylan leaned back in his bed and thought a moment. "Did he even know her?"

"Apparently, Jake isn't who we all thought he was. He changed his name a few years back. His real name is Mark Gordon, and he used to date Stacy. She broke up with him right before she started dating you. They have him on tape going to Stacy's apartment the night she was murdered, shortly after you left."

Dylan's eyes grew big, "I'm actually going to be cleared?"

"Yeah. There is so much more, too. He shot Sarah and the clerk that works at the antique shop, then he kidnapped Megan and took her to Mexico."

"Wow! A lot has happened since I've been in a coma."

"You're not kidding."

"Poor Megan. I'm glad my name is going to be cleared, but I'm sorry that her life is being destroyed in the process. That's not what I would have wanted."

"She knows that. We are just going to have to be there for her."

chapter 38

D r. Newcombe opened his desk drawer and pulled out a bottle of pills. He had trouble opening the bottle because his hands were trembling so much. He threw two pills into his mouth and swallowed them without water. Then, when he was finally able to stop shaking, he pulled himself together and placed a call to Ryan.

"Mr. Finch, this is Dr. Newcombe from the Ohio Psychiatric Institute. I'm calling to give you an update on your client, Jake Harbor."

"Oh, yes. Hello, doctor. I didn't expect to hear from you so soon."

The doctor's throat tightened, "I have some bad news for you."

"Really? I already know my client committed the crimes he is being charged with. How much worse could things possibly get?"

"Oh, much worse, I'm afraid. Jake has multiple personalities and has committed other crimes."

Ryan leaned back in his chair and exhaled, "Let me guess, he murdered Stacy Richards?"

"Yes. How did you know?"

"I've been investigating her death. I just filed an appeal for another client serving time for her murder. Do you know who the other personality is and why he killed Stacy?"

"Yes, his name is Mark Gordon. Apparently, he used to date Stacy. He saw her out that night with another guy. He got drunk and then went over to her place to try and get her back. When she refused him, things got physical, and she pulled a knife on him. He said he didn't want to kill her, but he had no choice. I believe Mark's personality split to help him deal with what he did that night."

"Are you telling me that Jake doesn't remember killing Stacy?"

"I'm sure of it. I just told him. He was in shock and couldn't believe it."

"Is that how he passed the lie detector test?"

"Yes, Jake had no clue what Mark did." The image of Mark's hands around his neck came back to Dr. Newcombe's mind. "Oh, and I had the pleasure of meeting Mark today."

"How can you tell them apart?"

"You can definitely tell them apart. Mark is incredibly angry. He attacked me, and I had to have the guards restrain him."

"Are you okay? Did he hurt you?"

Dr. Newcombe rubbed his neck. "I'm okay, just a little shaken up. I was fortunate the guards came in when they did, or things could have been much worse. I just wanted to let you know that I will be putting this information in the report I file and submit to Judge Lucas, and I also have to report it to the police."

Ryan exhaled, "I understand. What are you going to recommend?"

"I am going to recommend that Jake's trial take place in a mental health court to be sure that his mental health needs are taken into consideration and to warrant a fair trial."

"Thank you, doctor."

"You're welcome. I'm sorry I didn't have better news."

"It's okay. I appreciate you letting me know. Will you send me a copy of the report you're sending to the judge?"

"Sure, I'll send that to you later today. Take care."

"Thank you. You too."

When Ryan got off the phone, he immediately called Megan.

"Hi, are you home? Can I come over and talk to you?"

"Yeah, I'm home. What's up? Do you have an update on Jake's case? You can tell me over the phone."

"I'd rather tell you in person. I'll be right over." He hung the phone up before Megan could say anything else.

Ryan grabbed his suit jacket off the coat rack and headed out the door, stopping at Julie's desk on his way out.

"Somethings come up. I need you to cancel the rest of my appointments for today."

"Okay," Julie said but couldn't get another word in. Ryan was already out the door.

It took him no time at all for Ryan to get to Megan's house. Megan was looking out the window anxiously waiting for him. She rushed to the door, opened it, and walked out onto the porch as soon as she saw Ryan pulling into her driveway.

She wrapped her arms around her body to keep herself warm from the cold winter day and watched Ryan exit his car and approach the porch.

Ryan yelled, "Get inside. It's cold out here."

"What is so important you couldn't tell me on the phone?" she asked with concern in her voice.

Ryan ran up the steps, grabbed Megan, spun her around, and dragged her inside. "Let's talk inside. You're going to catch your death out here."

"What is it?" she asked as she closed the front door.

Needing a minute to get the nerve up to tell her, he asked, "Can I get a cup of coffee?"

"Sure, I'm sorry, please come in."

Ryan followed her into the kitchen, then took a seat at the counter and watched as she filled the coffee pot.

"How do you take it?"

"Cream and sugar."

After she started the coffee maker, Ryan said, "There is no easy way to tell you this, so I'm just going to come out and say it. Jake has multiple personalities."

Megan let out a nervous giggle, "What? Stop playing, Ryan. That isn't funny. Here I thought you had something serious to tell me." Ryan wasn't laughing. She could see that he was serious. "I would know if my husband had multiple personalities."

"How long have you known Jake?"

"Four years, why?"

Ryan fidgeted with the salt and pepper shakers in front of him. "You probably never met his other personality."

Megan stared at Ryan but said nothing. Ryan continued, "Think about it. It explains why he doesn't remember doing such horrible things. He had no idea he committed those crimes."

Megan's mouth sank into a sad smile. "Poor Jake. He is a good man; he didn't deserve this." Her brow rose in a slow arch. "What is going to become of him?"

"His psychiatrist is going to recommend he be tried in a mental health court in order to assure this illness is addressed."

Megan took a second to digest everything she was just told. "It all makes sense now." She poured a cup of coffee for Ryan, then brought it over to him and placed it on the counter.

Ryan cleared his throat. "I'm sorry, Megan. As Dylan's lawyer, I have to recommend that Dylan be released from prison and that Jake be charged with Stacy's murder. And one more thing, I can't represent Dylan and Jake. It would be a conflict of interest. Dylan was my client first; my commitment needs to be with him. I can recommend a colleague of mine, George Ramsey. He recently left our firm to work at another. He is an excellent lawyer. Jake will be in good hands."

Megan came around the counter, hugged Ryan, and cried into his shoulder.

"I'm so sorry, Megan." Ryan ran his hand up and down her back, comforting her as she cried. "I'm so sorry."

chapter

39

It took over an hour for Ryan to get Megan to stop crying, and he felt comfortable enough to leave her alone. She walked him to the front door and promised him she would call him if she needed anything. As soon as he got to his car, he called Sarah to give her an update.

"Hey, Sarah. It's Ryan. I have some news."

Sarah's raised her voice in excitement, "Me too. Dylan is awake."

"Oh, how did that happen? Never mind. Are you at the hospital?"

"Yes, Michael and I are here with Dylan now."

"I'll be right there. I'll update all of you when I get there."

"Okay, see you soon."

When Sarah got off the phone, she said to Dylan, "That was Ryan. He's on his way over to give us an update on your appeal."

"I hope it's good news," Dylan said.

It took no time at all for Ryan to get to the hospital and give Dylan the good news. "Hello, everyone," Ryan said as he entered the room. "I'm glad to see you're awake. How are you feeling?"

"I feel great. Michael has just been updating me on what has been going on the last four weeks. It's been a crazy month for everyone, you included, I'm sure."

"Yes, for all of us. Did he tell you we think Jake killed Stacy?"

Dylan shook his head in disbelief, "Yes, I can't believe it."

"Believe it because it's true. I just got a call from Jake's psychiatrist; he said that Jake suffers from multiple personalities and that he admitted to murdering Stacy. I'm just waiting for a copy of the report he is going to be sending the judge and the prosecutor, and then I am going to request that you be exonerated for Stacy's murder."

"Really?!" Jenna exclaimed.

Ryan shook his head. "Yes, really."

Jenna jumped to her feet and hugged Dylan. "Oh, Dylan. That's great news! It's finally over. You're not going back to prison."

"I can't believe it. I've wanted this for so long. I started to give up on the idea that I was ever going to be released."

Ryan placed his hand on Dylan's shoulder and said, "Just hold tight for a little while longer. It should all be over soon."

"How long?" Dylan asked.

"Hopefully, as early as Tuesday."

Dylan had a look of gratitude in his eyes. "I don't know how to thank you."

"You just did, my friend. I'm sorry you ever had to spend a single day in prison." He shrugged his shoulders and exhaled, "I just came from Megan's house. I had to break the news to her about Jake's multiple personalities."

"Oh, poor Megan. I need to see her. I have to tell her how sorry I am that this happened. I wanted to learn the truth about who killed Stacy Richards, but I never thought that the truth would destroy the lives of people I love," Sarah said.

"I'm sure she knows that. No one could ever have predicted this. We just need to be there for her; she could really use a friend right now," Ryan said.

Sarah looked at the clock, then said, "It's getting late. I'll pay her a visit tomorrow."

"Yes, it's been an exhausting day. I'm sure she is tired. I know I am. I'm going to go now. I'll be in touch, Dylan. As soon as I hear back from the judge, you'll be the first to know."

"Thank you," Dylan held his hand out to Ryan. Ryan took his hand and then pulled Dylan into a hug, "You're welcome."

"I'll walk you out," Sarah said, and the two left the room and headed to the elevators.

"What's going to happen to Jake?" Sarah asked on the way to the elevator.

"Best case scenario, he is sentenced to a psychiatric ward." They reached the elevator, and he pressed the down button.

"And the worst case?"

Ryan looked away from her and focused his gaze on the elevator doors. His voice dropped, "He gets the death penalty."

Sarah's eyes filled with tears. She gulped down the lump in her throat. "You can't let that happen."

Ryan reached for Sarah's hand. "There's something else I need to tell you. I can't represent him. It would be a conflict of interest. I told Megan I will refer his case to one of my old colleagues. He's very good. Maybe even better than me."

The elevator arrived, and Sarah got on with him to ride it down to the first floor. There was a custodian on the elevator when they got on. They rode in silence until the elevator stopped on the second floor and the man got off. "I will call him tomorrow and give him an update on the case. His psychiatrist is going to recommend that Jake be tried in a mental health court. If his lawyer can get the judge to agree, the death penalty will be off the table."

"I hope so."

chapter

40

It was Tuesday evening, and Megan was lying on the couch, a movie blaring from the television, the sound of other voices helping her to feel a little less alone. Her eyelids were so heavy, unable to fight sleep any longer; she closed them and drifted off to sleep. She barely slept a few minutes when her cell phone vibrated and woke her out of her slumber. She looked over at her phone lying on the coffee table and read the Ohio Correctional Facility. She quickly sat up and reached for it, then had second thoughts, *What are you going to say to him?* she thought and pulled her hand back. *Don't be a fool; you have to talk to him sometime. Answer it.*

"Hello."

"Will you accept a collect call from Jake?" the operator asked.

"Yes."

Megan heard a deep sigh before Jake said, "Hi, baby, how are you?"

"I'm okay," a lump formed in her throat. She struggled to hold back her tears.

"I miss you so much."

"I miss you too. What is your lawyer saying about your trial?"

"I only have eight minutes. I don't want to talk about the trial. I just want to hear your voice. Do you still love me? I can get through anything as long as I know that you still love me."

Megan started to cry, "Yes, I will always love you."

"That's good, baby. You don't know how happy that makes me." Jake sighed, "I'm so sorry for everything. I'm sorry for the things I've done. I'm sorry for letting you down, for letting myself down, and for ruining our lives. I won't ask for your forgiveness; I don't deserve it. Just know for what it's worth, I never meant for any of this to happen."

"I know, Jake. I know." They sat in silence for a few moments, then she said, "I keep thinking I'm having a bad dream and I'm going to wake up any moment, but it's not a dream."

"I wish I could take it all back, but I can't. I don't even remember doing it." A fellow prisoner tapped him on the shoulder. "We only have another minute. I love you, Megan. I need you to know that. I will always love you."

"I love you too, Jake." The phone went dead.

The next day when Megan awoke, she felt awful. Every bone in her body hurt, and depression had taken over. She pulled the covers over her head to blind her eyes from the sunlight that filled the room and tried to force the thoughts of her current situation out of her head. She lay there for another thirty minutes, unable to fall back to sleep, when she heard someone repeatedly ringing her doorbell. When she didn't answer the door, they started pounding on it.

"Go away!" she yelled and stumbled out of bed and over to the window. She pulled aside the curtains and peered out. There were half a dozen news vans parked outside of her house, and multiple journalists and cameramen stood on her lawn, hoping to get the next big story. As she closed the curtains, she got a glimpse of Sarah's car in her driveway. She threw on her robe and went downstairs to let her in.

She unlocked the door and opened it just enough for Sarah to squeeze through as reporters shouted questions at her.

"Hey, how are you feeling?" Sarah asked, handing Megan a cup of coffee and a bag from Dunkin Donuts.

"I've been better." Megan accepted the coffee, then turned and headed to the kitchen.

When they got to the kitchen, Sarah said, "Ryan told me about Jake. I'm so sorry, Megan. You have to know that I never wanted anything like this to happen." She put her arms around Megan and gave her a hug. She just stood there and did not return her hug.

When Sarah released her, Megan said nothing and went over to the sink and opened the window blinds.

"Are you mad at me?" Sarah asked.

"I don't know what I am; I'm numb. I'm still trying to process all of this." Megan went over to the kitchen table, pulled out a chair and slid into it, and said, "What am I going to do, Sarah?"

"You're going to take things one day at a time, and Michael and I are going to be here for you," Sarah said and took a seat across from Megan.

"I need to see Jake, but I don't know what to say to him or how to act. Should I be mad at him? Should I feel sorry for him? You didn't see him in Mexico. He has no idea what he did. Can you imagine finding out that you are a monster? How could I not know? I was married to him. Does that make me a monster, too? People will never believe me that I didn't know." She put her elbows on the table and then covered her face with her hands.

Sarah pulled Megan's hands away from her face and looked her in the eyes. "Who cares what people believe? Your family believes you. We didn't see it either. Jake was a good person with a good heart. We all loved him."

A thought had just occurred to Megan. "Oh my God. Dylan's going to hate me!"

Sarah shook her head, "He doesn't hate you."

"Yes, he will."

"He's awake, and he doesn't hate you." Megan gave Sarah a look of surprise, and Sarah continued. "He can't believe Jake is responsible for all of this. He knows about his multiple personalities. I think he feels sorry for him, and he certainly doesn't blame you."

Megan got up from her chair. "I need to talk to him. I need to tell him I'm sorry."

"He knows. There will be plenty of time for you to talk to him. Right now, you need to rest. Come on; you're going back to bed." She guided her out of the kitchen and to the stairs.

"I can't sleep. It's better if I keep busy. I'm going to the hospital to talk to Dylan." She staggered up the stairs to shower and change, and Sarah followed her.

"If you insist on going, I'll drive you."

Sarah made Megan's bed and tidied up her bedroom as she waited for Megan to shower. Ten minutes later, Megan came out of the shower, looking clean but no better than she had before.

"Are you sure you're up to this?" Sarah asked. "Maybe we should go later."

"I'm sure. Let's go." Megan put her hair in a ponytail, put one of Jake's baseball caps on her head, and then grabbed her keys off the dresser. "We can take my car; it's in the garage."

Sarah held her hand out, and Megan put the keys into it. When they got downstairs and into the kitchen, Sarah asked, "Have you eaten anything today?"

"No."

Sarah grabbed the Dunkin Donut bag off the table on the way out. When they got into the car, she handed Megan the bag and said, "Eat."

The press ran beside the car snapping pictures of Megan as she used the baseball cap to shield her face. Sarah backed out of the driveway and then looked out the rearview mirror and saw the reporters and cameramen scurrying to their vans and then following their car. "Damn, they're following us. Don't worry; they won't let them in ICU."

Megan said nothing and just stared out the car window. When they reached the hospital, Sarah went to the top floor of the parking garage so that she could park close to the elevators. "Are you ready for this?" Megan shook her head.

"I'll get out first. Don't get out of the car until the elevator doors open, then make a dash for the elevator."

Sarah got out of the car, walked to the elevator, and pressed the down button. The press remained planted outside of the passenger side door waiting for Megan to show her face. The elevator doors opened, but Megan couldn't see past the people, microphones, and cameras in her face.

She was about to open the door and make a dash for the elevator when suddenly the press backed away from her car. She looked out and saw Chase push a camera down to the ground and out of the way. Then he opened her car door and held his hand out to her. Megan took his hand and then shielded her face in his shoulder as he wrapped his arm around her and led her to the elevator.

When they reached the elevator, some of the press attempted to get into the elevator, and Chase pushed them out of the door opening while Sarah pressed the close door button. Once the elevator doors closed, Sarah asked, "What are you doing here?"

Megan pulled her face away from Chase's chest and looked up at him. "Ryan asked me to keep an eye on Megan. He thought she might need some protection." He smiled at Megan, then asked, "You okay?"

"Yes, thanks to you."

When they reached the ICU floor, Chase said, "You guys go see Dylan. I'll stay here and take care of the press."

Megan looked at Chase, unsure of what to do. "Go ahead. They won't come after you. I promise."

Dylan was sitting up in bed, a tray of food in front of him. He smiled at Sarah and Megan when they appeared at his door. "Hey."

"Hey," Sarah said, "You look good."

"I feel good. First food I've had in a month. I just wish it tasted better." He put the fork down on the tray.

Megan came closer to the bed and handed him the Dunkin Donuts bag. "Here, have this."

He opened the bag and beamed at the sight of the chocolate-frosted donut. Sarah reached for the bag and asked, "Are you allowed to have this?"

Dylan yanked the bag away from her, "Who cares? I'm having it." He pulled the donut out of the bag and took an enormous bite out of it, leaving chocolate smears on both sides of his cheeks. Dylan and Sarah laughed and then stopped suddenly when they realized that Megan was crying.

Dylan turned his attention to Megan, and she said, "I'm sorry. I didn't know."

Dylan put his donut down, wiped his face on a napkin, and then reached for her hand, "I know."

"I'm sorry about everything." Megan wept for a second and then continued, "For cutting you out of my life, not believing in your innocence, and for letting you sit in prison because of my husband. Can you ever forgive me?"

Dylan pulled her into a hug, "Yes. You're my sister. Nothing's going to come between us ever again."

Megan stayed in the comfort of his arms for several minutes before she drew herself away from him and said, "We had you all wrong. You are a good person, you know that? How can you not be bitter? How do you not hate me?"

"Oh, I was pissed for a long time. I blamed everybody for my situation. I took my frustration out on everyone around me. I started a lot of fights and got an ass beating a few times, but then I got tired of fighting, and something inside me changed. I prayed to God to help me prove my innocence, and the next day, Sarah came into my life."

Dylan winked at Sarah. "I made myself a promise that day. If I got out of prison, I would never take life for granted again, and I wouldn't waste any precious time on being bitter. I just want to be happy. I want my life back, but I want it back better than it was before. If being incarcerated has taught me anything, it has taught me how important it is to have people you love in your life. I love you, Megan, and I want you to know that I'm here for you. We'll get through this together."

"Thank you," Megan said with tears streaming down her face, then she rested her head on his shoulder.

chapter
41

Jake thrashed on his cot, beads of sweat formed on his forehead; he was having the nightmare again. His hands were wrapped tightly around Paul's neck, and he squeezed as hard as he could. He smirked as he watched the color of Paul's face change from red to white, and then his body went limp. He released him and let his lifeless body fall back into the couch.

Someone was shaking him. "Jake, wake up! You're having a nightmare."

Jake's eyes flew open. He jumped to his feet, his hand in a fist inches away from his cell mate's face.

"Whoa, whoa. Take it easy; it's just me," Sonny said, taking a step back away from Jake.

Jake was trembling, "Sorry, man." He pulled the perspiration-soaked shirt over his head and let it drop to the floor, then went over to his dresser to retrieve another one.

"It's okay. I'm going back to sleep. Try and keep it down, would you?" Sonny said, then climbed back into his cot.

"I'll try," Jake said, pulling a dry shirt over his head.

It was almost dawn. Unable to fall back asleep, Jake lay in bed thinking about what he would tell Dr. Newcombe at his appointment later that day.

"How are you doing today?" Dr. Newcombe asked Jake after the two of them took their seats across from each other.

"Not good. What in the hell did you do to me?" Jake spat at the doctor and crossed his arms over his chest.

The guard in the corner of the room took a step forward, and Dr. Newcombe raised his hand to him to let him know he should remain there. "Tell me what's going on, Jake."

"I've been having nightmares ever since you hypnotized me. I keep having a dream that I strangled a man. It feels so real."

Dr. Newcombe wrote some notes down on his pad and then looked up at Jake. "Do you think it is real?"

Jake huffed and raised his voice in anger, "I don't know. You're the doctor, you tell me."

"It is possible that now that you are aware of your altered personality, your brain is showing you what Mark did. I'm afraid it is one of the repercussions of knowing about your multiple personalities. I believe it is probable that you did strangle that man. I will need to hypnotize you again to know for sure."

"No way!" Jake jumped to his feet, and the guard grabbed his stun gun and came charging at him.

"Sit down!" the guard demanded.

Jake put his hands up in the air, "Okay. I'm sitting down." He took a seat back on the couch.

"Don't get up again," the guard warned and took a few steps back.

Jake sighed and then said, "You can't put me back under; it will only make things worse."

Dr. Newcombe removed his glasses and studied him, "Don't you want to know what happened?"

"No, why would I want to learn that I am a monster? How do you think that makes me feel?" Jake said in an undertone.

"I don't know. How do you feel?"

Jake shook his head in frustration, "Oh, come on, man. It makes me feel awful. I never dreamed that I could murder anyone. I still can't believe it. My entire life is ruined. I have a wife. How can I look her in the eyes knowing what I've done?" He dropped his head down and mumbled, "I'm so ashamed."

"Do you want to take responsibility for what you've done?"

Jake thought about it a second then replied, "Yeah, but it's so hard. It's as if you are asking me to take responsibility for someone else's actions."

"I understand. If you are going to accept responsibility, first you must learn everything you have done. Think about the families of the people you murdered. They deserve closure, don't they?"

Jake started to get up from the couch to pace and then thought better of it when he saw the guard give him a look. "I feel like this whole thing is a bad dream that I can't wake up from. I don't even know who I am anymore."

"What do you mean?"

"Who is the real me? Am I Mark, or am I Jake?" A look of torment showed on his face. "Am I a good person or a bad person?"

"Are you asking for my professional opinion?"

"Yes."

"I believe you are a good person. You didn't intend to kill Stacy. You were drunk, and things got carried away. Your mind split to help you deal with what you did. You managed to live a crime-free life up to that point and then again after your mind split because deep down, you are a good person. I think that Mark was dormant until he felt threatened that what he did was going to be discovered."

"Can I get a glass of water?" Jake gulped through a dry patch of words.

"Sure." Dr. Newcombe got up and poured Jake a glass of water from the pitcher on his desk. Then he went back to his seat, placed the glass of water on the coffee table in front of him, and slid it over toward Jake.

Jake raised his eyebrow and stated, "You're afraid of me."

"After last time, I'm not taking any chances."

"Do you think there is help for me?" his eyes pleaded.

"Yes. But it's not going to be easy. You are going to need to face the reality of what you've done and stand up to Mark. Show him you are strong enough to take control of your life and that you don't need him anymore."

"What life? I've lost everything. I'm going to spend the rest of my life in prison."

"Maybe so, but do you want to have to deal with him forever? He's not going to go away until you stand up to him. I'm going to be honest with you; if you don't deal with this now, I'm afraid your mind might split again, and you will develop another personality."

Jake's mouth dropped open; that had never occurred to him. "Okay, I'll do it."

"Alright. Lie back on the couch and try to relax."

Jake lay back and put his feet up.

"Now close your eyes and imagine you are lying on a blanket in a pasture surrounded by flowers. It is warm, and the sun is shining down on you. You can hear a waterfall somewhere in the distance. You get up from the blanket and follow the sound. It takes you to a cliff, where you find the waterfall underneath a beautiful vibrant rainbow. You see a bottle with a note in it floating in the water below and want to know what it says. You take your first step down the mountainside, and you start to fall deep into hypnosis. Slowly, you take another step, still focusing on the bottle below. You take another step, and then another. With each step, you go deeper and deeper under, until you feel like you are no longer walking. It is as if you are floating in air."

Jake's body went limp, and one arm fell off the edge of the couch, his hand resting on the floor.

"Very good. Now, I need to speak to Mark. Is he there?"

"Yes."

"Good, very good. Now Mark, who is this man Jake keeps dreaming about?"

"Nobody important. Just another scumbag I rid the world of."

"You killed him?"

"Yes."

"Who was he? What did he do that made him a scumbag?"

"Paul Nelson. He was a stalker, a real pervert."

Dr. Newcombe wrote his name on his notepad. "How do you know him?"

"I hired him to steal the tape. The incompetent fool didn't lock it up, and it was stolen. I had to kill him; he knew what I look like. He would have squealed to save his own behind."

"Have you killed anyone else besides Stacy and Paul?"

"I should have killed Jenna, but that bitch Sarah messed everything up for me. She couldn't leave things alone. She had to stir up trouble. I should have killed her too."

"Are you there, Jake?" Dr. Newcombe asked.

"Yes."

"Stand up to him. Are you going to accept these things he is saying about the people you love? Tell him you're not going to put up with this any longer."

Mark said, "He can't. He's a pushover. That's why I had to take control of things."

"That's enough, Mark!" Jake shouted.

Mark broke out in laughter. It was an evil, wicked laugh. "Whoa! You put on your big boy pants today? You going to take control now? Where were you the whole time I was handling things?"

"Yeah, I'm taking control. I'm tired of you messing everything up and hurting my family. You murderer!"

"That's good, Jake. Tell him to leave," Dr. Newcombe affirmed.

"Stay out of this!" Mark demanded.

Jake yelled, "No! You stay out of this, Mark. No one needs or wants you here. I won't allow you to be here anymore."

"Mark, what are you going to do now?" Dr. Newcombe asked.

"Mark, are you there?"

"He's gone," Jake replied.

"Good job! Jake, do you still see the bottle in the water?"

"Yes, it's there."

"Okay, good. Can you reach it? Pull it out of the water."

"I'll try." Seconds later, he said, "I got it."

"Good, now open it."

"Okay."

"What does the note say?"

"It says, THE TRUTH SHALL SET YOU FREE."

"You did it, Jake. You stood up to him. You can come back now. Start making your way back up the mountainside. As you take your first step, you will start to wake up. When I count to ten, you will be fully awake. One, two, three. You are becoming aware of your surroundings. Four, five, six. Focus on the sound of your breathing. Good! Seven, eight, nine. When I say ten, you will open your eyes. Ten!"

Dr. Newcombe snapped his fingers, and Jake opened his eyes. "How do you feel?"

"Alright. What did you find out?"

"What I expected. You strangled that man. His name was Paul Nelson."

Jake shook his head in disbelief. "Did I murder anyone else?"

"I don't think so. You did really good, Jake. You confronted him. You told him you didn't want him in your life any longer."

"Is he gone?"

"For now. It's not that simple. I will teach you some exercises you can do to help keep him away. The more you do them, the stronger you become, the longer he will stay away, until eventually, if all goes well, he will stay away forever."

Dr. Newcombe looked up at the clock on the wall. "Our time is just about up. I want to see you again on Friday. I'll teach you some of the therapy techniques then. I'm going to prescribe you something to help you cope with things." Jake shook his head, and the doctor continued, "It's nothing too strong, just something to help with stress."

Dr. Newcombe wrote a prescription out on his prescription pad and then ripped the page off the pad. "In the meantime, if you have any more nightmares, I want you to stand up to Mark. You may not be able to change reality, but you can change your dreams. Okay, I'll see you on Friday."

The doctor and Jake got to their feet. The guard came forward and put handcuffs on Jake's wrists, and then Dr. Newcombe handed the guard the prescription. Dr. Newcombe patted Jake on the back before they left.

chapter

42

Dylan was just waking up when Dr. Knolls came to see him, first thing on Monday morning. "Good morning, Dylan. How are you feeling today?"

Dylan raised the bed up to a seated position. "I feel great, doc. I'm getting stronger every day."

"I'm not surprised. I don't know how you did it, but your blood count is coming up. I'm moving you out of ICU and to a regular room."

"Really?"

"Yes. No promises, but if your blood count continues to rise, you're not going to need the new medication. We'll need to keep an eye on you for a couple of days, but after that, you should be able to be discharged."

Dylan grinned, "That would be awesome!" He thought about what the doctor said and then frowned.

"What's wrong?"

"I haven't been exonerated yet. I don't want to go back to prison."

Dr. Knolls placed a hand on Dylan's shoulder, "Let's just take things one day at a time. How about we start by getting you out of this bed?"

Dylan threw the blanket off his legs, "Sounds good."

Dr. Knolls helped Dylan sit up on the side of the bed. Then he disconnected Dylan's heart monitor, helped him into a chair, and reconnected the monitor. "How's that feel?"

Dylan grinned, "I feel like a whole new person."

"Glad to hear that, but promise me you will take it easy. We don't want you to have another heart attack."

Dylan made a cross with his finger over his heart and said, "Cross my heart."

"Good. I'll check on you later."

Dylan was sitting in the chair doing a crossword puzzle when Jenna came to see him.

"Wow! Look at you," Jenna said, surprised to see Dylan out of his bed.

"I got good news. My blood count is coming up. I'm being transferred to a regular room. I may not need the experimental drug."

"That's awesome!" She bent down and gave him a hug. He held her in his arms for a moment. When she pulled away, their eyes locked, and he planted a real kiss on her lips. The kiss was electric and sent heat down his body, instantly arousing him as passion grew deep inside of him. It had been a long time since he was aroused by a woman. He missed the feeling of a woman's touch more than he remembered.

A nurse came into the room unnoticed and coughed to let them know she was there. Jenna pulled away, her face red with embarrassment.

The nurse rolled a wheelchair in front of Dylan and asked, "Are you ready to go?"

"Yes," Dylan answered and readjusted himself to hide his erection. The nurse paid him no mind as she transferred his IV from the bed pole to a pole on the wheelchair. Once situated in the wheelchair, he reached his hand out to Jenna and held her hand tightly in his as the nurse rolled him out of the room. He refused to let go the entire way to his new room and repeatedly looked up at her and smiled to reassure himself that she was still there.

Dylan was impatient for the nurse to leave so they could pick up where they left off, but that wasn't to be. As soon as the ICU nurse left, his new nurse came in to introduce herself and take his vital signs. When the nurse wasn't looking, Dylan winked and grinned at Jenna, causing her to blush. Just before the nurse left, Sarah and Michael entered the room, and Dylan rolled his eyes at Jenna and dropped his head back onto his pillow.

"Hey there, brother!" Michael said, strolling into the room.

"Hi, guys," Dylan said to Michael and Sarah.

Sarah and Michael visited for twenty minutes, and then Jenna stood and said, "I have to go. I have an appointment."

"Are you coming back?" Dylan asked anxiously and reached his hand out to her.

"I'll try," she said and took his hand.

He pulled her into him and kissed her, not caring that Michael and Sarah would see. He placed his hand on the back of her head and kissed her with a yearning from deep inside. When he released her from his kiss, he whispered into her ear, "I'm not finished with you."

"I'll walk you out," Sarah said to Jenna.

Michael waited until they left and then said, "Wow! It looks like you and Jenna are getting pretty close. You think maybe you should take things a little slower?"

"No, I've lost too much time already. I love her. I've always loved her. I'm not wasting another minute. I'm going to marry that girl."

"Whoa, whoa! Don't you think you should get your life in order before you start thinking about marriage? You haven't even been released from prison yet. You need to get a job. What can you even offer her right now?"

"I know I have a lot of things to figure out first. I'm just telling you I'm not going to let her go this time. I'm going to make her my wife."

"If you say so," Michael said, nodding his head.

"I need you to do me a favor," Dylan said.

"Anything. What do you need?"

"Can you pick something up from the post office for me?"

"Sure."

"Thank you. I'll call my sister today and ask her to send it to me right away. I'll tell her to put it under your name, so you won't have any problems picking it up. I'll let you know when you can pick it up."

Michael tilted his head and asked curiously, "What is it?"

Dylan smirked, "You'll see."

Sarah returned from escorting Jenna out with Ryan by her side. "Look who I found in the parking lot."

"Hi, Dylan. Hi, Michael."

"Just the man I want to see," Dylan said, "Do you have any news for me?"

"Yes, Jake confessed. The judge had no choice but to drop the charges against you. You're not going back to prison." Ryan walked over to the door and handed the guard a folded piece of paper.

The guard took it and asked, "What's this?"

"Your walking papers. Dylan is being released."

The guard read the papers and then took his cell phone out of his pocket and called the prison to confirm. After he got off the phone, he walked up to Dylan and extended his hand to him and said, "Congratulations. Have a good life."

Dylan shook his hand and said, "Thank you."

After the guard left, Sarah hugged Dylan and said, "It's finally over. You are free."

When she pulled away from the hug, Dylan said, "It's all because of you," with tears swelling up in his eyes.

chapter

43

It was the morning of the first day of Jake's trial, and Megan woke up with her stomach in knots. She hadn't seen Jake in the three months since he was arrested and dreaded seeing him today. She attempted to visit him on several occasions but always chickened out at the last moment because she was unsure of what she would say to him. She still loved him very much but was conflicted because of the things he had done. She didn't want to love a murderer.

She got out of bed and made her way to the bathroom; her stomach began to turn, and she let out a belch causing bile to rise in the back of her throat. She ran to the toilet and threw the lid up just in time and vomited into the bowl. She sat on the floor for several minutes with her head resting on her arm on the side of the toilet and prayed, *Lord, please help me get through this. I need to be strong for Jake.*

When she was finally able to pull herself together, she went to the sink and rinsed her mouth out and washed her face. She patted her face dry with the hand towel lying on the sink and then looked at herself in the mirror. *You can do this!*

She went back into the bedroom and looked at the clock on her nightstand and realized that she only had thirty minutes before Sarah and Michael would be picking her up for the trial. She rushed to her closet, pulled one of Jake's favorite dresses off the rack, tossed it onto the bed, then went back to the bathroom and turned on the shower.

Twenty minutes later, she was standing in the kitchen freshly showered and dressed, looking somewhat presentable thanks to her ability to apply makeup. She was filling a coffee pot with water when she heard a car pull into her driveway. She poured the water into the coffee machine, placed the pot on the burner, then went to answer the door. She opened the door and attempted to smile but had to bite her lip to keep herself from crying when she saw the look of pity in Sarah and Michael's eyes.

Sarah stepped into the foyer and put her arms around Megan and said, "Oh, honey. It's going to be okay."

Megan put her head on Sarah's shoulder and wrapped her arms tightly around her. "I don't know how I am going to get through this."

Sarah pulled herself out of the hug and looked into Megan's eyes. "One day at a time, and we will be here for you every step of the way."

Michael asked, "Is that coffee I smell?"

"Yes, I just made a pot. Do you want a cup?"

"I would love a cup," he said.

"Me too," Sarah said.

The three of them went into the kitchen, and Sarah asked Megan, "Have you had breakfast?"

Megan replied, "No, I don't think I could eat anything. I was sick on my stomach this morning."

"I'm sure it's just your nerves, but maybe it's best if you don't eat anything. How about a cup of coffee?" Sarah asked, opening the cabinet to retrieve the coffee cups.

"Yeah. I'll have a cup. Maybe it will help calm my nerves."

Sarah poured three cups of coffee and carried them over to the table, then went to the refrigerator to get the milk. They sat at the table and drank their coffee for several minutes, giving Megan a chance to calm her nerves a little bit.

"Do you feel any better?" Sarah asked, reaching over and putting her hand on top of Megan's.

"A little."

"Good. We better get going," Sarah said, stood up, collected the coffee cups, and brought them over to the kitchen sink.

Megan stared out the car window as Sarah and Michael made small talk on the drive over to the courthouse. Her nerves started to get the best of her again.

"Can you pull over, please?" Megan asked.

"What?" Michael asked, not sure what she said because he was listening to Sarah speaking.

"Pull over!" Megan yelled with urgency.

He pulled to the side of the road, and Megan flung the car door open and jumped out even before the car had fully stopped. She barely made it out of the car before she started gagging and spewed the coffee she just drank all over the grass. Sarah grabbed some napkins out of the glove compartment and quickly joined Megan on the side of the road. She stood over her and rubbed her back as Megan continued to heave.

When Megan was done throwing up, Sarah handed her a bunch of napkins so she could wipe her mouth.

"Oh, honey, you got some on your dress," Sarah said, taking a napkin from Megan and wiping a spot on her dress.

Megan started to cry. "I can't do this."

Sarah asked, "Do you want to go home?"

Megan shook her head and said, "No, I need to be there."

When they finally got to the courthouse, they were ten minutes late for the trial.

"I'll drop you guys off and then park the car," Michael said, "Save me a seat if you can."

chapter 44

Jake's lawyer elbowed him in the ribs and whispered, "Pay attention." Jake turned his head back around to face the front of the courtroom and tried to focus his awareness on what was going on in front of him, but he couldn't stop thinking about Megan and worrying that she wasn't coming. *I can't believe she's not coming,* he thought and cast his eyes downward, no longer hearing what the judge was saying. Just then, the doors flew open, and Megan and Sarah hurried into the packed courtroom and scanned the pews for a place to sit.

Jake's heart stopped beating for a moment when he turned his head back around and saw his wife rushing down the aisle. She was even more beautiful than he remembered. It was all he could do to restrain himself; he wanted to jump over the railing and run to her and hold her in his arms. He watched as she found a seat a couple of rows behind him, and then finally, when she made eye contact with him, he smiled at her, and she blushed and looked away.

His lawyer elbowed him again, and he turned his attention back to the judge.

"We are here today to determine the sanity of Jake Harbor because he has pleaded guilty by reason of insanity. Is that still your plea, Mr. Harbor?"

"Yes, your honor."

"I have ordered a psych evaluation of Jake Harbor and hold a copy of the findings report here in front of me. Have you both had an opportunity to read over the report and make yourself aware of the findings?"

"Yes, your honor," replied the prosecutor.

"Yes," Jake's lawyer responded.

"Very well. The prosecutor may call his first witness."

"I would like to call Dr. Peter Newcombe to the stand." All eyes turned to watch as Dr. Newcombe stood, buttoned his suit jacket, and made his way to the witness stand where he was sworn in and then took a seat.

"Good morning. Would you please state your full name and give the jury your credentials?"

"Good morning. My name is Dr. Peter Newcombe. I am a clinical psychiatrist at the Ohio State Psychiatric Institution. I have a Ph.D. in Psychology and have worked in the field of psychology for thirty-two years. The last ten of them at the Ohio State Psychiatric Institution."

"Thank you, doctor. I understand that you have evaluated Jake Harbor's mental capacity. Is that correct?"

Dr. Newcombe cleared his throat and moved closer to the microphone. "Yes, I have."

"And what is your professional opinion of Mr. Harbor's state of mental being?"

"It is my professional opinion that Jake Harbor suffers from Dissociative Identity Disorder."

The prosecutor looked over at the jury and then said, "For the benefit of the jury and anyone else who is not familiar with this term, would you please explain what dissociative identity disorder is?"

"Sure, most people commonly refer to dissociative identity disorder as multiple personalities."

After hearing this, several jury members turned their attention to Jake, and he dropped his head down to his chest.

"And in your opinion, how many personalities does he have?"

"Two."

"And how did you come to determine this?"

"I used hypnosis."

"What did you learn by putting Jake under hypnosis?"

"Jake was not aware of the crimes he committed. He was even able to pass a polygraph test. I suspected that he might have multiple personalities, and once I put him under hypnosis, I was able to speak to his other personality."

"Could you please speak up? Does this other personality have a name?"

Dr. Newcombe raised his voice, "Yes, his name is Mark Gordon."

The prosecutor paced back and forth in front of the jury. Then walked back to the witness box and asked, "And what did you learn from speaking to Mark Gordon?"

"That he killed Stacy Richards."

"How did you learn this?"

"Mark admitted it to me."

"And what did you do with this information?"

"I put it into the report and submitted it to the judge, then I called Ryan Finch, Jake's lawyer at the time, and told him, and I also reported it to the police."

"Thank you. I have just one more question for you. Do you think that Jake is dangerous? I guess what I am really asking is do you think that Jake could kill again?"

Dr. Newcombe looked over at Jake and swallowed the lump in his throat before responding, "If provoked, yes."

"Thank you. No further questions, your honor."

The prosecutor walked back to his table and took a seat, then the judge gave the defense the opportunity to cross-examine the witness.

George Ramsey, Jake's lawyer, rose from the table and slowly strolled in front of the jury box and up to the witness stand, keeping the jury and everyone in the courtroom in suspense, wondering what he was going to ask the doctor.

George waved his hands in the air and rolled his eyes, "Dr. Newcombe, are you telling me that you want the jury to believe that Jake Harbor killed Stacy Richards, but it wasn't really him, it was Mark Gordon?"

"Yes. I know that it seems hard to believe, but that is what I am saying happened."

"And you expect us to just take your word for it?" He pointed a finger at Jake, "Are you telling me that this man, a professional businessman, functioning in society, married for three years, has multiple personalities, and no one noticed it? Not even his wife? Is that what you want us to believe?"

"Yes, but don't take my word for it. You can see for yourself. I recorded our hypnosis sessions."

George Ramsey said, "Ladies and gentlemen, I present to you Exhibit A." He walked over to the projector and then nodded to the bailiff, who dimmed the lights, then he pressed the play button. The entire courtroom sat in silence as they watched the video of Jake as he transformed into Mark Gordon.

Jake had never seen the video before. His mouth dropped open when he watched his personality change, and he became someone else, someone who scared him. He saw raw anger he never knew he was possible of. He turned his head around to look at Megan and wished that he hadn't; he would never forget the look of fear he saw on her face. The video ended with his attack on Dr. Newcombe and him being restrained. The lights were turned back on, and Jake looked over at the jury box and saw the look of disgust on the faces of the jury. They were repulsed by him.

Jake's lawyer walked over to the witness box, "Dr. Newcombe, could you please explain to the jury what it is that we just witnessed?"

"Sure. What you just witnessed was Mark Gordon taking over the body of Jake Harbor. Jake was not aware of what happened under hypnosis or when Mark takes control of his body."

"In your professional opinion, has this ever happened before?"

"Yes. There are three other cases of this happening that I am aware of, but that is only because these are extreme cases. There are hundreds of cases of people with multiple personalities doing things that they don't recall doing."

"Can you give us an example, please?"

"Sure. There have been cases where a person has gone somewhere and done something and doesn't remember doing it. I once had a patient end up in Las Vegas, and he didn't know how or why he went there. He didn't remember any of it because he drove himself there under his other persona."

"Okay, I think we understand. Is there a cure for multiple personalities?"

"No, there is no cure, but with therapy and medication, Jake can reduce the chance of these occurrences."

"Have you had much success with this?"

Dr. Newcome sighed, "No, but that is only because I've personally only had three other cases like his, but I've read several medical journals which have documented the success."

"Why weren't you successful with the three other cases?"

"Because the clients were not forced to enter therapy, and they both decided against it."

"Why would they decide against it?"

"Because it requires many hours of therapy, and they didn't think they had the time to commit to it. And frankly, I'm not sure they wanted to believe they had dissociative identity disorder. It is not an easy thing to accept."

"Thank you, Dr. Newcombe. That is all the questions I have for you."

The judge looked at the clock on the wall; the time was 4:17. He said,

"The court will adjourn for the day and resume tomorrow morning at nine a.m." He picked up his gavel and pounded it against the wooden sound block and then rose from his seat and left the courtroom.

After the judge's exit, the jury rose and left next. Jake stood up and turned to face Megan, who was still seated behind him. A guard quickly approached him and put Jake's hands behind his back and cuffed them. Jake mouthed the words "I love you" to Megan and looked her straight in the eyes, and then he was escorted out of the courtroom.

Megan stayed in her seat and watched Jake leave with tears rolling down her cheeks. Sarah and Michael stayed seated next to her and waited as everyone left the courtroom.

"Let's go home," Sarah said and grabbed Megan by the arm and pulled her up.

chapter

45

Megan was quiet on the drive home; she couldn't get the image of Jake saying "I love you" to her out of her head. It broke her heart to see him in shackles, unable to go to him and hold him. Still thinking about Jake, her stomach started to turn; she was going to be sick again. *Oh no!* she thought, *Please, Lord, it can't be.*

"Can we make a stop at the drug store? I'm not feeling very well," Megan asked Michael.

"Sure, we go right past a CVS on the way home."

"Thank you," Megan said, calculating the date of her last period in her head and getting more worried by the minute.

Michael pulled into a parking space right in front of the CVS entrance, and Megan said, "I'll be right back," and got out of the car.

"I'll come with you," Sarah said, following her into the store.

Megan walked past the aisles, reading the signs above them, and then turned down aisle three.

"I don't think that is the right aisle," Sarah said and watched as Megan walked over to the pregnancy test.

Sarah walked over to Megan and put her arm around her shoulder, "Oh, honey. Do you think you might be pregnant?"

Megan started to sob, "I don't know. I hadn't thought about it until today. With everything going on, I didn't realize that I missed my period the last several months."

"It's going to be okay," Sarah said, rubbing her back as Megan picked a pregnancy test off the shelf. "We'll get through this together."

Megan purchased a two-pack of pregnancy tests, and the two women left the store and joined Michael in the car.

"Everything okay?" Michael asked when they got into the car. "You took a while."

"Yeah, everything's fine. Let's just go home," Sarah said to her husband and turned the radio up.

When they got back to Megan's house, the two ladies went straight to the upstairs bathroom, leaving Michael alone in the living room. He made himself comfortable on the couch and picked up the tv remote and flicked it on.

Sarah and Megan went into the master bathroom, and Sarah read the instructions on the box to Megan as she peed on the pregnancy test stick.

"It says to put the cap back on the stick and place it on a flat surface. The results can be read after three to five minutes. Two lines means positive, and one line is negative."

Megan placed the test on the counter and washed her hands. "What am I going to do if I am pregnant, Sarah? How will I run the store and take care of a baby all by myself?"

"You won't be by yourself. You have me and Michael to help you."

"There couldn't be a worse time for this to happen," Megan said and glanced down at the test and saw two dark lines glaring up at her.

Sarah put her arms around Megan and held her as she cried. "It's okay. We will help you. You'll see, this baby is going to be the best thing that has ever happened to you."

Megan wiped the tears from her cheeks and said, "I'm so scared."

"You don't have to be. You're not doing this alone. You have so many people around you who love you."

Megan closed the lid on the toilet and sat on it. She dropped her head, placed her hands over her face, and said, "What am I going to do?"

Sarah got on her knees next to her and pulled her hands away from her face and said, "The first thing you are going to do is call the doctor tomorrow morning and make an appointment. I'll go with you if you want."

Megan nodded and said, "Thank you."

"Let's go downstairs, and I'll make you something to eat." Sarah took Megan's hand and pulled her up on her feet.

Megan opened her mouth to protest, and Sarah cut her off, "You haven't eaten anything all day. It doesn't matter if you throw it up; you need to try."

"Okay. I'll be down in a minute. Just let me clean up a little," she said and grabbed a tissue from the tissue box, then blew her nose.

"All right," Sarah said and left the bathroom.

"Are you hungry?" Sarah asked Michael as she came down the stairs overlooking the living room.

"I'm starving," Michael said, rubbing his stomach.

"Let me see what I can whip up."

"I'll eat anything," Michael said and jumped off the couch and followed her into the kitchen.

Ten minutes later, Megan came into the kitchen. She had changed out of her dress with throw up on it and was wearing sweatpants and a t-shirt. Her face still blotchy from crying, her mind going in a million directions. She had just found out that she was pregnant, but somehow, she felt different already.

"I'm making burgers." Sarah smiled at her, then flipped one of the burgers over in the pan.

The smell of the meat made Megan's stomach turn over. She swallowed the lump in her throat and said, "Smells good," to Sarah, not wanting to hurt her feelings. She looked at Michael and tried to determine whether Sarah had told him the news. She couldn't tell but had the feeling that he didn't know. When Sarah didn't bring it up, Megan was sure that he didn't know and avoided the topic as well.

They sat down to eat, and Megan managed to eat half of her burger and two spoonsful of potato salad while they talked about Jake's trial.

"Are you going to finish that?" Michael asked, pointing to her half-eaten burger.

"No, you can have it," Megan replied and pushed her plate over to him.

Sarah shot Michael a look, "You already had two. You can't possibly still be hungry."

Michael responded by grabbing the burger and taking a huge bite of it.

The two women laughed until Megan started to cry again.

chapter

46

Dylan didn't sleep at all last night. After three days of his blood count improving, Dr. Knolls said that it was back to normal, and he was going to release him from the hospital. He could hardly control his excitement as he made plans in his head for his future with Jenna. By 8 a.m., he had already eaten breakfast and was pacing the halls of the hospital, waiting for Michael to arrive.

He stopped walking and turned his head and waited for the elevator doors to open each time he heard the elevator stop on his floor. After doing this for the past forty-five minutes, he was about to call Michael again when the door opened, and Michael stepped off the elevator. He rushed down the hallway and greeted him, "What took you so long?"

"What do you mean? It's only ten o'clock. I bet Dr. Knolls hasn't even released you yet."

Dylan grabbed the bag from Michael's hands and asked, "Did you bring everything?"

"Yes, I brought you some new clothes and sneakers."

Dylan rummaged through the bag and asked, "That's great, but did you bring the package?"

Michael followed Dylan into his room and said, "Yes. I picked it up yesterday. It's in there."

Dylan placed the bag on his bed and pulled out the small package. He quickly ripped open the padded envelope and pulled out a small ring box.

"Is that what I think it is?" Michael asked.

Dylan opened the box and exposed the most beautiful two-carat diamond ring Michael had ever seen. His mouth dropped open in awe, and he said, "Where did you get that?"

"It was my grandmother's. My sister was already married when my grandmother passed away, so she left it to me. She loved Jenna so much. She told me she wanted her to have it. I was only in high school when she died; marriage was the last thing on my mind. I thought she was senile, asking me to give it to Jenna. I didn't even know if I loved her. My grandmother said she knew I loved Jenna; she could see it in my eyes. She said one day I would realize it, and when I did, it would hit me like a ton of bricks. I'm so happy that she was right and that I get to give her ring to Jenna."

"Jenna is going to love it."

"I hope so. I know exactly how I want to ask her. Will you help me pull it off?"

"Of course. What do you want me to do?"

"Okay, here's what I need from you."

Dylan sat on the bed and went over his plan with Michael, and by the time he was done, Michael had a whole list of things he needed to do. "I better get going if you want me to get all of this done."

"Thanks, Michael, and remember what I said. Don't tell Sarah. I don't want her to accidentally slip."

"Not a word, I promise. Okay, I'll be back later to pick you up."

"Great!"

Michael left to run the errands, and Dylan went into the bathroom to get dressed. He took the ring with him, not wanting to let it out of his sight. He heard Jenna call his name when he was dressing. "I'll be right out," he yelled to her through the door and put the ring into his front pocket.

When he came out of the bathroom, he was wearing just his jeans and socks because he was unable to put his shirt on with the IV in his arm. His face lit up at the sight of Jenna, his heart skipped a beat, just like it did the first time he saw her in high school. He had the same butterflies in his stomach he had as a young schoolboy. *I can't believe I'm getting a second chance with her. I'm not going to mess it up this time. I'm going to marry this girl.*

He leaned in and planted a kiss on her lips. "Hey, baby. I missed you."

She wrapped her arms around him and hugged him tightly. "I missed you too. I'm so happy you are going home today."

"Me too." He placed his head against hers and ran his fingers through her hair and was immediately aroused. He pulled himself away. *No, not now. Save it for later. When the time is right.*

"So, what are your plans after you get out of here?"

"Michael will be by later today to pick me up. I'll be staying with them until I can find a job and save up some money for my own place."

"You could stay with me?" She batted her eyes at him.

"Thanks, but Michael and I are just getting to know each other again. I think I should spend some time with him and Sarah, don't you think? Besides, you have a roommate, remember?"

Jenna frowned, "Yeah, you're right. I just thought maybe we could be alone."

"I'm sorry, please try and understand. Sarah is so excited to have me stay with them. I don't want to disappoint her."

He saw the look of rejection on her face and put his arm around her. "We'll have time to be alone soon. I promise." It broke his heart to disappoint her, but she would understand everything soon enough.

chapter 47

After two weeks of trial and three days of deliberation, it all came down to this moment. Jake paced his holding cell and wiped his sweaty palms on his pants, then took a seat on the cold steel bench and dropped his head toward his chest. He placed his hands over his face and rested his elbows on his knees. He stayed this way for a long time, until the sound of footsteps approaching his cell brought him back to reality.

He looked up and saw his lawyer and a guard standing on the other side of the bars. "The jury has reached a verdict," his lawyer said as the guard unlocked the cell door and slid it open. Jake slowly got on his feet, took just one step forward when his knees buckled, and he started to go down. The two men each grabbed an arm and caught him before he hit the floor.

"Jake, take it easy," his lawyer said as they eased him back onto the bench. "Take a deep breath. It's going to be okay."

Jake sighed and shook his head, "No, it's not."

They gave him a couple of minutes to get his composure, and then his lawyer put his hand out to Jake and helped him up, "You need to get dressed. We have to be in court in an hour."

Jake ran his hand over the razor stubble on his face and said, "I need to shave."

He changed out of his orange jumpsuit and into a suit and tie, cleaned himself up the best he could, and was ready to go in no time at all. He looked in the mirror and hardly recognized the man staring back at him.

Megan was loading the dishwasher when she got the call from Jake's lawyer, shortly after 2 p.m. on Tuesday afternoon. The jury had reached a verdict. She needed to get to the courthouse right away. The first thing she did was call Sarah.

"They reached a verdict."

"We're on our way. We'll pick you up."

"Thanks. I'll see you soon," Megan said, then ran upstairs to change her clothes.

Fifteen minutes later, she was sitting in a rocker on the front porch waiting for Sarah and Michael to pick her up. She looked up at the sky and watched the sun move behind the clouds. She thought of Jake and worried what the future would hold for him, then looked down at her stomach and placed a hand on her belly. *Don't worry, baby. Mommy will take care of you.*

When Michael pulled the car up to the front of her house, she smiled at Sarah sitting in the passenger seat and thought, *I don't know what I would do if I didn't have them in my life.*

Sarah got out of the car and opened the back door for her as Megan made her way down the stairs. "How are you feeling?"

"I'm okay. I managed to eat a little bit today." Megan climbed into the back seat of the car.

"That's good," Sarah said and closed the car door.

"Hi, Megan," Michael said.

"Hi. Thanks for picking me up."

"You're welcome." He looked up at the dark clouds and said, "I hope the rain holds out until we get there."

The weather did not cooperate; the rain went from a drizzle to a downpour in a matter of minutes. As they turned the corner and pulled onto Courthouse Drive, all they could see was a sea of media vans and reporters everywhere.

Michael pulled up in front of the building and said, "Wait here." He jumped out of the car and opened the trunk. He retrieved an oversized umbrella and opened it, then went around to their side of the car. He opened Megan's door as Sarah was already getting out of the car. Megan got out of the car with her head down. Michael put his arm around her; she put her head into his shoulder, shielding her from the reporters.

The three of them huddled together under the umbrella and shuffled their way to the building as the reporters shoved microphones in their faces and shouted questions at them. It was difficult to see two feet in front of them with all the cameras flashing before their eyes.

When they entered the building, Megan and Sarah shook the rain off and removed their coats while Michael headed back out to park the car. A security guard stepped forward and held his hands up, pushing the crowd back. "If you don't have a pass to sit in the courtroom, you're going to need to wait outside."

They went through the metal detector, then gathered their belongings and went into the crowded courtroom. All eyes were on them as they hurried down the aisle and took their seats in the first row behind the defense table. Once seated, Megan exhaled and folded her hands on her lap to keep them from shaking.

Moments after they were seated, Megan looked up just as the side door opened and Jake appeared; their eyes locked on each other, her heart started to race. He gave her a weak smile and made his way to his seat, keeping his eyes on her the entire time. She was shocked to see how much he changed in such a short amount of time. He lost so much weight; his cheeks sunk into his face; dark circles under his eyes; he appeared so much older than he had before this whole ordeal began.

"All rise," the bailiff proclaimed. Everyone got on their feet and watched as the judge made his way to his bench and took his seat and then said, "You may be seated."

Everyone took their seats, and the judge turned to speak directly to the jury. "Have you reached a verdict?"

The foreman stood and said, "Yes, we have, your honor," then handed a folded piece of paper to the bailiff.

Megan held her breath as she watched the bailiff carry the paper to the judge, and he opened it and read it. Sarah reached over and took Megan's hand in hers.

"Will the defendant please rise?"

Jake stood up and cast his eyes over to the jury box, giving them one last look, begging for compassion.

The judge asked the foreman, "On the count of first-degree murder of Stacy Richards, how does the jury find the defendant Jake Harbor?"

"Not guilty, your honor."

"On the count of second-degree murder of Stacy Richards, how does the jury find the defendant Jake Harbor?"

"Not guilty by reason of insanity."

The courtroom erupted with gasps and chatter. The judge pounded his gavel on the sound block, "Quiet!" He banged the gavel again, "I will not tolerate such outbursts in my courtroom!" The room immediately became silent. Once the judge had everyone's attention again, he said, "Given the verdict that has been reached today, I hereby find that the defendant, Jake Harbor, be committed to the custody of an Ohio Secured Mental Health Facility for an indeterminate period of time, until he is found to be mentally stable and no longer a threat to society."

He then turned to the jury and said, "Thank you, Jury, for your service today. Court is adjourned."

The bailiff called out, "All rise," and everyone stood up and watched as the judge left the courtroom. As soon as he was out of the courtroom, pandemonium broke out.

chapter

48

The nurse pushed a wheelchair into Dylan's hospital room and asked, "Are you ready to go?"

Dylan smiled, jumped off the bed, and clapped his hands together, "Let's do this."

"Hop in," the nurse said.

"No, thanks, I'd rather walk."

"Hospital policy. If you want to get out of here, you need to get in the wheelchair." She pushed the chair closer to him.

"This is silly," Dylan said and took a seat in the wheelchair.

"Is someone picking you up?"

"Yes, my brother just went to get the car."

When they reached the main entrance of the hospital, Michael wasn't there yet. Dylan sat in the wheelchair and looked around; he heard a bird chirping and looked up in a tree and saw a red cardinal. He smiled and took a deep breath of fresh air and never felt more alive.

Michael pulled into the circular driveway, put the car in park, and hopped out to help Dylan, but he was already out of the wheelchair and had opened the car door.

"Thanks for picking me up, bro," Dylan said after the two of them were seated in the car.

"You're welcome." Michael held out his fist, and Dylan gave him a fist bump. "What do you want to do on your first day of freedom?"

"Would you mind taking me to get a haircut and then shopping? I need to get some new clothes and a few other things."

"Sure, I know a great barber. He will fix you up." Michael pulled out of the driveway.

Dylan smiled at Michael, "Thanks."

After several hours of shopping, Dylan was satisfied with the new wardrobe he had accumulated.

"Can we get something to eat? All of this shopping is making me hungry," Dylan asked as he placed the shopping bags into the trunk of Michael's car.

Michael slammed the trunk closed. "I thought you would never ask."

They went to a local bar around the corner from the mall, known for having great food. They took a seat at the bar and ordered two beers while they looked over the menu.

Dylan took a big guzzle from his beer mug, then slammed it back on the bar. "Wow! Do you know how long it has been since I've had a beer?"

Michael patted Dylan on the back and said, "Enjoy it, man. You deserve it. I'm sorry we never got a chance to have a beer together before this." He frowned, "You missed out on so much."

"I know, and I am not going to miss out on anything else ever again." Dylan took another swig of his beer. "Prison changes a man. I'm not the same person I used to be. Some men lose themselves when they spend time in prison, but I like to think that I found myself. I got my priorities straight now. I know what is most important to me now. Family is everything. You and Sarah are my family now. I'm so glad you are back in my life."

Michael's eyes swelled with tears, "Me too." Michael cast his eyes downward and fiddled with the bottle of ketchup on the bar, then sighed. "Listen, I know I told you I was sorry before, but I need to tell you again. I feel awful about the way I treated you. I was a stupid ass. Can you ever forgive me?"

Dylan didn't answer because the bartender came over and delivered their food. He placed two plates in front of each of them and asked, "Two more beers?"

"Yes," they answered in unison.

The bartender took the empty beer mugs and refilled them at the beer tap in front of them. Dylan took a bite of his burger and waited for the bartender to bring them their beers and walk away.

"It's okay, man. I get it. It's in the past. The way I see it, we're even. You saved my life, and I saved yours."

"I didn't save your life. It was Sarah."

"Close enough. She's your wife." Dylan took another gulp of his beer and became profoundly serious. "Can I ask you a question?"

"Sure, anything."

"How did you manage to marry her? I mean, she is so far out of your league it isn't funny. Did you blackmail her or something?"

Michael laughed and punched Dylan in the arm, almost knocking him off the barstool. "What?! She's lucky to have me. I'm a great catch, you know. Many of women were disappointed when I was taken off the market."

Dylan laughed, "If you say so."

Twenty minutes later, Michael got a call from Sarah. "Hey, are you guys still at the hospital? I thought you would be home by now."

"No, we're at Larry's Place having a beer. I took Dylan for a haircut and shopping for some clothes."

"Hi, Sarah," Dylan yelled in the background.

"Okay, well, it sounds like you guys are having fun. I just wanted to see what time you would be home."

"We're okay. We'll be home soon."

Three hours later, Sarah answered the door when someone rang the bell.

"Oh, hi, Jenna. How are you?"

"I'm good. Is Dylan here?

"No, he's out with Michael."

"Do you know when he will be back? We are supposed to have dinner plans."

"They should have been back by now. They are at Larry's Place having a beer. That was a long time ago. Come with me." She grabbed Jenna by the elbow. "I think we need to go and get them."

When Sarah and Jenna got to the bar, it was after six, and the bar was crowded for happy hour. They walked into the entrance of the bar and searched the crowd for Michael and Dylan.

"There they are," Sarah said and pointed to the bar where Michael and Dylan were seated with one arm around each other singing "*Take me Home, Country Roads*" by John Denver. They weaved their way through the crowd and up to the bar.

"Hi, guys. Having fun?" Sarah asked.

"Sarah, what are you doing here?" Michael asked and hugged his wife.

"Jenna," Dylan slurred his words. "Have a seat, baby." He got up and stumbled. "Do you want a drink?"

"No, thank you. Maybe you better keep the seat."

"No, a true gentleman always lets the woman sit." Dylan pushed her into the seat and elbowed Michael to do the same.

Michael jumped up and offered Sarah his seat.

Dylan leaned over and kissed Jenna on the cheek. "You smell good."

"Thank you. Have you had anything to eat?"

"We had lunch. I didn't eat dinner. I thought we were having dinner together?"

"I think maybe we will have to do that dinner some other night. You are pretty drunk. Maybe you should go home and sleep it off."

"Nooo! I bought new clothes. And I got a haircut." He ran his hand through his hair. "Do you like my haircut? I got it for you."

Jenna smiled at him, "Yes, you look very handsome."

"If you think I look handsome now, just wait until you see me in my new clothes."

The bartender came over, "Can I get you ladies something to drink?"

Sarah said, "No, thank you. Can we get the check?"

"Sure thing." The bartender left to get their check.

"I'm sorry, we didn't mean to stay this long," Michael said to Sarah.

"It's fine," Sarah said, "We'll leave your car here and pick it up tomorrow." Sarah paid the check and said, "Come on, guys. It's time to go."

Jenna got up and wrapped her arm around Dylan's waist. He placed his arm over her shoulder, and she helped him walk through the crowd. He gazed at her and whispered in her ear. "I love you. I'm going to marry you."

She stopped walking for a moment, caught off guard by what he had just said, and looked up at him. He gave her a big cheesy grin and shook his head.

chapter

49

Dylan opened his eyes and waited for his vision to come into focus. He looked around the room, took in his surroundings, and tried to remember where he was. "Ouch!" He put his hand on his head to ease the pain and stop the room from spinning, then sat up and put his feet on the floor.

He sat on the side of the bed with his hands over his face for several minutes resisting the urge to throw up. When he was unable to fight it any longer, he ran out of the bedroom and down the hall to the bathroom and slammed the door behind him. After throwing up multiple times, he rested his head on the side of the toilet and cursed alcohol.

He splashed cold water on his face and gargled with mouth wash, then looked at himself in the mirror. That was when he remembered his dinner plans with Jenna. "You jerk. How could you mess this up?" he said to his reflection in the mirror.

He opened the medicine cabinet, found a bottle of aspirin, and took two of them, and then turned the shower on and undressed. Ten minutes later, he descended the stairs and followed the smell of coffee coming from the kitchen.

"Good morning," Sarah said as he shuffled his way to the breakfast bar and took a seat.

"Morning," he mumbled.

"Coffee?" she asked, holding up the carafe.

"Yes, please."

She got a coffee cup out of the cabinet and poured him a cup of coffee, then slid it in front of him. He touched her arm as she was moving her hand away and said, "I'm sorry about last night."

"That is not necessary, but you might want to apologize to Jenna." Sarah sighed, "She said something about a special dinner date you had planned?"

Dylan folded his arms on the counter and placed his head in them. "I know. I wanted last night to be so special, but I messed everything up."

"Yeah, you messed up big time," Michael said, coming into the kitchen.

Dylan raised his head and looked at Michael, who looked as hungover as he did. "It's all your fault. Why did you let me get so drunk? You knew I had plans with Jenna."

"Hey, I didn't force the beer down your throat. I asked you several times if you wanted to leave, and you said just one more. I'm sorry if I was having a good time with my brother that I haven't spent any time with in years."

Sarah put her hands on her hips and raised her voice, "That's enough, you two. You're both to blame. Sit down, Michael. I'll make you guys something to eat, and then you can help Dylan figure out a way to make things up to Jenna."

"How mad was Jenna when she left last night?" Dylan asked Sarah.

"She wasn't mad; she was disappointed."

"Oh, great! That's even worse," Dylan said, and Michael patted him on the back and shook his head.

"I should call her," Dylan said, getting up from his chair.

Sarah said, "Sit down. Your breakfast is almost done. You can call her after you eat." Michael gave Dylan a look of warning, and he took his seat.

After breakfast, Dylan thanked Sarah and then said, "I better get this over with," then went upstairs to call Jenna.

The phone rang several times, and Dylan was afraid she was ignoring him. He was about to hang up when she answered, "Hello."

"Hi. Are you mad at me?"

"No, I'm not mad." She sighed, "But, if I'm being honest, I was a little disappointed. I was really looking forward to having some alone time."

He sighed, "I'm disappointed in myself. I was so excited to spend my first night of freedom with you, and then I had a couple of beers, and I don't know what happened. I haven't had a drink in years, and I guess it went right to my head." Dylan nervously paced the room. "Let me make it up to you? What are you doing tonight?"

"I'm going out of town for work. My flight leaves in two hours."

"Damn, how long will you be gone?" Dylan asked sounding disappointed.

"Two weeks."

"I'm so sorry. I guess I really messed things up."

"Don't worry about it. You can make it up to me when I get back." Dylan could hear sadness in her voice. A car horn honked. "My Uber is here. I have to go. I'll call you when I get to Denver."

"Okay. Bye, Jenna."

"Bye."

When Dylan got off the phone with Jenna, he went back downstairs and plopped onto the couch where Michael was watching the morning news.

"How did it go with Jenna?"

"Terrible. She's going out of town for two weeks. She's on her way to the airport now."

"Oh, damn. I'm sorry, that really sucks."

"Tell me about it."

chapter 50

Megan placed her clammy hand on the door handle and waited. When the buzzer sounded, she pulled the door open and stepped into the psychiatric hospital. She scanned the lobby, taking in the environment on her way to the front desk. Two young people sitting on the couch, a checkerboard between them, looked up at Megan and smiled. She gave them a quick wave and flashed a smile as she glided past them and stopped at the reception desk.

"May I help you?" the pleasant woman with a friendly face asked.

"Yes, I have an appointment to visit Jake Harbor?"

The woman grabbed the clipboard off her desk and asked, "Your name?"

Megan cleared her throat, then responded, "Megan Harbor."

The receptionist eyed the list, then placed a check next to her name and handed her the clipboard, "Please sign here."

Megan signed her name with a shaky hand and gave the board back to the woman.

The receptionist turned to the security guard and said, "Can you please take Mrs. Harbor to the visitation room?"

Megan had hoped she would be asked to take a seat and wait so that she could calm her nerves a bit, but that was not the case. Before she knew it, she was ushered into the recreational room and stood face-to-face with Jake. He had lost even more weight than the last time she had seen him in court but still managed to take her breath away, despite the weight loss and dark circles under his eyes.

He pulled her into an embrace, held her tightly, and whispered into her ear, "I missed you."

"I missed you too," she said, fighting to hold back tears.

He let her go, then took her hand and guided her to a quiet corner of the room. He pointed to the recliner, and she took a seat, then left her to retrieve another chair from a table nearby. She watched as he strolled across the room with confidence; she loved the way that he always took control of things. *What am I going to do without him? How am I going to raise this baby without him?* she thought to herself.

He placed the chair directly in front of her and took a seat, then took both of her hands in his. "Thank you for coming. How are you?"

"I'm doing okay. How are you?" She looked around the room, "How is this place?"

He shrugged his shoulders, "It's better than prison, but I wish I were at home with you."

She just shook her head.

"I've been thinking," Jake said. "I don't like the fact that you are living in that house all alone. Do you think you should sell the house and move in with Sarah and Michael?"

"I don't know. I hadn't thought about it. I've had other things on my mind."

"I know." He cast his eyes downward. "I'm sorry. I know this is a lot to take in."

Her hands started to fidget. She pulled them out of his grip. "You don't understand. I have something I need to tell you."

Just then, two men started arguing. A burly male aid rushed across the room and yelled, "Hey, that's enough over there. You two separate." He put himself in between the two men and diffused the situation.

Jake turned his head back to Megan, took her hands in his again, and looked her in the eyes, "You know that you can tell me anything, right? I may be stuck in this place, but I'm still here for you."

Megan sighed and said, "I'm pregnant."

Jake placed a hand on her stomach and didn't say anything for several seconds.

"I know it's a lot to take in right now. Timing couldn't be any worse," she said. He still said nothing. Unsure of what he was thinking, she said, "I'm keeping it."

Finally, he broke his silence, "What if it has mental issues? What if it's hereditary?"

She hadn't thought about that. "I don't know, Jake. I don't know."

He reached over and hugged her, "I'm happy about the baby. Really, I am. I'm just worried, that's all."

chapter 51

Dylan was sitting on the couch, his feet resting on the coffee table, watching an old black and white movie when Michael came home and slammed the front door behind him. He made his way straight to Dylan and threw an envelope on the table. "This is for you," he said and walked away.

Dylan picked up the envelope and followed Michael into the kitchen. "What is this?"

"Why don't you open it and see?" Michael said as he got a beer out of the refrigerator.

Dylan opened the envelope. It was a plane ticket to Denver. He looked up at Michael with confusion.

"What?" Michael put his hands up in the air. "You've been moping around the house for the past five days. I can't take it anymore. Pack your bags. I'm taking you to the airport."

Dylan stood there and said nothing, his heart racing as thoughts of seeing Jenna ran through his head. He stared down at the ticket, "The plane leaves in two hours?"

"Yup! You better get packing." Michael took a swig of his beer.

Dylan raced out of the room and headed upstairs to pack. In no time at all, Dylan was packed and seated in the car as Michael drove him to the airport. He reached his hand into his coat pocket for the third time to reassure himself that the ring was still there.

"Do you have the address of the hotel?" Michael asked.

"Yes, she's staying at the Marriot in downtown Denver. Do you think she will be surprised to see me?"

"I'm sure she will."

Michael pulled up to the airport gates and put the car in park, then helped Dylan retrieve his luggage out of the trunk. He gave his brother a hug and said, "Text me when you get there."

"I will."

Michael got back in the car and was about to drive away when Dylan knocked on the passenger window. Michael rolled the window down and said, "Did you forget something?"

"I just wanted to say thank you and I'm glad to have you back in my life."

Michael beamed and held his fist out to him. Dylan gave him a fist bump, and Michael said, "You're welcome. Now get the hell out of here before you miss your flight."

Dylan quickly turned and rushed towards the airport entrance. He wasn't looking where he was going and bumped into a man pushing a cart full of luggage, knocking the bags off the cart.

"Hey, watch where you're going," the man yelled, frowning at him.

"Sorry, I'm so sorry," Dylan said, bending down and picking up the luggage. He threw them back on the cart and hurried into the building. The plane would be leaving soon.

When he got through security and made his way to Gate 8B, the plane was already boarding. "Wait, wait, I'm coming." He yelled to the flight attendant standing at the desk. Panting from his run, he handed her his ticket, and she said, "You just made it. We were about to close the door."

"I know, I know." He scurried through the entrance and down

the ramp to the airplane. The plane was packed; everyone was already seated, with only a few open seats. It took him no time at all to put his luggage in the overhead compartment and take his seat.

"Hello," he said to the elderly couple sitting next to him.

"Hi, sonny," the little woman smiled at him.

Excited and nervous about seeing Jenna and possibly proposing to her, Dylan chatted non-stop with the friendly woman the entire flight. He told her everything, including going to jail and missing out on so much of his life. He told her that he couldn't wait to start living again, and the first step in doing that was getting Jenna back. He reached into his pocket, took the ring out, and showed it to her. "Do you think she will like it?"

Her eyes swelled with tears, and she patted him on the arm, "Oh, honey. She's going to love it."

"I hope so," he smiled.

When the plane landed, Dylan helped the aging couple with their luggage and walked beside them as they made their way down the ramp. When they exited the gate, the couple's daughter and son-in-law were waiting for them. The lady introduced him to her family and then gave Dylan a hug, "Good luck, Dylan. I hope you and Jenna have a great life together."

"Thank you. It was a pleasure meeting you both."

Dylan claimed his luggage, exited the airport, and hailed a taxi.

"Where are you heading?" The taxi driver asked Dylan as he grabbed his bag and lifted it into the trunk.

"The Courtyard by Marriott."

"Great. Hop in."

On the way to the hotel, Dylan suddenly yelled, "Stop! Stop here."

The driver pulled the car over, and Dylan said, "Wait here. I'll be right back." He swiftly jumped out of the car before it had fully stopped and ran down the sidewalk up to a flower stand outside of a grocery store. When he got back into the taxi, he was carrying two dozen red roses.

The driver looked at Dylan through the rearview mirror and smiled. "Those are beautiful."

Dylan looked down at the flowers and said, "I'm going to propose tonight."

"Congratulations!"

When Dylan got to the hotel, he checked the time on his phone; it was 6 p.m. *Good, Jenna should be getting done work by now.* He went to the men's room. He changed his clothes, combed his hair, and put on some cologne, then stared at himself in the mirror. *"You got this!"*

He exited the bathroom and went to the front desk, where an attractive young woman smiled at him, "May I help you?"

"Yes, I'm here to visit Jenna Morris. Can you tell me what room she is in?"

"I'm sorry, sir, that is against company policy. I can call her room and announce your arrival."

Dylan lowered his head and frowned, "I was hoping to surprise her."

"I'm sorry. How about I call her and tell her she has a guest waiting for her in the lobby, but I don't tell her who it is?"

Dylan gave the woman a half-smile, "Okay."

The woman went back to her computer and asked, "What was her name again?"

"Jenna Morris."

She punched her name into the computer and then picked up the telephone and dialed her room number. After several rings, the woman hung up, "I'm sorry, sir. There was no answer. If you like, you could go have a drink at the bar, and I'll try her again later?"

"Okay."

"We can hold your luggage for you if you'd like?"

"That would be great," he said and walked around the desk to where the bellhop was. He gave the man his luggage and the flowers to hold, then made his way to the restaurant to find the bar.

He entered the restaurant and scanned the bar looking for a seat. He smiled when he saw Jenna sitting at the bar having a drink. He didn't move; he stood there for a couple of seconds and watched her. She wasn't alone. When she smiled at the man sitting next to her, Dylan's heart sank. *That's my girl.* Paralyzed by his emotions, all he could do was watch as the man leaned in and kissed her.

He wanted nothing more than to go up to the guy, pull him away from Jenna and punch him in the face. But what good would that do? Instead, he turned and ran out of the restaurant then out of the hotel. He kept running down the sidewalk until he was out of breath and couldn't run any longer. He bent over panting, his hands on his waist, and tried to catch his breath.

When he was finally able to breathe normally, he stood up and looked around the city. *What am I going to do now?* He spotted a bar across the street and took off towards it. The bar was dark and dreary, perfect for how he was feeling.

The bartender made his way over to him just as he took a seat at the bar. Before the bartender could even ask, Dylan said, "I'll have a shot of jack."

He downed the first shot and said, "I'll take another."

The bartender poured him another shot, "Bad day?"

"Yeah, you could say that." He downed the second shot and slammed the shot glass on the bar. "I'll have a beer."

Dylan sat hunched over the bar, drowning his sorrows in his beer, and didn't notice that someone had taken the seat next to him.

"Hey, I remember you," the woman next to him exclaimed.

Dylan looked up and into the eyes of one of the flight attendants from his plane ride there.

"Do you remember me?"

He smiled at the pretty woman and said, "Yeah, I do. Can I buy you a drink?"

"Sure. I'd like that. My name is Rachel, by the way."

"Dylan. It's nice to meet you, Rachel."

Two hours later, Dylan placed his arm around Rachel's shoulder and looked her in the face, "You're so pretty."

"Thank you." She motioned to the door. "You want to get out of here and get something to eat?"

"Sure." He raised his hand and said, "Bartender, we'll take the check."

Just then, Dylan felt his phone vibrate in his pocket. He took it out and read the text; it was Michael.

"Where you at? You were supposed to text me when you got there."

Dylan frowned and texted him back, *"I'm here."*

When he got off the phone, Rachel said, "Before we go, there's something I have to ask you."

The bartender placed the check in front of Dylan. He pulled out some money and placed it on the bar, next to the check. "Ask away."

"You aren't married, are you?"

"Nope," he slurred. "I'm totally free and available," he stumbled off the stool, took her hand, and said, "Let's go."

They walked hand in hand down the street, looking at the storefronts, then stopped in front of Tony's Pizza. "How does pizza sound?" he asked.

"Sounds delicious," she said.

Dylan reached for the door and opened it, then waited for Rachel to enter first. She took one step towards the door, then gyrated towards him, leaned in, and kissed him.

He let go of the door, grabbed her by the waist, pushed her up against the brick wall, and planted a kiss hard on her lips. He pressed his body up against hers and couldn't contain the heat that generated between his legs. He needed to be with a woman; he needed it now.

He ran his fingers through her hair, then moved his lips over to her neck, taking in the scent of her perfume while he continued to kiss her. He was still kissing her neck when he heard footsteps approaching. "Excuse me."

He broke away from Rachel and said, "Oh, sorry." They moved away from the entrance to let the family of four enter the pizza place.

"Let's go," he said to Rachel, taking her hand in his. "Where are you staying?"

"The Hilton, it's right next door."

They were both starving, but there was something they wanted more than food. They entered the lobby of the Hilton and smiled at the man already on the elevator when they got on. Rachel pressed the 17th-floor button and noticed the 6th-floor button was already lit up.

"Have a good evening," the man said as he exited the elevator.

"You too," Dylan said and waited for the doors to close before pulling Rachel into his arms again. He lifted her off the ground and placed her bottom on the handrail, then slipped his tongue inside of her mouth. He squeezed her voluptuous breast, then he slid his hand between her legs. He had dreamed about this moment for so long, but in his dreams, it was always Jenna.

The elevator dinged, and the door opened on their floor, bringing them back to reality. As soon as Rachel unlocked and opened the door, Dylan firmly grabbed her and started kissing her again, pushing her backward and onto the bed. The urgency to be with a woman was growing deep inside of him. If he didn't have her soon, he thought he would explode.

He stood and unbuckled his belt and removed his pants. The whole time, his eyes were on Rachel; he watched as she removed her blouse and bra. His eyes grew wide at the sight of her naked body. *God, she was beautiful!* He struggled to get his pants off in haste. She laughed at him when he almost fell because he didn't take his shoes off before trying to remove his pants.

His phone started to ring and fell out of his pocket onto the floor while he fought to remove his pants. He looked down at it and saw Jenna's face appear on the phone. His heart broke at the sight of her face. He loved her so much. He turned to face Rachel and said, "I'm sorry, I can't do this."

Dylan wandered the streets of downtown Denver, not knowing where to go or what to do next. Sick to his stomach at the thought of what he had almost done, he longed for the numbness of the alcohol to return. He walked for several miles in new dress shoes, not meant for walking, and knew that blisters had formed on his feet.

He spotted a park bench, drifted over to it, and took a seat, then removed his shoes and socks and inspected the fresh red blisters on each of his heels. He pulled his phone out of his pocket, put it to his ear, and played the message from Jenna.

"Hey, it's me. I just wanted to tell you I miss you. I can't wait to see you again. Alright, well, it's late. I'm going to bed now. Goodnight, Dylan."

He played the message over and over, his heart thundering in his chest. He couldn't get the sight of someone else kissing her out of his head. After he had enough torture, he lay back on the bench and went to sleep.

He felt a poke in the ribs, "You can't sleep here." He opened his eyes; it was morning. A police officer was jabbing him in the side with his nightstick, "Did you hear me? You can't sleep here."

Dylan sat up and wiped the sleep out of his eyes. "Sorry, sir. I'm leaving." He reached down and grabbed his socks and shoes and started to put them on. *Ouch!* His heels burned as soon as the shoes made contact with his feet.

Dylan made his way back the way he came. The police officer watched his every move to be sure that he left. He walked a short distance and then placed his hand to his coat pocket; the ring was gone. He frantically checked all his other pockets; it wasn't there.

He stopped, took off his shoes, then started to run at breakneck speed. Out of breath, he didn't stop until he reached the hotel. He slid his feet into his shoes and winced in pain, knowing that he had torn open his blisters. He barreled through the lobby and slammed his hand on the elevator button.

When the elevator doors opened, he pushed his way in before the people on the elevator could exit and got a dirty look from more than one of the people. He pushed the 17th-floor button, then checked the time on his phone. It was 9:35. *I hope I'm not too late.*

He pounded on the door of room 1705 and yelled, "Rachel, it's Dylan. Open up."

When there was no answer, he pounded again and again. The door next to her room opened, and a man poked his head out and shouted, "Hey, buddy. You want to keep it down, some of us are trying to sleep."

Defeated, Dylan raised his hand to the man and said, "Sorry, I'm leaving."

"Good," the man said and slammed his door.

Dylan stopped at the desk in the lobby and asked the man, "Can you please tell me if the woman in room 1705 has checked out?

"Certainly, sir." He punched a couple of buttons on the computer and said, "Yes, sir. She checked out early this morning."

Dylan dropped his shoulders, turned away from the man, and mumbled, "Okay, thank you."

He left the hotel and went to a coffee shop across the street. He ordered a cup of coffee and then contemplated what to do next. He used his phone to book a flight home for later in the day and then texted Michael. "I'm coming home."

After breakfast, he walked back to the Marriott to get his stuff. He approached the bellhop and gave him a ticket for his luggage. The man returned with his luggage and the flowers. The sight of the flowers was like getting kicked in the stomach all over again. He grabbed the flowers and carried them over to the check-in desk and handed them to the same woman who helped him the day before. "Here, these are for you."

Confused, she took the flowers, smiled, and said, "Thank you."

He went over to where several couches were and placed his luggage on a coffee table, then unzipped it and took out his sneakers. He changed his shoes, put the dress shoes into his luggage, and closed it back up, then went outside and hailed a cab to the airport.

He took a seat at the airport gate and replayed the trip over and over in his head and couldn't believe how badly things went. Not only did he lose Jenna, but he lost his grandmother's ring too. He just wanted to get home and forget the trip ever happened.

chapter

52

Megan turned down her street and sighed when she saw the press camped out in front of her house. She laid a hand on the horn, then threw her hands in the air. "Get out of the way," she yelled at the reporters and cameramen blocking her driveway. She inched the car forward, and they slowly stepped to the side, allowing her to pull into the driveway.

She turned the engine off and sat there for a few seconds, trying to shield herself from the cameras flashing in her face. She took a deep breath, then threw open the door and pushed a reporter backward in the process. "No comment," she cried out and made her way to the trunk to get her groceries.

"Are you going to divorce the murderer?" a reporter shouted at her, then forced a microphone in her face. She grabbed the two bags out of the trunk and slammed it closed, then scurried to the porch. In her haste to get away from them, she tripped and spilled her bags of groceries all over the place.

"Please leave me alone," she begged in barely a whisper. She sank to her knees and collected her items as silent tears rolled down her cheeks.

"Leave her alone," Sarah yelled, racing up to the porch to help her sister-in-law. "Get out of here before I call the police."

The crowd of reporters backed away and let Sarah through. She held her hand out to Megan and pulled her up on her feet, then took the house key from her and guided her to the front door. Sarah unlocked the door and guided Megan into the house and over to the couch, then went back outside to get the groceries.

When she returned, Megan said, "They won't leave me alone. They follow me everywhere. I need to get out of here for a while."

"You could come and stay with us."

"They would only follow me there. I need to go somewhere far away from here."

"Good idea. You know I can work from anywhere, and Michael hasn't gone back to work yet. We should go on vacation, get away from the craziness for a while. Where do you want to go?"

Megan got up from the couch and started to pace as she thought about where she wanted to go. A thought jumped into her head; her face lit up, and she made a turnabout. "I got it! We should go to Mexico. I already have an apartment there. It is so beautiful there. You're going to love it."

Sarah hesitated, "Are you sure you want to go there? Won't it bring back too many memories?"

Megan thought about it for a minute, and a look of contentment came over her face, "I'm sure. That's where I want to go."

"Okay, when do you want to go?"

"As soon as possible."

Sarah jumped up from the couch and said, "I'm going to go. I need to talk to Michael. I'll call you as soon as I talk to him and let you know what he says." She made her way to the front door.

"Great. In the meantime, I'll look for flights."

Sarah put her hand on the doorknob and started to turn it.

"Sarah."

She turned to face Megan. "Yeah?"

"Thank you."

Sarah beamed, "You're welcome."

chapter

53

Michael and Sarah were sitting at the breakfast bar in the kitchen discussing the idea of going to Mexico when they heard the front door open. They looked at each other with confusion and headed into the living room, and stopped in their tracks when they saw Dylan walk through the door. They could tell something was wrong by the look on his face.

"What are you doing back so soon?" Michael asked Dylan.

"I don't want to talk about it," he barked.

Sarah rolled her eyes and went upstairs, giving them time alone.

"Come on. You look like you could use a beer?" Michael said and went into the kitchen.

Dylan put his bags in the corner next to the stairs and followed behind.

"Did you see Jenna? What happened?" Michael cracked a can of beer open and placed it in front of Dylan.

"Oh, I saw her alright." He took a guzzle from his beer.

"She wasn't happy to see you?"

"She didn't see me."

Michael's eyebrows moved into a judgment position, "You're not making any sense. You said you saw her."

"I saw her at the bar." His nostrils flared, "She was kissing another guy."

Michael's eyes widened, "Really?"

Dylan shrugged his shoulders and said, "Yup," then took another swig of beer. "That's not all. I lost the ring."

Michael sank into a seat at the kitchen table. "Oh, Dylan. How the hell did you do that?"

A look of despair washed over Dylan's face. "I was pissed. I got drunk. I met this girl. I don't know what happened, but before I knew it, I went back to her hotel."

Not liking what he was hearing, Michael sighed and said, "Go on."

"I haven't been with a woman in so long. I wanted to get back at Jenna. But I couldn't do it. I left. I slept on a park bench, and when I woke up the next morning, the ring was gone."

"Do you think you were robbed?"

"I don't know. It's possible. I went back to her hotel to see if it was there, but she already checked out." He dropped his head in defeat.

Dylan's phone started to ring. He pulled it out of his pocket and saw Jenna's face appear, then swiped decline and dropped the phone on the counter.

"Are you going to talk to her? Let her explain?"

Dylan glared at Michael. "I don't want to hear anything she has to say. I know what I saw. I just wish she hadn't led me on. I thought we had a second chance at love, but obviously, I was wrong."

Michael placed a hand on Dylan's shoulder, "I'm sorry, Dylan. Do you know what you need?"

Dylan lifted his head and looked up at Michael, "What?"

"A vacation. I think we could all use a vacation. Megan needs to get away. We're going to Mexico. You should come with us."

Dylan took a moment to think it over, then said, "I'm in."

chapter

54

Megan placed a Closed Until Further Notice sign on the antique shop window, then went to the office to collect the mail and pay some bills. When she finished, she checked the time; it was almost seven, and Jake would be back in his room for the night.

Not permitted to make outgoing calls, Jake jumped at the phone when it rang, "Hello."

At the sound of his voice, Megan closed her eyes and inhaled deeply, "Hi."

"What's wrong?"

"Nothing, it's been a rough day, that's all. I just needed to hear your voice. How are you doing?"

"I'm fine, but I'm worried about you. How are you feeling?"

"I'm okay, I have a lot of morning sickness, but honestly, I could use some time away. The press is relentless; they are everywhere. That's why I'm calling. I'm going away for a while. I need to get my head straight."

"By yourself?"

Megan could hear the concern in his voice, "No, with Sarah and Michael and maybe Dylan."

"Oh, good. Where are you going?"

"Back to Mexico, we still have the apartment. I might as well make use of it."

"I think that's a great idea."

"Me too. How is your therapy coming along?"

"I'm getting more memories back, and I don't like what I'm learning about myself. It's really hard for me to accept the fact that I did horrific things. It's like someone else did them, but that someone else was me." He hesitated a moment, "I don't want to talk about it. Can we talk about something else?" He fell back onto his bed, "Let's talk about the baby. I still can't believe you are pregnant. I thought you were on the pill?"

"I was. It must have happened that night in Mexico. We left without our luggage. I didn't have my pills. Now that you've had some more time to think about it, how are you feeling about us having a baby?"

"I'm still nervous about my mental issues being hereditary, but honestly, I'm so excited. I can't wait to see who he looks like."

Megan placed a hand on her stomach and grinned, "What do you mean he? What if it's a girl?"

"Oh, no. No girls. Not if she's beautiful like you. I couldn't take that."

Megan went on and on for a while, babbling about the baby until finally, she realized that Jake wasn't listening to her. "What's wrong?" she asked.

"What are you going to tell the baby about me? When he gets older, he's going to learn the truth. I don't know if I could bear that."

"I'm going to tell him or her that you are a good man and that you were sick, and you love them very much. Don't worry, Jake. We'll figure it out. I promise you; I won't paint you out to be a monster."

"I don't want you to tell him who his father is."

Megan's temper rose, "No way."

"Please hear me out. The world is cruel, Megan. His life will be much easier if no one knows who his father is. I can't be there for him; let me do this one thing for him. I want you to stay in Mexico, make a new life for yourself. Make a better life for him. I want you to marry again and give the baby a real father."

"No, Jake. Please don't ask me to do that."

"You don't have to make a decision today. Go to Mexico and relax, and while you are there, promise me you will think about it."

"No. I can't.

Jake's heart constricted in his chest. "Please, Megan. After you've had some time to think about it, you're going to realize it is the right thing to do for you and the baby."

Not wanting to talk about it any longer, Megan said, "It's getting late. I'm still at the shop. I better be getting home now."

"Okay, Megan. I love you."

"I love you too. Goodnight."

"Goodnight."

chapter 55

Jenna hadn't heard from Dylan in days. She sent him multiple texts and left numerous messages, but he didn't get back to her. A rock formed in the pit of her stomach. *Something must be wrong. I'll call Sarah.*

Sarah's phone went straight to voicemail. "Hey, it's Jenna. Is everything okay with Dylan? He's not getting back to me. I hope he's not sick. Please give me a call. I'm really starting to worry. Okay, thanks. Bye."

She waited another day for someone to get back to her before she took matters into her own hands. She stood at the entrance of the hotel restaurant and searched the room for her boss. She spotted him sitting alone at a table eating breakfast, then took off toward his table. He placed his coffee cup back onto its saucer and looked up at her. "Oh, good morning, Jenna. Would you like to join me?"

"Thank you," she said and took a seat across from him. "I'm sorry for disturbing your breakfast, but I was hoping I could have a word with you?"

"Of course," he waved the waiter over.

The waiter gave her a friendly nod and handed her a menu. She waved the menu away and said, "Just coffee, please."

"I think the conference is going well, don't you?" her boss asked.

"Yes, it's going great. I made quite a few contacts. I plan on following up with them in a couple of weeks."

"That's good. Keep me in the loop." He picked a piece of bacon up from his plate and took a bite.

The waiter returned with her coffee. "Thank you," she said and smiled thinly. She cast her eyes downward and picked at her fingernails. "I hate to ask this, but there's something I have to take care of. Would you mind if I went home a day early? There's a red eye that leaves tonight."

"I don't mind." A look of concern flashed across his face. "Is there anything I can do to help?"

"No. It's something I have to do myself. Thank you very much." She got on her phone and booked the flight she previously saved. Then she finished her coffee and updated him on the progress she made at the conference.

The boss checked his watch and said, "We better get going. The first presentation will be starting soon." He paid the check, and they left together. When they reached the conference room, she made it a point to excuse herself to say hello to one of her colleagues, so she didn't have to sit with him for the next several hours.

She didn't retain much of what the speaker was saying. Her mind was raced with thoughts of Dylan, imagining the worst, as she stared forward at the speaker but not really seeing him. She checked her phone multiple times to see if anyone had gotten back to her and was disappointed each time that she did.

Somehow, she managed to get through the excruciating long business day but still had many hours until her flight would be leaving. She packed her bags and went down to the lobby to grab some dinner. On her way to the bar, she heard someone call out her name, "Jenna."

She turned to see who called her name and saw a familiar face beaming at her. He waved her over, "Jenna, please join me for dinner."

She made her way over to his table and smiled. "Hi, Noah. Are you sure? I don't think I will be good company right now."

He got out of his seat and pulled her chair out for her, "Let me be the judge of that."

She took her seat and said, "Okay. Don't say you weren't warned."

The waitress came over to the table, and Noah said, "You look like you could use a glass of wine."

She nodded her head, and Noah turned to the waitress and said, "The lady will have a glass of chardonnay."

After her drink arrived, he said, "Now, tell me. What is making you so sad tonight?"

"It's Dylan. Something's wrong. I don't know what, but I can feel it in the pit of my stomach. He's not answering my text or phone calls. I haven't heard from him in days. I'm flying home tonight. I need to find out what is going on."

He reached his hand over and placed it on top of hers. "Maybe he is cheating on you. He's not worthy of your love. I would never take you for granted. You know that, right?"

Jenna pulled her hand out of his. "Noah, please. I can't do this right now. I'm really worried about Dylan. What if he is sick again? He might be back in the hospital."

Noah dropped his shoulders and leaned back in his chair. "I'm sorry. Okay, let's think about it. If he were in the hospital, someone would have called you. Wouldn't they?"

"Yeah, I like to think so, but I don't know. I called Sarah, and she's not getting back to me either." She bit her lip, "I can't take it anymore. I need to know what is going on."

"Well, you're going home tonight, and you'll figure it all out soon enough. No sense worrying about it until then. Let's enjoy our dinner, and I will try my best to get your mind off of Dylan." He cast her a full-dimple smile and batted his baby blues at her in a playful manner.

Jenna chuckled and reached for her glass of wine. Over the next two hours, she feasted on a steak dinner and finished a bottle of wine. During that time, Noah even managed to make her laugh and forget about Dylan for a while.

"Well, I better get going. I need to get to the airport. Thank you for dinner, Noah, and for listening to my problems."

He got up and went behind her and pulled out her chair, "You're welcome." He leaned into her from behind and whispered into her ear, "It was my pleasure."

They walked together to the elevator, and he asked, "How are you getting to the airport?"

"I'll take an Uber."

"Let me take you. I have a rental car."

"No, I couldn't impose. It's getting late, and you have to get up early for the conference tomorrow. I'll just take an Uber."

"Nonsense, I insist."

"Okay, if you're sure I'm not putting you out."

"I'm sure. I want to do this for you. It will give me one last chance to change your mind about Dylan and come back to my hotel room with me." He grinned and winked at her.

"That's not going to happen. I told you before. I love Dylan." Jenna got off the elevator on her floor, and Noah followed her to her room. She scanned her keycard in front of the reader and opened the door. "Just let me get my bags. They are already packed."

She used the television to check out of her room and left her key on the table. "Okay, all set."

Noah grabbed her luggage and said, "Let's go."

Denver International Airport was only a short distance away, and the city traffic was light due to the hour of the night. The airport was only a couple of miles down the road from their hotel. Noah took the ramp onto I-70 and was telling Jenna a funny story about his childhood when suddenly Jenna yelled, "Get over, this is the exit."

He jerked the car to a quick right so he wouldn't miss the exit and saw the brown pickup truck a moment too late. He applied his brakes and swerved the car to the left, just before he heard and felt the impact of the crash. Instinctively, he threw his arm across Jenna's chest as if somehow, he could soften the blow. The last thing he saw was Jenna's face right before the hood of the truck crashed into the passenger side door, crushing her.

chapter

56

Dylan was sitting on the balcony of Megan's apartment in Mexico nursing a beer and watching the sunset when the sliding door opened, and Sarah stepped out. "Care for some company?"

He tried his best to give her a sincere smile, "Sure, have a seat."

She took a seat alongside of him and gazed at the orange rays of sunshine that appeared to be disappearing into the aqua blue sea, then took a deep breath of sea air. "It's so beautiful here. I can understand why Megan wanted to come back."

"Yeah, me too. How is she doing?"

"She's doing a little better. This place has a good effect on her. What about you? How are you doing?"

Dylan didn't turn and face her. Instead, he kept his eyes focused on a couple walking along the beach holding hands. "I'm a free man; I should be happy right now. As hard as I try, I can't stop thinking about Jenna." His face turned red, "I guess Michael told you what happened when I went to Denver?"

She placed her hand tenderly on top of his. "Yeah, I'm really sorry about that. She keeps calling me. She's really worried about you. What do you want me to tell her?"

"Nothing," Dylan snapped at her and pulled his hand away. "Let her worry. I don't owe her any explanation. She kissed another guy; she made her choice. I won't compete for her. He can have her." He crossed his arms in front of his chest.

"Maybe you should talk to her to get some closure?"

"No, I don't need closure. I was a fool to fall so fast. I thought it was our second chance at love. I was wrong. I just need a little time. I'll get over it." He took the last swig of his beer and stood up. "I need another beer," he said, then went into the apartment.

Oh! Dylan. You got it bad. I don't think you're going to get over her as fast as you think.

"There you are," Michael said, coming out onto the balcony. "I was looking for you." He squeezed into the same lounger as her, positioned her between his legs, and wrapped his arms around her.

She leaned her head against his chest. "I was just telling Dylan; Jenna keeps calling me because he won't talk to her. I feel bad; she's really worried about him. Someone needs to tell her what is going on."

"Stay out of it, Sarah. You can't fix everything. She kissed another guy. She made her choice. You should feel sorry for Dylan, not her," Michael said with a firmness in his voice.

"I know. I do feel bad for Dylan, but I think they both need closure. He needs to tell her what he saw and how he's feeling, so he can get past this."

"No, that's not what he needs. Guys don't like talking about their feelings. What he needs is to find another woman. That will do wonders for his ego."

Sarah punched him in the shoulder, "That is not what he needs. Is that what you would do if it were me?"

"Yeah, that's exactly what I would do, but first, I would kick the guy's ass."

Sarah laughed at her husband, "Yeah, right." She sighed and looked up at him. "How did everything get so complicated?"

"I don't know, but you know what?"

"What?"

"This past year has taught me to never take anything for granted because it can all change in a minute. I also learned that there is a silver lining in every situation if you are willing to look for it."

She tilted her head up to him and lifted one eyebrow, "What do you mean?"

"Well, look at all of us, I got sick and almost died, but it was because of this that I got my brother back in my life. Dylan got sent to prison for something he didn't do. He lost so many years of his life, but because he helped me, he was given a second chance at living. Megan lost her husband through all of this, but she is being blessed with a baby. I know that none of this has been easy, and it's not the ideal way we would want things to turn out, but there is always something to be thankful for." His eyes fixed on the sunset as he watched a seagull soar high into the sky.

"Yeah, you're right. I'm so thankful to have you back." She leaned in and kissed her husband. "I don't think I could have gone on without you."

"I'm not going anywhere. You're stuck with me. I love you."

"Can you promise me something?"

"Anything."

"No more secrets?"

"No more secrets," he repeated.

Sarah sighed, "When I found out about Dylan, I was crushed that you didn't confide in me. I questioned whether I even knew who you were and whether our marriage was real. I wondered if there were any other secrets you were keeping from me."

"I'm sorry. It was wrong to keep that part of me from you. I promise, no more secrets."

"Good." She closed her eyes and listened to the sound of the ocean. They sat in silence, and Sarah drifted off to sleep.

chapter

57

They had been in Mexico for almost a week, and Megan was starting to feel much better. There were no reporters following her around, and she had her family to lean on for support, but she knew that they would have to go home eventually. With no income coming in, she had practically depleted their entire savings account. She needed to get her business up and running again real soon, or she would lose everything. She had a plan. If it worked, she could stay in Mexico and still run the business.

"Good morning," Megan said to Michael and Sarah as she walked into the kitchen, then poured herself a cup of coffee. "Is Dylan up yet?"

"Yeah, he went for a walk on the beach. He's been gone for a while. He should be back soon," Michael replied.

"Thanks." She took a seat at the table across from them.

Sarah said, "Megan, I hate to bring this up, but have you given any thought to when you want to go back home? Michael has a doctor's appointment in a couple of days. I could send him home alone and stay here with you if you need me?"

"No, that won't be necessary. I've been thinking about going home soon. I need to reopen the antique shop. We should start looking for flights."

Just then, the front door opened, and Dylan walked in.

"Can I have a word with you?" Megan asked Dylan.

"Sure." Dylan took a seat at the table.

"We'll let the two of you talk," Sarah said and got up from the table, "Come on, Michael. Let's go sit on the balcony."

When they were gone, Dylan asked Megan, "What's up?"

"I was wondering, have you thought much about what you are going to do for a job?"

"A little. I've been checking out the job openings on Indeed. I'm going to start applying for some of them when we get back. Sarah and Michael have been great, but I can't keep sponging off them forever. I would like to get my own place eventually."

Megan nodded her head in agreement then said, "I have a proposition for you. How would you like to run the antique shop for me?"

They fell silent for a moment, then Dylan said apprehensively, "But I don't know anything about running a store?"

"I could teach you." Megan jumped to her feet and paced the kitchen. "I'll handle all of the paperwork, taxes, payroll, and all that stuff. I just need you to run the store. I have a couple of great employees who can help you out too."

"I don't understand why you need me. I don't want you to feel indebted to me. I'll find work." Dylan went to the refrigerator and got some orange juice out of it.

"I don't. I need you. I don't want to go back." She hesitated, and Dylan turned to look at her. She continued, "I want to stay here. I need someone to run the shop. I really need some income coming in. I could go home with you and teach you how to run the store and then come back here and do everything else remotely."

Dylan shook his head, "I don't know. Can I have some time to think it over?"

"Sure, I'll tell you what. Why don't you come to the shop and let me show you around, and then you can make your decision?"

"Okay, I can do that."

Megan was feeling good about going home and getting things straightened out, and then she was hit with another blow. The four of them were eating dinner and discussing the flights available when the doorbell rang.

"I'll get it," Megan said and went to answer the door.

She opened the door and found herself face to face with a young man she had never seen before, "Megan Harbor?" he asked.

"Yes?"

He handed her an envelope, "You've been served," then quickly turned and walked away without another word.

She looked down at the envelope with a puzzled look on her face, then spun around to face her family. She opened the envelope and read the large bold letters that ran across the top while everyone held their breath and watched.

Megan walked over to the couch and sank into it, despair hitting her hard.

"What is it?" Sarah asked.

Megan's eyes brimmed with tears, "Jake wants a divorce."

chapter 58

Noah opened his eyes and focused on the fluorescent lights shining above him. He listened to the sounds of the busy emergency room, and the memory of the car crash came back to him. *Jenna.* He shot up in his bed and was struck by a throbbing pain in his head. He reached his hand up and touched his bandaged forehead. *Ouch.* "Nurse," he yelled. "Nurse," he hollered again and pressed the call button on the side of his bed.

Moments later, his nurse pushed back the curtain and came into his bay. "Did you need something?" she asked.

"The woman I came in with, how is she?"

"She's pretty banged up. They're prepping her for surgery now."

"But will she be alright?" he asked wide-eyed.

"I don't know the extent of all of her injuries. She took the brunt of the crash. I can have her doctor come and see you when he gets a chance."

"Thank you. I need to see her." He swung his feet around the side of the bed and immediately became dizzy. "Whoa," he put his hand to his head to stop the spinning.

"Take it easy there. You hit your head pretty hard. No quick movements. I need to check with the doctor to see if it is okay for you to see her." She pushed him back against the bed. "You lie back down and rest, and I'll be back in a little bit."

When she left his bay, Noah heard her say to someone on the other side of the curtain. "He's awake now."

Two police officers entered the bay, and Noah rolled his eyes and dropped his head against the pillow. *Great.*

"Mr. Rogan, my name is Officer Jackson. Would it be okay if we have a word with you?"

Noah sighed, "Yes."

"Can you tell me what happened tonight?"

"I was taking Jenna to the airport. We were busy talking, and I almost missed the exit. She hollered for me to get over, and I did. I didn't see the truck coming. I tried to swerve, but he hit us anyway."

The officer was writing this down in a small notebook. He looked up from the notebook and gave Noah a stern look, "Were you drinking tonight, Mr. Rogan?"

"I'm not going to lie, yes. I had a couple of glasses of wine. But that is not what caused the accident. I told you, I got over at the last minute and didn't see the truck."

The officer shook his head, "And you don't think the alcohol might have impaired your response time?"

"No, I don't." Noah folded his arms across his chest. "I'm not saying any more without my lawyer."

Noah became even more agitated when his nurse came back and informed him he couldn't see Jenna because she had already been taken up to surgery.

He called his lawyer.

chapter

59

Jenna survived the two-and-a-half-hour surgery and awoke in agony. She tried to speak but couldn't open her mouth. She didn't remember what had happened or why she was in the hospital. She touched the nurse's arm and pleaded her for help with her eyes.

"Hold on, honey."

The nurse left her room and came back with a small whiteboard and a black marker and handed them to her, "Here you go."

Jenna wrote "What happened" on the board and showed it to the nurse.

"You were in a car accident. You broke your jaw. The doctor had to wire it shut so it heals properly." The nurse handed Jenna a mirror.

She looked at herself in the mirror. Her face was covered with bruises; she placed a hand on her mouth. It was coming back to her now. She wrote "Noah?" on the board and looked at the nurse curiously.

"He's okay. He's still in the emergency room. We called your sister. She's flying out to see you."

Jenna shook her head in approval then wrote, "My phone?" on the whiteboard.

The nurse walked over to a small closet in the corner of the room and said, "It's here, with the rest of your things." She took the phone out of a bag and then gave it to Jenna.

Jenna wrote, "Thank you."

"Are you in any pain?"

Jenna nodded yes.

"I'll see if we can increase your pain meds." The nurse left the room, and Jenna got on her phone. She texted Sarah, *"I've been in an accident. Please text me back. I'm worried about Dylan."*

Her cell phone immediately started to ring, and Sarah's name came across the screen. Jenna declined the call and shot her another text. *"I can't talk. My jaw is wired shut. Please tell me, is Dylan okay? I haven't heard from him in over a week."*

"Dylan is fine. But what about you? What happened?"

"I was in a car accident. I'm pretty beat up. I'll probably be in the hospital for a little while. Why won't Dylan talk to me? Is he mad at me?"

"Oh, Jenna. He flew to Denver to surprise you. He saw you kissing another man."

Jenna furiously typed out her next text message. *"Oh, no! That was Noah. I work with him. We dated on and off again before Dylan came back into my life. He saw me telling Noah that I couldn't see him anymore. I told him I love Dylan. He gave me a kiss goodbye and wished us good luck."*

"I knew there had to be an explanation. I told Dylan he needed to talk to you, but he was being stubborn. He's a mess right now, he's so hurt."

"I need to explain to him. Do you think he will talk to me?"

"Leave it to me. I'll take care of it."

"Please don't tell him about Noah. That needs to come from me."

"I won't. Take care of yourself, Jenna. I'll see you soon."

chapter 60

Dylan was loading some dishes into the dishwasher when he heard the front door slam, and Sarah yelled, "Dylan, where are you?"

"I'm in the kitchen," he called back to her.

She rushed up beside him and sighed, "I know you told me to stay out of it, but I texted Jenna."

He clenched his jaw, a flash of anger came over his face, then he raised his hand to her, "Stop! I don't want to hear it!" He placed his hands over his ears and scrambled away from her.

"She's hurt. She's in the hospital," Sarah blurted out.

Dylan stopped in his tracks and turned to face her, wide-eyed.

"She's been in a car accident. She's in the hospital. I don't know any more."

"I have to see her." He ran out of the kitchen to go pack.

"I'll check the flights." Sarah smiled and yelled back at him.

Ten minutes later, he came down the stairs and found Sarah sitting on the couch with her laptop over her legs. She tapped a button on the computer and said, "You're booked."

"What time is my flight?"

"The first flight I could get was 7 a.m. tomorrow."

"Thank you." He took a seat next to her on the couch, "Do you think I should call her?"

"No, she's not in any condition to talk."

Dylan stood and paced the room, wringing his hands, his head filled with worry. Sarah went to him and placed a hand on his shoulder and tried to reassure him, "She's going to be okay."

"I hope you're right."

The next morning, Dylan placed his carry-on bag into the overhead compartment of flight 722 to Denver, then settled into his seat and closed his eyes. He hadn't gotten any sleep the night before; he couldn't stop worrying about Jenna. He got in touch with the hospital, but they would not give him any information on her condition because he wasn't family.

Exhaustion had finally gotten the best of him. When he opened his eyes, he heard the pilot inform the flight attendants to prepare for landing. He only brought the one carry-on bag, so he didn't need to claim any baggage. He exited the plane and navigated his way through the crowd at break-speed to hail a cab.

"Where to?" asked the cab driver.

"Saint Joseph Hospital."

The closer he got to the hospital, the worse he felt. His stomach formed a knot, and he thought he might be sick. *What if she doesn't make it?*

He paid the cab driver and entered the hospital, then went directly to the woman sitting behind the desk in the main lobby. The woman gave him a visitor pass to room 217. When he got off the elevator, he discovered her room was right next to it. He rounded the corner to enter her room, and his heart dropped.

Sitting by her bedside, holding her hand, was the man that kissed her that night at the bar. The man looked up at the sound of footsteps approaching and locked eyes with Dylan. He smiled and said, "You must be Dylan."

Stunned, Dylan just nodded his head. After he had a moment to pull himself together, he looked over at Jenna and his eyes filled with tears as he was overcome with emotion. He was not prepared for what he saw. Covered with cuts and bruises, her jaw wired shut; she looked broken.

The man got to his feet. "She's resting. Would you like to go grab a cup of coffee and talk?"

It was then that he noticed the man had several bruises too. He wanted nothing better than to punch this guy in the face, but he wanted answers more. "Sure," he said and followed the man out of the hospital room. When they got onto the elevator, Noah held his hand out to Dylan and said, "I'm Noah, by the way."

Dylan did not take his hand, and Noah finally pulled it away.

"I can understand why you are mad at me. I feel terrible about the accident."

"Were you driving?" Dylan asked through clenched teeth.

Noah raised a hand to Dylan. "Just let me explain."

Dylan eyed him narrowly and asked again, "Were you driving?"

Noah dropped his head and replied, "Yes."

Dylan grabbed him by the shirt and threw him up against the elevator wall. The elevator dinged, and the door opened. An elderly woman stood there with her mouth open, and Dylan saw the look of fear in her eyes. He released Noah and stepped out of the elevator, and Noah followed him.

"Look, I get it. You love Jenna, but you got to know I would never do anything to hurt her. It was an accident. If you'd just let me explain."

Dylan poured himself a cup of coffee, paid the cashier, then walked away from Noah and took a seat in the cafeteria. A short time later, Noah joined him at the table with his own cup of coffee.

Dylan cleared his throat. "I'm sorry. I shouldn't have grabbed you. I can be a little overprotective sometimes."

"It's okay. I get it. If she were my girlfriend, I would want to rip your head off too."

"She's not my girlfriend." Dylan took a sip of coffee.

A crease formed on Noah's eyebrows, "Wait, I don't understand. Jenna's not your girlfriend?"

"I thought she was, but I guess she wasn't as serious about me as I was about her. If she were, she wouldn't have been with you."

Noah raised a finger to Dylan, "Wait a minute. So, you're saying you're not in love with Jenna?"

"No, I'm not saying that. I do love her. I've loved her my entire life, since we were kids. I came to Denver to ask her to marry me, but then I saw you kissing her."

"I think there's been a misunderstanding. Jenna and I work together. We dated on and off again for several months, but that was before you came back into her life. That night, when you saw me kiss her, she broke it off with me. She told me we couldn't date anymore because she was in love with you. Do you know where we were going when we had the accident?"

Dylan shook his head.

"I was taking her to the airport. She was going home early because she was worried about you. She thought that you might be back in the hospital."

Dylan covered his face with his hands and dropped his head.

After a few moments, he removed his hands and looked at Noah.

"It's all a misunderstanding. She loves you, Dylan."

chapter
61

Jenna lay in the hospital bed, dozing in and out of sleep, when she felt a gentle touch caressing her hand. She opened her eyes; she was so groggy, she stared at the man before her and thought she was dreaming.

Dylan smiled at her and whispered, "Hi."

Her eyes twinkled, then darted to the whiteboard on the counter. She pointed to it, and Dylan brought it to her. "Here," he said, handing it to her.

She removed the attached marker and frantically started scribbling on the board, then flipped it around so he could read it.

It read, "I'm sorry. Please let me explain."

"It's okay. Noah told me everything. I'm the one who should be apologizing. I'm a stupid jackass. Can you ever forgive me?"

She nodded and blinked, sending a single tear rolling down her cheek.

His face grimaced, "Will it hurt if I hug you?"

She shook her head, and Dylan softly wrapped his arms around her. She pulled him closer, hugged him tightly, and rested her head on his shoulder.

"I'm so sorry, baby. I love you," Dylan exclaimed.

When he pulled away from their embrace, she made her hands form a heart and then pointed to him.

"Look at you, you're all banged up, and it's all my fault. I wanted to surprise you. I should have told you I was coming. If I had let you explain, you wouldn't have left early and gotten in a car accident."

She shook her head and wrote on the board, "I love you, Dylan. I can't believe we have a second chance to be together. I'm not going to mess that up."

He read it and smiled, "Me either."

Jenna spent two more days in the hospital, then went back to her hotel with Dylan. He doated on her every whim and need, except her desire for them to be together. It killed her to sleep in the bed next to him and not make him hers. She placed a hand on his leg and sensuously ran it up his thigh.

He stopped her just before she reached his manhood, "No, not like this," he said, pulling her hand away from his body.

She shrugged and moved away from him. Then she got out of bed, went into the bathroom, and forcefully shut the door behind her. When she got out of the bathroom after taking a shower, Dylan was not there. She clicked the television on and then got dressed. A few minutes later, Dylan came back, carrying two cups of coffee, a blueberry muffin, and a smoothie.

"I got you a coffee," he said, handing her the cup as a peace offering.

She took the coffee from him, then he placed his arms around her, wrapping her in a bear hug. "Don't be mad at me. You have no idea how much I want you right now. I am not going to make love to you until you are all better. I don't want to hurt you, and I want it to be perfect."

Her heart melted. *He is so sweet. How can I be mad at him?*

She nodded that she understood, then he said, "Good." He gave her a kiss on the forehead, then released her and went over to the small table under the window. "I got you a smoothie, too. I hope you like strawberry?"

She nodded and joined him at the table.

"The doctor said you could fly home tomorrow. I booked us a 2 p.m. flight."

She nodded.

She wrote on the whiteboard, "What should we do today?"

He gave her a stern look, "Nothing. You need to rest."

"I'm fine," she wrote.

chapter

62

Megan threw the manilla envelope at Jake and said, "What is this?" She planted herself in front of him, folded her arms across her chest, and waited for an answer.

"I thought it was self-explanatory. I want a divorce," Jake replied smugly and picked the envelope up from the floor and handed it back to her. When she refused to take it, he placed it on the table and walked away from her.

She followed him, waving her arms in the air. "You can't be serious? I'm pregnant, for God's sake. You seriously want to put me through a divorce right now?"

He shrugged his shoulders, "You need to go on with your life."

Her eyes burned with fury, "That's it. After all we've been through. Just like that, you want to throw the towel in and call it quits."

He turned and faced her, placing both hands on her shoulders. "You have to face it, Megan. I'm not getting out of here. Our life together is already over. Don't contest it. You'll only drag things out. I've made up my mind. You can have everything, the house, the store, our savings. I don't need any of it in here. All I want is a divorce." He walked away from her.

A lump formed in her throat. She struggled not to cry. She had never seen him so cold before. She went over to him and touched his arm. He immediately pulled it away from her.

"How can you be so mean?" She looked at him curiously and wondered if it was Mark she was talking to. "Where is my husband? I want to speak with Jake!"

He suddenly became enraged, "Don't you dare go there!" He moved toward her with his fist in the air. She flinched and turned her head away from him, preparing herself for the blow, but it never came.

He picked the envelope back up and shoved it into her chest. "Sign the papers," he said. She wrapped her arms around the envelope, and he brushed against her shoulder as he left the room.

She stood there in shock for a minute, then wiped her tears with a shaky hand and left with as much dignity as she could with all the residents staring at her.

Jake went back to his room and slammed the door behind him. He walked over to his dresser and swung his arm across it, sending everything crashing to the floor. Then he threw himself on his bed and pushed his face into his pillow and screamed. That was the hardest thing he ever had to do in his life. It broke his heart to be so cruel to her, but he knew that would be the only way she would divorce him and go on with her life.

Two weeks later, he got a call from his lawyer telling him that Megan had signed the papers.

chapter

63

Dylan spent the next two weeks in training. Megan taught him everything he needed to know about opening, closing, and running the antique shop. He spent his days at the store and his evening at Jenna's apartment, looking after her, and he had never been happier in his life.

Jenna was healing nicely; her bruises were gone, and she was no longer in pain. Dylan was finding it harder and harder to restraint himself. He wanted nothing more than to make her his, but he promised himself he would wait until her jaw was better.

He had never taken so many cold showers in his life. He went years without being with a woman in prison, but this was different; he didn't have to look at Jenna every day when he was in prison. She was so sexy without even trying. He counted down the days on a calendar, waiting for six weeks to pass so Jenna could have her jaw unwired.

One day when Jake and Megan were closing the store, Megan said, "I booked a flight to Mexico yesterday."

Dylan dropped the money he was counting back into the register and shot her a look, "So soon?"

She nodded, "You're ready. I've stayed longer than I wanted. I need to get away from here."

Dylan hated seeing Megan so unhappy the last several weeks. He felt helpless that there was nothing he could do to make her feel better. He knew she desperately wanted to go back to Mexico, and that was something he could help her do.

"I was thinking," Megan said. "How would you like to have your own place? Don't you and Jenna want some privacy?"

He went back to counting the money. "I would love to get my own place, but I don't have enough money saved up yet. Jenna has a roommate, so I can't move in there. I'll figure something out. I just need a little more time."

"You could move into my house? I'm going to need someone to look after the place while I am gone."

Dylan took a minute to think it over. "Are you sure?"

She nodded, "You would be doing me a favor. I don't want to rent it out to a stranger and have to worry about collecting the rent and making repairs. What do you say? I think it's a win-win for both of us."

Dylan smiled, "Okay, but only if I can pay rent. You are doing so much for me already."

"Of course. If you could cover the mortgage and pay for your utilities, that would really help me out. The mortgage isn't bad, we put forty percent down, so it's manageable." She let out a sigh of relief, then hugged him, "Thank you. I don't know what I would do without you."

He wrapped his arms tightly around her, "No, I don't know what I would do without you."

Two days later, Dylan drove Megan to the airport, then went to the shop for his first day on his own. He was in the office in the back preparing next week's schedule when Hope, one of the workers, popped her head in and said, "There's someone here to see you."

He looked up from the schedule. "Who is it?"

"Sorry, I didn't ask."

"Okay, I'll be out in a minute." He put the computer in sleep mode, then turned his head side to side, stretching his neck, then got up from the desk.

He walked into the front of the store, where a woman was standing with her back to him. "Can I help you?" he asked the woman.

She turned around and smiled at him, "You are a hard person to track down, you know that?"

It was Rachel, the flight attendant from Denver. Dylan's face turned red, and he shot a look over at Hope to see if she was watching him. He grabbed Rachel by the elbow and pulled her away from the checkout counter. "What are you doing here?"

"I wanted to talk to you. Is this a bad time?"

"I'm working. I can't talk here. Would you like to go next door and grab a cup of coffee?"

"Sure."

"Okay, just give me a minute." He went back to the office and grabbed his jacket, then stopped at the counter and told Hope, "I'm taking lunch now. I'll be back in an hour."

Hope replied, "Okay, I'll be here. Have a good lunch."

They walked to the coffee shop next door and got a table. After the waitress took their order, Rachel placed a ring box on the table and slid it over to him, "I think this belongs to you."

His entire face lit up. "I didn't realize I lost it until the next morning. I ran back to your hotel, but you had already checked out. I didn't even know your last name. I can't believe you found it and came all the way here to bring it back to me. It was my grandmother's; it means so much to me. How did you find me?"

"It wasn't easy. I only knew your first name and the flight you were on. I looked you up and found your last name, then I Googled your name." A look of sympathy showed on her face, "I found the articles about your past. I'm sorry for everything you've been through."

He sent her a half-smile, "Thanks."

"I couldn't find an address for you. The credit card you used was under another name, Michael Evans."

Dylan nodded, "That's my brother."

"I went to his house, and he told me where I could find you. Sorry it took me so long to get here. I had to wait until my next flight to Ohio. I would have called you to let you know I had it, but I didn't have a number for you."

"That's okay. I'm just so happy to have it back. You don't know what this means to me." He touched her arm and tapped it.

She tipped her head sideways and hesitated, "Can I ask you a question?"

"Sure." He leaned back into the booth.

"What happened? I guess what I mean is why were you with me? You were carrying around an engagement ring, yet somehow you ended up in a hotel room with me."

"I came to Denver to surprise Jenna and ask her to marry me. When I got to her hotel, I found her at the bar kissing another guy. I was so hurt. I didn't want to feel anything, so I got drunk. Really drunk. Then I met you, you were so beautiful, and I wanted to get even with her." He cast his eyes downward, ashamed of himself, "I'm sorry. I didn't mean to use you."

She nodded for him to go on.

"It was all a misunderstanding. She had been seeing Noah before she and I got together. She was breaking it off with him." He beamed, "Told him she couldn't see him anymore because she loved me. He kissed her goodbye and wished us well. Now, thanks to you, I can give her the ring again."

"I'm glad. I can see that you love her very much."

"I do."

"Well, I better get going. My flight leaves in a couple of hours."

Dylan paid the bill and walked her to the door. When they left the restaurant, he gave her a hug and said, "Thank you."

She said, "You're welcome," then Dylan turned right, and she went left.

He walked away from her with a lightness in his heart and his hand on the ring in his pocket. Suddenly, on impulse, he turned and looked back, at the same time as she did, then smiled and waved goodbye.

chapter
64

The day had finally arrived for Jenna to have her jaw unwired, and Dylan was busy making plans for a celebration. If all went well, it was going to be a night they would never forget.

At 3:15, the bell on the antique store door jingled, letting him know that someone had entered the shop. His eyes shot to the entrance to see who it was, and his face lit up when he saw Jenna walk through the door with a beautiful smile on her face. He rushed to her side, lifted her off the ground, and spun her around in a circle, "Look at you. You're so beautiful." He planted a kiss on her lips and could feel her go weak in his arms.

Remembering where they were, he murmured breathlessly in her ear, "I can't wait until tonight," then released her. He took her hand and led her to his office in the back. When he had her all to himself, he shut the door and picked her up, focusing his eyes on her pouty lips, then he sensuously licked his, sending goosebumps down her entire body. He slowly lowered his head to meet hers and sucked her bottom lip into his mouth as the tension of his desire reached the point of explosion.

There was a knock on the door, "Dylan? I can't get the register drawer open again."

He broke away from their kiss and sighed. "I'll be right there," he yelled out.

He placed her back on the ground and straightened his shirt, "Damn, woman. You got me so tangled up in knots, I can't think straight."

She shot him a devious smile, "Good."

He opened the door and said, "I got to get back to work. You better get out of here, or I'll never be able to get my work done. I'll pick you up at seven?"

"I'll be ready," she said, following him to the front of the store.

He spent the rest of the workday distracted with thoughts of Jenna and had to repeat several tasks more than once, but eventually, he was able to close the shop for the night.

He made a quick stop at the florist and dry cleaners before rushing home to shower and change. He stepped out of the shower and wrapped a towel around his waist, then stood in front of the mirror and took his time shaving, not wanting to nick himself. He combed his hair, slicked it back with gel, then left the bathroom to put on his evening attire.

He dressed in black dress pants and a crisp white shirt, then looped his belt around his waist before putting on his black socks and dress shoes. When he was finished dressing, he put on his black sports jacket, grabbed the ring box off the dresser, and placed it in the pocket of his coat. He stood in front of the dresser and was pleased with what he saw in the mirror, then he sprayed Jenna's favorite cologne on his neck and smiled at his reflection, "You got this!"

He made the short drive to Jenna's apartment and stood at her front door, nervously clutching the flowers he brought for her, then rang the bell and waited. A few moments passed before the door opened. Dylan's eyes widened, and his mouth dropped open. Unable to find his words, his lips formed a kissing position, and he said, "Phew."

He stood speechless for several moments, then pushed the flowers toward her, "These are for you."

"Thank you," she took the flowers and said, "You look great."

His eyes ran up and down her tight-fitted red dress, which accentuated her every curve, and said, "You look incredible."

She opened the door further, "Would you like to come in?"

Not trusting that he could control himself, he said, "I better not. We don't want to be late for our reservation."

"Okay," she turned away from him. "Just let me put these in water and get my things."

Dylan drove to the restaurant with one hand on the steering wheel and the other placed on her lap, holding her hand. "How does it feel to have your jaw back?"

"It feels great. You don't know how excited I was to get it unwired."

"I can only imagine. It must have been hard."

"It wasn't that bad. The worst part was not being with you." She seductively rubbed her fingers over his hand and up his arm.

He glanced her way and sighed. "Oh, I know exactly how hard it was. I promise you that after tonight, I will never make you wait again."

They reached the restaurant and checked their coats at the door, then followed the hostess to their table. Dylan was filled with pride as he observed other men watching Jenna make her way across the room. He pulled the chair out for her, then took a seat across from her and placed his hand on his pocket to feel for the ring.

They ordered dinner and a bottle of wine and made small talk for a while, then suddenly, Dylan became quiet.

"You're not even listening to me," she said.

"I'm sorry." He took a gulp of water and tried to get his nerve up to tell her something. "There is something I need to tell you."

Jenna placed her fork down and gave him her full attention, "Okay."

"I love you very much, and I can't wait for us to start a life together, but I don't want there to be any secrets between us. We already know how a misunderstanding can damage a relationship. I don't ever want that to happen again."

"Me either."

He hesitated and exhaled deeply, "That night when I saw Noah kissing you, I was so hurt. No, I was more than hurt. I was devastated. I got drunk."

A waiter came over and refilled their water glasses. Dylan looked up at him and said, "Thank you." When he left, he continued, "A flight attendant came into the bar, we had a few drinks. I got really drunk. I'm not blaming my behavior on the alcohol. It was more about not being with a woman in so long and wanting to get back at you."

He could see the hurt in her eyes as she held up her hand and asked, "Did you sleep with her?"

"No. We almost did, but I couldn't do it."

She exhaled, "Okay, that's all I need to know."

He reached across the table and took her hand in his, "I didn't tell you this to hurt you. I needed to get it off my chest before I asked you something."

He released her hand and got up from the chair and went by her side. He reached into his coat pocket and got down on one knee.

Jenna began to tremble, knowing what he was about to do.

The chatter in the restaurant went silent, the wait staff stopped serving, and all eyes turned to look at them.

"Jenna, you stole my heart when we were just teenagers, and you've had it ever since. Out of all the mistakes I've made in my life, letting you get away is the one I regret the most. I can't believe I've been given a second chance with you, and if you will have me, I promise to never mess it up again. I love you, Jenna. I don't have a lot to offer you other than my unconditional, eternal love."

He opened the ring box and held it up to her with shaky hands, "Will you marry me?"

She shook her head and let the flood gates open on her tears. He placed the ring on her finger, swooped her up in his arms, and sealed the deal with a gentle kiss while the entire restaurant broke out in applause.

The owner of the restaurant came over to their table carrying a bottle of their best champagne. He held the bottle out to Dylan and said, "I understand congratulations are in order."

"Yes," Dylan beamed. "She said yes."

He looked at the bottle of champagne and said, "Thank you, but do you mind if we take the bottle to go? I'm driving, and I've already had a few." The owner patted Dylan on the back and winked at him, "Of course. No problem. I'll have the wait staff pack it up for you."

Several people came over to their table to congratulate them while they waited for their check and to-go bag. When they were finally able to get out of the restaurant, they practically ran to the car in their eagerness to get home. He placed the bag into the trunk, closed it, then took her into his arms, pushing her up against the car.

He kissed her and slipped his tongue into her mouth, and tasted the sweetness of her desire. He pulled her coat and dress off her shoulder in one quick movement and glided his tongue down her neck and nibbled on her shoulder as he pressed his manhood against her body. He wanted to take her right there in the parking lot, under the stars and moonlight, but somehow found the strength to pull himself away from her. "Let's go home."

He drove back to his place, parked the car, and said, "Wait here." He jumped out of the car, got the bag out of the trunk, and ran into the house. It seemed like forever before he finally came back to get her. He opened her car door and said, "Sorry I took so long."

She took his hand and got out of the car. He placed his arm over her shoulder, and they walked to the porch. When they got to the front door, it was already open; he swooped her up into his arms and carried her inside. In the living room, there was a fire burning in the fireplace, candles illuminated the room, the bottle of champagne was chilling in a bucket on the coffee table next to a plate of chocolate-covered strawberries.

Her eyes brimmed with tears as the romantic atmosphere warmed her heart. "I love you," she said and kissed him.

He carried her to the couch and set her down, then poured two glasses of champagne. They raised their glasses in a toast, and Dylan said, "To our first night of bliss."

They stayed on the couch kissing and exploring each other's bodies like they did when they were teenagers so many years ago. When they reached the peak of their arousal, and Dylan couldn't contain himself any longer, he gathered her up into his arms and carried her to the bedroom. He swung the door closed with his foot, and they did what lovers do best.

Over and over again!